Books in the AGENCY Series

Eve of War
The Favor
The Cure
Marque
Reprisal

Books in the PANTHEON Series

Hecate
Tridyma

Books in the COLONY Series

QUANT
ARCADIA
GALACTIC SURVEY
SILK ROAD
LOST COLONY
EARTH

Books in the EMPIRE Series

by Richard F. Weyand:

EMPIRE: Reformer
EMPIRE: Usurper
EMPIRE: Tyrant
EMPIRE: Commander
EMPIRE: Warlord
EMPIRE: Conqueror

by Stephanie Osborn:

EMPIRE: Imperial Police
EMPIRE: Imperial Detective
EMPIRE: Imperial Inspector
EMPIRE: Section Six

by Richard F. Weyand:

EMPIRE: Intervention
EMPIRE: Investigation
EMPIRE: Succession
EMPIRE: Renewal
EMPIRE: Resistance
EMPIRE: Resurgence

Books in the Childers Universe

by Richard F. Weyand:

Childers
Childers: Absurd Proposals
Galactic Mail: Revolution
A Charter For The Commonwealth
Campbell: The Problem With Bliss

by Stephanie Osborn:

Campbell: The Sigurdsen Incident

Reprisal

An Agency Thriller

by

RICHARD F. WEYAND

RICHARD F. WEYAND

ISBN 978-1-954903-16-6
Printed in the United States of America

Cover Credits
Cover Art: Luca Oleastri and Paola Giari,
www.rotwangstudio.com
Back Cover Photo: Oleg Volk

Published by Weyand Associates, Inc.
Bloomington, Indiana, USA
June 2023

REPRISAL

CONTENTS

Status Meetings 1
Brain Trust 9
Febo And Varley 19
Military Planning 29
Febo And The Aliens 39
A Plan Comes Together 49
Erias 60
Pilot School 68
The Marines 77
Reconsideration 84
Ladyhawke 93
Departure 102
To Earth 110
The Aurora Project 119
Vauxhall Arrival 128
Intermezzo 135
The Resistance 143
Applying The Pressure 154
Convergence Of Forces 162
The Effect Of The Cure 171
Countermeasures 179
First Blood 186
Oh-Four-Hundred Hours 194
Dogfight 203
Melee 210
Denouement 215
Reconstruction 221
Preparing For Departure 229
To Earth, Again 237
To Mardouk 245
Naval Construction And Destruction 255

Isabela Febo....267
Earth Planetary Police....277
Gearing Up....286
Fanning The Flames....293
The Fire Spreads....305
The Chairman....310
Changes....315
Ten Years On....319
One Hundred Years On....323
Author's Afterword....331

Status Meetings

King Albert XIV of Vauxhall and his son, Crown Prince James, were meeting in the king's office in the royal palace just outside the downtown area of the capital, Vauxhall City, on the planet of Vauxhall.

"Good morning, Father."

"Good morning, James. Time for another quarterly update on our project?"

"Yes, Father."

"Well, I hope it's some news finally. These have been disappointing so far."

"Oh, we have progress this time. On two fronts, actually."

"Excellent. What's first?"

"Materials. We have successfully managed to embed a single carbon nanotube mesh in stainless steel."

"A single layer? Isn't the cluster material multiple layers?"

"Yes, but it's the breakthrough they needed. They think it will be much easier to get to the multiple-layer mesh now that they have managed one layer. It's a case of refining and repeating the process."

"I see. Timeframe to production of multiple-layer mesh?"

"Probably on the order of six months or a year. These things are hard to predict, but they're confident of progress at this point."

"Very well. And the other front?"

"Strategy. That is, how we build a force to defeat the cluster's navy."

"Did your idea of smaller attack ships pan out with the Navy people?"

"Yes. Oh, they were dismissive at first. All of the wars fought in the core worlds to establish the current kingdoms were played out with big starships maneuvering against and pounding on each other. That's where their thinking was. And the musings of the prince in their affairs was greeted with, shall we say, a certain amount of pushback."

The king nodded.

"Do it like we did it before. Hidebound, but traditional Navy thinking."

"Yes, Father. Absolutely. Then I reviewed wet-navy history for them. From two thousand years ago."

"I always told you to study history, James. It comes in handy, because people who don't know what went before have no guideposts to the future."

"Yes. They were shocked. We had actually played out once again in the colonies the development of wet-navy strategies from old Earth. Bigger ships, bigger guns, bigger losses."

"And your argument?"

"I introduced them to the concept of the aircraft carrier."

The king chuckled.

"In this case, spacecraft carrier. I suppose."

"Yes, Father. A stand-off ship whose small and expendable attack ships carry the offensive to the enemy, while the large and expensive vessel remains out of harm's way."

"Did that turn the tide?"

"No, of course not. They did commit to gaming out the scenario on the simulators, however. That was what turned the tide. They became positively enthusiastic at that point."

"Simulations proved the point, James?"

"Yes. There were a couple of people who were open to the concept, and they played the red team in the simulations. They had some early victories, but they refined and enhanced their designs until they were consistently prevailing over the best effort the big-ship navy types could throw at them."

"So do we have designs we can pursue once our materials people come up with a multiple-mesh solution?"

"Yes, Father, though they continue to refine them. We will have some pretty clever things to build up once the materials work is in place."

"What about this new hyperspace drive of theirs? Do we know what's going on with that?"

"I don't have as much progress to report there, Father. It doesn't seem to be a major refinement. It's not new ships, after all, but existing ships being refitted somehow. That speaks to a relatively minor change, though with big consequences. What it is not is a major shift that requires keel-out changes."

"But our people are working on it?"

"Yes, Father. And we have picked up some intelligence that is giving us some direction."

"Excellent. So we are perhaps two years away from giving these cluster people some serious payback?"

"Two or three years, Father. Things always take longer than one would wish."

"That's all right, James. I'm prepared to be patient."

The king nodded, then continued.

"But I will have my reprisal at last."

Isabela Febo, the long-time Chairman of the Council of the Association of Planets, turned off her display after watching the latest meeting between King Albert XIV of Vauxhall and his son.

Febo had hoped it would take them longer to reproduce the cluster's technology with regard to carbon nanotube reinforced stainless steel. That they had done it in a bit less than two years was troubling, but the facts were the facts. They had done it, and multiple-mesh versions were on the horizon.

Their strategy of small attack ships to go after the big heavy cruisers of the cluster's combined navy was also troubling. Febo had started her own people looking at the history of carrier warfare in the wet navies of old Earth when James had previously brought it up, and she had no doubt about their heavy cruisers' vulnerability to that sort of attack.

The ability of the Agency courier ship *Jasmine* to disable the Vauxhall heavy cruiser HMS *Prince Alfred* more than two years ago had spoken to the danger, after all.

Febo's people were also looking at counter-measures, and she expected a report soon on that.

The fact, however, was that the cluster currently had the advantage. The question was, Did they push that advantage now, and, if so, how?

"Good morning, Isabela," said Michael Corliss, the Speaker of the Assembly of the Gaston Alliance.

"Good morning, Michael. Congratulations on your election results."

"Thank you, Isabela. The electorate is pleased with my party these days, and so I have another several years of these enjoyable telephone calls with you."

Febo chuckled. She and Corliss liked each other, and got along well. The results of their cooperation had accrued to both of their benefits with their electorates.

"Well, Michael, I am afraid this call will be less enjoyable than most. Have you seen the recording of the latest meeting between King Albert and Crown Prince James?"

"Oh, yes. It was brought to my attention by the people we have monitoring the king's office stream. They are making better progress now than I had hoped, based on their previous meetings."

"Yes, they've had some recent breakthroughs that are troubling."

Febo paused, then continued.

"You know, it occurs to me, Michael, that the king erred in writing those letters of marque against our people. It was the mission to overturn that decision that resulted in our placing your QE transmitter bug in his office. If he had set off on this path initially, we would not even know of their progress against us."

"Yes, but now that we know, we have decisions to make, Isabela."

Febo nodded.

"Do we move against them while we have the advantage? And if we decide to do that, how do we even proceed?"

"That is certainly one set of decisions, Isabela. The other set concerns how we maintain an advantage going forward if they cannot be derailed."

"Not easy questions, Michael."

"No, but we are working on things, and I assume you are. I have some information I can share there, Isabela."

"I would love to hear it, Michael."

Corliss nodded.

"We have been doing our own simulations, assuming they deploy attack ships from carriers. We also went back and researched the history ourselves.

"The first conclusion is that the best defense against such attack ships appears to be to go after their carriers."

"That doesn't help our heavy cruisers, Michael."

"I think we need to increase the energy density of the point-defense guns on the heavy cruisers, Isabela. Give the heavy cruisers significantly increased defensive capability against these targets.

"But if you assume any war is going to be a war of attrition, you need to cost them the things that are expensive and hard to replace, and that is both the carriers and trained pilots for the attack ships. Whittle away at those things, and you win."

"How do you get past their point defense, and attacks by their attack ships on ours, Michael?"

"One word, Isabela. Maneuverability. We've been working the simulators hard, and winning with an attack ship always comes back to maneuverability. We think we have ways to make ships very maneuverable. Ways they may not have thought of."

"I see. Interesting. Well, I have something to share with you as well, Michael."

"Go ahead, Isabela. This should be good."

"Oh, it is. Michael. It is. In our simulations, things are helped out a great deal if the enemy can't see you until it's too late. Our materials people have come up with a major advancement. You know about carbon nanotube reinforced stainless steel, of course."

"Yes, Isabela. That's what they've been trying so hard to reproduce."

"Exactly, Michael. Well, our people have come up with a way to make it so the outside layer is exposed carbon nanotube, not stainless steel."

"So one layer of the carbon mesh is on the surface?"

"Yes, Michael. And carbon nanotubes absorb radar signals."

"Oh, ho! Now I see where that's going. You can reduce the radar signature, Isabela?"

"We have almost eliminated it, Michael. With this technology we can build attack ships with the radar signature of a dinner plate. Or less."

"Wow. All right. Now if we put that together with our increased maneuverability, I think we're getting somewhere, Isabela. Then where do we launch them from? Do we build carriers ourselves?"

"Some, I think. We probably should, Michael. My people are also looking at using the heavy cruisers as launch platforms. They won't have as large a parasite complement as a full-up carrier, but they would be able to defend themselves much better."

"All right. So it looks like we need to do the 'have my people talk to your people' thing, Isabela. To pull all of this together."

"That's where I was headed, Michael. And let's put the question of how do we derail them while we have the advantage on the table, too. Let's work it all, and see what they come up with."

"All right, Isabela. I'm with you."

"Thank you, Michael."

Gloria Dent looked up from her reading when Davian Varley got home on Friday to the high-end condo they owned in downtown Somerset, on the planet Wilbourne. The sun was just heading toward dusk, and the royal palace of King Ferdinand IV shone in the early evening light, north across the city park from their picture windows.

"Oh, you look beat. How about a drink?"

"Thanks, Gloria. I could use one."

Dent set her roll-up display aside and went over to the bar. She came back over to where Varley had collapsed on his armchair, looking out to the west.

Dent handed him his drink, and Varley sipped and sighed.

"Oh, that's welcome. Thank you."

"Sure, Davian. What's happened? What's going on?"

"I haven't been able to tell you, Gloria, but now I can."

"Tell me what?"

"I'm finished."

"Finished? What do you mean finished?"

"I finished the job. I'm done."

"What about the clinical trials?"

"Complete."

"The sign-offs and approvals?"

"All in hand."

"And the manufacturing modules? The testing of those?"

"Complete. Released to manufacturing."

Dent flopped into the neighboring armchair.

"My God, you *are* done. That's everything, isn't it?"

"Yes. Absolutely everything."

"So now what do we do, Davian?"

"Anything we want, Gloria. I'm resigning my position. There's no reason to work anymore."

Varley looked around the condo as if seeing it for the first time.

"No reason to stay here, for that matter, Gloria. We can go anywhere you want."

Dent stared off into the west, her eyes out of focus.

"I'm not even sure where that would be, Davian," she said absently. "I've never had that option before."

"Well, you do now, Gloria. The royalties will start rolling in soon. There's no financial bound on our freedom anymore. We can go wherever you want. Do whatever you want."

Dent turned back to him.

"Let me think about it, Davian."

"Of course, dear. Just let me know. Whatever you want, I'm good."

Brain Trust

"Hi, Bert!"

"Hi, Gloria. What's going on?"

"Davian and I are taking a vacation. We decided to go over to Mardouk and visit all you guys."

"What about his work?"

"Done."

"Done? He's completely done with the RDT addiction cure?"

"Yep."

"What about the fabrication modules?"

"Done. Signed off. Released to manufacturing."

"No shit."

"Yep. So we're taking a vacation for a change. First time off in two years."

"Interstellar? That's some vacation, Gloria."

"Not really, Bert. I mean, it used to be. It was two weeks to Crossroads, a layover, then two more to Mardouk. Not anymore. All the liners run the X-3 drive now. It's under two weeks' travel time to Mardouk from here."

Mangum nodded. Febo had decided to release the X-3 drive to commercial spacing, both passenger and freight. She just couldn't justify holding up the economic advantages for the military secrecy. A stronger economy made for a stronger military anyway.

"Well, it'll be great to see you guys."

"Yeah, we're looking forward to it. Some time in the capital. Then out to the beaches for a while."

"How's Davian going to feel about being on the ocean again, Gloria? Last time wasn't pleasant."

Varley had been held for eighteen years – without charges – on Anacapa Island in Southern California, before Mangum and company had shown up and released him.

"No, he's good, Bert. I think he's made his peace with all that. Finishing his work has really capped all that off for him."

"Wow. That's great."

"Yeah. So what's the name of that place you told me about? The place where you stay when you go to the beach. It sounds about perfect."

"I'll send you the info, Gloria. Including which cabin to ask for. It's not cheap, but it's secluded. And you can still call them to pick you up in an electric cart for transfer to the main resort buildings for meals. Assuming you don't just want to get room service."

"Thanks, Bert. Well, plan on seeing us in a couple weeks. We're on the *Wilbourne Adventure,* leaving tomorrow."

"First class?"

"Yes. Of course. Money is no longer a problem, Bert."

Mangum nodded. Varley, with some prodding from Mangum, had negotiated royalties on his prior work. He was already well compensated as the director of the research unit of the Evans Group that had completed the work on the cure for RDT addition. Those royalty payments on Varley's initial work back on Earth, though, would really add up.

"We'll see you then, Gloria. Good spacing."

"Good afternoon, Mr. Grant."

"Good afternoon, Madam Chairman," said Henry Grant, the Director of the Association Intelligence Agency. "How may I help you this afternoon?"

"Things on Vauxhall are proceeding apace, Mr. Grant. They have reverse engineered embedding carbon nanotubes in stainless steel, and are working on an aircraft-carrier-type concept for starships to take on our Navy."

"I see, ma'am."

"So we are proceeding along two fronts, Mr. Grant. One is to upgrade our Navy to fight their new concept. The other is to work on some way to take them down before it comes to war."

"Take them down, ma'am?"

"Yes, Mr. Grant. Topple the regime. It is a corrupt, feudal system that, over the long term, will come to blows with us in any case. We are structural antagonists in a political sense. They will fight us, sooner or later, rather than allow us to continue as we have."

"I see, ma'am. And our role?"

"I want you to be working on both problems, Mr. Grant. Toppling the regime is much more in your wheelhouse, but I want you involved in the Navy business as well. It was your organization that came up with the solutions to the Abelon Crisis and the Crossroads Affair, and I want those same people involved. They have insight, and I want them thinking about both problems."

"Which people in particular, ma'am, if I could ask."

"Of course, Mr. Grant. I want Mr. Mangum, Ms. Dent, Ms. Stavros, and Mr. Portnoy involved. Ms. Stickney, too, I suppose, since she and Mr. Portnoy have apparently become a couple."

"They are all very close to Serp Kendall and his wife, Marge Schofield, as well, ma'am."

"Include them. Put Kendall and his wife on your payroll as analysts. I want them all briefed in. This is going to be a very involved business, and I want all our best people involved. I need options, Mr. Grant."

"Of course, ma'am."

"Your people should be reviewing the current status of Vauxhall's preparations, and our Navy people's analysis so far. Also Gaston's analysis. I will forward all of these to you."

"Thank you, Madam Chairman."

"Good day, Mr. Grant."

Bert Mangum and Elina Stavros had Serp Kendall and Marge Schofield for dinner later that week. They all ordered from room service in The 909, the luxury condo building in which both couples had top-floor units.

Sam and Jules were there as well, in their utility personas. They had just put Frankie to bed. They ordered a couple of large 'Mangum Specials,' ham and pineapple pizzas.

"Well, this will be fun," Schofield said when they all had drinks. "I watched the sunrise this morning out of our east-facing windows, and will see the sunset tonight out of your west-facing windows."

"I always liked the sunsets better," Stavros said. "No offense, Marge."

Schofield laughed.

"None taken, Elina. Some of us are just early birds."

"So what's going on, Bert?" Serp Kendall asked. "You sounded like you had an agenda for tonight."

The former independent freighter captain – given the irregularity of some cargoes, some might say smuggler – shifted in his chair to face Mangum.

"Yes, Serp. There are some things going on, and we could use your help."

"Who's 'we' in this case, Bert?"

"Well, now I need you and Marge to promise me you'll keep all this confidential, Serp. I need to tell you some things that really shouldn't get around."

"Sure, Bert. Who would we tell, anyway?"

Mangum looked to Schofield.

"Yes, Bert. I promise to keep your confidence."

"All right. Elina and I work for something called the Agency for Interstellar Trade. That's a front. It's actually the Association Intelligence Agency."

"The Agency doesn't exist, Bert," Kendall said.

"Correct. That is the official position of the government."

"Got it. What do you do for them, Bert?"

"I am the head of field operations for the Agency."

"No shit."

"No shit, Serp. I was an agent for over a decade, then got promoted to the head of field operations when Elina and I started a family. Elina is the assistant head of field operations."

"So how does this relate to us, Bert?" Schofield asked. "Why tell us?"

"We want to hire you. Both of you. As analysts. We have some very difficult times with Vauxhall ahead, and the chairman wants all the input she can get from the people most knowledgeable about what's going on."

"The chairman?" Kendall asked.

"Chairman Febo."

"Holy crap."

Kendall looked over at Stavros, and she just nodded. He looked back to Mangum.

"All right, Bert. We don't really need the money, but we're willing to help. We like it here. Much better than all those kingdoms run by hereditary morons. How do we help?"

"I'm going to be sending you background materials. You're going to be included in briefings. We will occasionally get together and talk about things. You and us and Claude and Phyllis. Sam and Jules. Gloria Dent, too."

"Dent is here on Mardouk? I thought she was in Somerset, over on Wilbourne."

"She was. Gloria and Davian Varley will be here next week. So that's our brain trust. The ten of us."

"I thought Varley was working on the cure for RDT," Schofield said.

"He was. He's done. It's all in the pipeline now."

"Wow."

"Yes, and that's potentially one of our weapons against Vauxhall."

Kendall nodded. That would throw a wrench in things over there. Big time.

"So Claude and Phyllis and Gloria are all in the Agency, too, Bert?"

"No, Serp. Claude is. As an agent. Phyllis and Gloria both work for Gaston's Bureau of Intelligence and Espionage. Chairman Febo and Speaker Corliss of Gaston are working this whole thing together."

"Gaston *and* the Association of Planets?"

"Yes, and Wilbourne, Villacqua, Abelon, and Lyons. All six of the cluster star nations are in cahoots on this whole deal."

"Damn," Kendall said.

"And we're their brain trust on this?" Schofield asked.

"Part of it anyway, Marge."

Schofield looked to Stavros, who nodded.

"We've pulled the bunny out of the hat for them before, Marge."

Schofield turned back to Mangum.

"Well, all right, Bert," Schofield said. "If you think we can help."

There were four liners that made the round trip from each

of the six capital planets of the cluster nations to the Crossroads space station. The round-trip had been four weeks, so they managed one weekly departure from each end of these legs. One took a liner to Crossroads, then a liner to your destination. Depending on the layover – which could be up to a week – it took about five weeks to transfer from one cluster star nation's capital to another's.

Since the invention and deployment of the X-3 drive, however, the time in hyperspace went from almost two weeks to four days. With a day in normal-space transit at each end, it now took one week to get to Crossroads, and one more week to get to the other star nation's capital.

The four liners on each leg now made a departure every three days, so layovers at Crossroads were also reduced.

The same four liners with X-3 drives more than doubled the capacity for passenger traffic, but they didn't travel half-empty. Shorter transit times made travel more convenient, and the ability to carry more passengers in the same period of time reduced fares.

The end result was that space travel was more popular than ever.

Gloria Dent and Davian Varley arrived on Mardouk, the capital planet of the Association of Planets, just two weeks after leaving Wilbourne. They checked into the Ashur Park Plaza Hotel, just down the block from The 909 on Park North Boulevard.

They had received an invitation from Bert Mangum for dinner during the day they spent in normal-space travel from the hyperspace limit to the planet, and accepted.

The alien shape-shifters Sam and Jules lived with Bert

Mangum and Elina Stavros, and Serp Kendall, Marge Schofield, Claude Portnoy, and Phyllis Stickney all lived in The 909 as well, so they were all there when Gloria Dent and Davian Varley showed up, guided to Mangum and Stavros's unit by a bellhop from downstairs.

It was a gathering of old friends. There were lots of hugs and handshakes when Dent and Varley showed up. For all that, Dent was surprised to get a big hug from Stickney, whose work persona had always been so prim and proper and aloof.

"It's good to see you, Gloria," Stickney said.

"It's good to see you, too, Phyllis. You're looking good."

"I'm great. On the way back from Vauxhall, I realized I liked my mission cover better than my work persona, so I switched."

"And that worked out?"

"Oh, yes. Marvelously. And Richard and I are so happy."

Portnoy was standing there, and saw Dent's raised eyebrow.

"My mission name, Gloria," he said. "And a very old persona as well. So with each other, we go by Richard and Susan."

"I see. Well, I'm very happy for both of you. I switched personas, too, in a sense, to marry Davian, and we couldn't be happier."

Sam and Jules were manning the bar. They knew – and remembered – the preferences of everyone there, and had drinks ready for Gloria and Davian when they meandered over.

Conversation was mostly people catching up, telling war stories of the assassination attempts from two years ago in response to the King of Vauxhall's letters of marque, and how things had gone for everyone since.

At six, everyone sat for dinner at a table for ten. Marceau's had clearly been there, with their table service and name-embroidered cloth napkins. Sam and Jules, in their utility personas, sat with the rest, and helped themselves when the dishes were uncovered.

"Wait," Dent said to Sam. "How do you guys eat anything from Marceau's? I thought you were allergic to onions."

"We are, Gloria. Raw onions. We did some careful testing of minor amounts, and cooking onions destroys the enzyme that gives us trouble. So as long as the onions aren't raw, we don't have any problems."

"Nice," Dent said. "And Bert doesn't have to put up with the smell of ham and pineapple pizza."

"Not a minor consideration," Mangum said, and everyone laughed.

Stickney turned to Dent.

"So why are you on Mardouk, Gloria? Is it all vacation, or are there business considerations as well."

Dent hesitated, glancing at Kendall and Schofield. It was an awkward moment as she considered what she could say. Mangum stepped into the pause.

"I should note that Serp and Marge are now on the inside. The Agency has hired them as analysts to assist with the upcoming difficulties with Vauxhall and the other monarchies."

"Ah, well. In that case," Dent said, "Davian is meeting with the chairman. She heard we were coming to Mardouk and asked to get together when we got on planet."

Varley nodded.

"On that subject, Elina, could you accompany me again? Gloria will be going as well, but I suspect your status will, once again, assist in avoiding the worst of the security concerns."

"I'd be happy to, Davian," Stavros said.

"Very good. I appreciate it. Chairman Febo has expressed a

desire to meet with me very early on in our visit, and actually suggested tomorrow morning."

"That will work for me, Davian. Just let me know."

Marceau's had outdone themselves once again, and dinner was excellent. A further hour of cocktails as they watched the city come alive for the evening below them, and then all made their goodbyes and headed home.

Febo And Varley

Elina Stavros met Davian Varley and Gloria Dent for breakfast the next morning in the lobby of the Ashur Park Plaza Hotel, east down the block from The 909.

"Morning, everybody," She said to the waiting scientist and his former BIE operative wife. "Let's go in for breakfast."

They went in and were seated, then made a trip through the buffet before talking about anything of substance. Stavros had directed the counter clerk to show them to a discreet table in the corner, and they could talk here.

"So, Davian. What does the chairman want to talk to you about? Do you know?"

"Not exactly, Elina. I expect some questions about how the effort went, and its current status. Perhaps a thank you for proceeding with the work on arrival here rather than go in some other direction. That sort of thing."

"So nothing really surprising, in either direction?"

"I wouldn't think so, but I don't really know. The chairman has many sources of information, and many considerations, of which I have no knowledge."

Stavros nodded.

"All right, Davian. Just checking. Sounds like a fun meeting."

"I hope so, Elina," Dent said. "Fun and boring. We had enough excitement a couple years back to last us for a while."

Varley nodded.

"'Nothing in life is so exhilarating as to be shot at without result.' Isn't that the ancient quote?"

Stavros chuckled.

"Yes, Davian. I think we all had our share of that particular exhilaration during those events. Let's hope life is boring going forward."

"What are the odds, though, Elina?" Dent asked. "Not good, I would think."

"We'll see, Gloria. We'll see."

The big government car picked them up at the hotel a half-hour before the meeting. They all piled in as the driver held the door open for them and the shotgun monitored his displays. The driver closed the door and walked back around the car to his door and got in. He eased the big car away from the curb and into light traffic.

It was a short drive to the Association government center west of the central park that The 909 and the Ashur Park Plaza Hotel faced. The car was waved through the security gates of the fenced compound of the executive building.

When they got to the side entrance portico of the executive building, there was a man waiting. The driver opened the car door and Varley, Dent, and Stavros got out.

"This way, please, Professor Varley."

They followed him into the building. Just inside the doorway there was a security screening station, with metal detectors and all the rest. The guards all wore Special Protective Services uniforms. Their guide got into line there.

Dent and Stavros, of course, were both armed, each with a primary firearm and a backup secondary. There was no way they were getting through even a casual security check.

But Stavros had been here before.

Stavros walked up to the supervisor of the security checkpoint, standing to one side watching the checkpoint. She handed him her card. He glanced at it and raised an eyebrow.

REPRISAL

ASSOCIATION OF PLANETS
Agency for Interstellar Trade

Elina Stavros
Asst Head of Field Operations

The security supervisor scanned her card with a display on a table to one side. Stavros' face came up with the barest minimum of information, the rest being classified higher than his level.

The supervisor knew damned well what the Agency for Interstellar Trade really was. The Association Intelligence Agency, or just The Agency. The Agency was the primary security for the chairman and the council, among other things. Which is to say, it was the superior to his own agency in providing security to the government.

And the Assistant Head of Field Operations was near the top of the Agency. Among its senior leaders.

The supervisor turned back to her.

"Yes, Ma'am. How may I help you?"

"We have a meeting with Chairman Febo. Take us to her."

"Of course, Ma'am. This way, please."

Stavros waved Dent, Varley, and their guide ahead, then followed them all past the security checkpoint and deeper into the building.

"Nice trick," Dent whispered back to her as they walked.

"All I did was let him know I was his superior," Stavros said.

"Like I said. Nice trick."

They took an elevator up to the top floor, the supervisor using a pass key to access that floor. In the elevator lobby on the top floor was another, more intrusive, checkpoint. The supervisor led them past that one as well, and down the hall to the outer office at the end.

"Visitors to see the chairman," he told the receptionist there.

The supervisor then turned around to Stavros.

"Ma'am," he said, then nodded and walked away, back to his post.

The receptionist turned to their guide.

"Professor Varley and his associates are on the chairman's schedule this morning," he told her.

She checked her display, then nodded.

"I'll be right back. Please wait here."

The receptionist went through a door to the inner office, and returned within a minute.

"The chairman will see you now. Right this way, please."

Isabela Febo got up and came around her desk to greet her guests. Davian Varley and Elina Stavros she had met before. The other woman must be Gloria Dent, both Varley's wife and his security, provided courtesy of the BIE.

"Professor Varley. How nice to see you again."

"Madam Chairman."

They shook hands.

"Miss Stavros."

"Madam Chairman."

"And you must be Gloria Dent."

"Yes, Madam Chairman. It's good to meet you."

Febo nodded and waved to a side seating arrangement of four armchairs around a coffee table.

"Please, everyone. Let's be seated."

They all sat, with Varley opposite Febo, and Dent and Stavros to either side.

"First, Professor Varley, thank you for agreeing to meet with me today."

"Of course, Madam Chairman."

"I wanted to personally express my gratitude to you for carrying on your work and creating a cure for RDT addiction we can use to clean up this scourge from the cluster."

"Of course, ma'am."

"I do have some questions for you about it."

"Yes, ma'am?"

"The cure you've passed through clinical trials, Professor Varley. This is the enhanced version we spoke of two years ago?"

"Narlaxatrophine-II. That is correct, ma'am."

"And it renders the patient incapable of becoming readdicted to RDT, Professor Varley?"

"Yes, ma'am."

"Excellent. The manufacturing modules have also been signed off to production, Professor Varley?"

"Yes, ma'am. They are in production right now, actually."

"Now, Professor Varley, are you sure the Narlaxatrophine-II being manufactured by the modules is identical to the drug on which you performed clinical trials?"

"Yes, ma'am. One hundred percent sure. The clinical trials were conducted with the drug as produced by the prototype manufacturing module."

"Ah. So there is no concern that the drug produced by the manufacturing modules will differ in some way, Professor Varley?"

"None at all, ma'am."

"Excellent. We now come to a harder question, Professor Varley. How are we to get our existing RDT addicts to line up for injection with this cure?"

Varley looked puzzled for a moment, then spoke up.

"I'm afraid I may have left you with a misconception at our

last meeting, Madam Chairman."

"How so, Professor Varley?"

"The enhanced version of the RDT addiction cure, ma'am? Narlaxatrophine-II? An additional enhancement over the original cure is that it can be orally administered."

"Orally administered?"

"Yes, ma'am. It is an odorless, colorless liquid that can be administered orally. Such as in a glass of water."

Febo's world flipped around and resettled on another axis.

"We can just add it to water, Professor Varley?"

"Yes, ma'am. Or put it in a beer or soft drink. Any of those methods will work."

"How precise does the dosage need to be, Professor Varley?"

"Not very, ma'am. It is essentially a – how would you say – a catalytic process. With a higher dosage, it proceeds faster, and with a smaller dosage takes longer. But the actual dosage range permissible is very wide."

"Does it harm someone not addicted to RDT, Professor Varley?"

"No, ma'am. But it will make them immune to RDT's effects, including addiction, thenceforward."

"So we could just put it in the water supply, Professor Varley?"

"Potentially, ma'am, but that is not the most effective. Most of a city's water supply is used for purposes other than as drinking water. As I understand it, industrial processes are the lion's share of water usage, with cleaning, irrigation, livestock, and other uses all ranking higher than drinking water."

"What then, Professor Varley?"

"Bars. Bottled water. Bottled beverages generally. But there is still the moral issue, ma'am. Is it morally just or justifiable to administer a medication to someone without their informed consent?"

Febo nodded. Not a minor issue, that. Could she simply introduce the addiction cure to the population at large, without information or consent? More to the point, *should* she?

"Your thoughts on the moral matter, Professor Varley?"

"I have considered the matter off and on over twenty years, Madam Chairman, and I'm afraid I do not have much insight to offer. It is, above all, a political question and not in my purview."

"Potentially also a military question, Professor Varley, if we were to use this cure against the stability of the core-world monarchies."

"That is a different situation, ma'am. Curing people of RDT addiction – even without their consent – is surely preferable to bombing them or otherwise pursuing military means against an enemy population."

"Yes, of course, Professor Varley. A different matter entirely."

Febo thought for a few seconds, then continued.

"Very well, Professor Varley. Thank you for coming in to see me today. It has been most enlightening."

"You are very welcome, Madam Chairman."

"And if I might ask one other favor."

"Of course, ma'am."

"We will be considering, over the next several weeks, what measures we might use to dissuade Vauxhall from pursuing military objectives against us. Some of these involve actually toppling the existing regime there. If you could make yourself – and you, Ms. Dent – available to your friends here for some of these discussions, I would appreciate it."

"Of course, Madam Chairman. It was, after all, my rescue which accelerated the inevitable conflict between the core worlds and the cluster. I would be glad to help in any way I could."

"Thank you, Professor Varley. It need not delay your well-earned vacation. I believe much of this could be done in virtual meetings as well as actual ones. It is your thoughts on the matter I wish to capture, after all."

"Thank you for that, ma'am."

At that, Febo stood up, and the other three followed suit.

"Thank you again, Professor Varley. Ms. Dent. Ms. Stavros."

Febo's receptionist, summoned by a call button Febo carried, came in then.

"If you would all follow me, please."

The government car was waiting under the portico of the executive building when they exited, shown to the door by their guide from before.

"You know, after that I could use a drink," Stavros said. "You guys want to pop 'round The 909 and join me for lunch?"

"Sure," Dent said, and Varley nodded.

"Driver. The 909, please."

"Yes, ma'am."

They rode to The 909 in silence, mindful that theirs were not the only ears in the car.

Mangum came out from the office to join them in the living room when they arrived at Mangum and Stavros' unit. Stavros went over to the bar and prepared drinks.

"Oh, my," Mangum said. "That good, huh?"

"It was, to use Madam Chairman's word, enlightening," Stavros said.

She explained the conversation to Mangum, who was thoughtful when she finished.

"Orally administered, eh?"

"Yes," Varley said. "I have been thinking in those terms for so long, it didn't occur to me to mention it until it was clear the chairman was unaware."

"That opens up a lot of possibilities," Mangum said.

"It sure does," Stavros said.

"Talk to me about that," Dent said.

Mangum was having a nightcap after his first ninety-minute sleep cycle, sitting in the living room with Sam and Jules. It was a habit he had picked up along the way, and he enjoyed watching the night life of the city shutting down and the city go quiescent for the deep part of the night.

"I thought that was an interesting discussion about using Davian's cure against the nobility and elites of Vauxhall, Bert," Sam said.

"Yes, it was, wasn't it. Sam, if we turned that drug loose on Vauxhall, the commoners would no longer be drugged into acceptance of their second-class status. It wouldn't even be possible anymore, since they would be immune to it going forward. All hell would break loose."

"I believe you're right, Bert. That whole society would become a pressure cooker, building up steam."

"Yes. It's no wonder they kept Varley imprisoned for eighteen years. He might have just arranged distribution himself."

"That's another question, though, Bert. How will we introduce the drug into Vauxhall? We need assistance on the ground there, I think."

"There must be an opposition, Sam. Some resistance group of some kind. We need to find them, and empower them with that cure. That will be an Agency mission, I suspect."

Sam nodded, and they continued to look out at the view for several minutes. At length, Sam stirred.

"Do let us know if there is any way we can assist in this effort, Bert. We have a vested interest in this one."

That surprised Mangum. Sam had come along with him when he was rescued from being marooned on the aliens' planet out of curiosity. For the sheer hell of it. And his participation in Mangum's missions had been for fun. Now Sam was in deadly earnest.

"Really, Sam?"

"Yes, Bert. Jules and I have become convinced that our planet will eventually be found by humans. The expansionism and curiosity of humans all but guarantees it. And we would much rather be a part of a democratic human civilization than a feudal one."

Mangum nodded. A feudal society always needed lots of underlings – commoners, peasants, serfs, whatever you called them – to hold up the very few in the nobility. One guess where the aliens would fit into such a society.

"Will do, Sam. I'll keep it in mind."

Sam turned from the windows to catch Mangum's eye.

"Thanks, Bert. It's important to us."

Military Planning

Bert Mangum had scheduled an afternoon meeting to work on the military problem. What was the cluster Navy to do to defend against Vauxhall's planned carrier-based force?

Attending were all ten of them. Mangum and Stavros, Portnoy and Stickney, Kendall and Schofield, Varley and Dent, and Sam and Jules. There was more than enough seating in Mangum and Stavros' cavernous living room. With Frankie down for his afternoon nap, this was the time to have it.

"Has everyone had a chance to read the background materials?" Mangum asked to get them started.

There were various nods and assents.

"Yeah," Kendall said. "Thanks for sending us those reports, Bert. We never really knew what happened on Earth when you guys got away. That was illuminating."

Stickney and Portnoy both nodded. Stickney had not been involved in that mission, and Portnoy, having been gut-shot by the Earth Planetary Police boarding party, had already been in the cooler when the escape from the HMS *Prince Alfred* was carried out.

"So the question before us today is, What do we do to counter Vauxhall's plans to deploy a navy-killer force against the consortium navy?"

"I think it's clear we need a fighter to go up against their attack ships," Portnoy said. "Get them before they get our ships."

"That's part of it, certainly," Stavros said. "We need some defensive force to fight them."

"You know," Kendall said, "I've been looking into the old

wet-navy tactics on Earth. Since Prince James brought it up in his meetings with his father. You know. And it seems the best defense against carrier-based planes, long-term, was to take out the carriers. You can shoot down other people's attack ships all day long, but if you want to hurt them bad, the thing to do is take out the carriers. Much harder to replace."

"That's interesting," Dent said.

"Yes, and not where my thinking was going," Mangum said. "What about their attack ships going after our cruisers, Serp?"

"Oh, I think you need to beef up the point-defense on the cruisers," Kendall said. "No doubt about it. That was what the wet navies did. Really build up their anti-aircraft defenses. And keep a combat air patrol in the sky above their carriers to defend them. But the big deal was to go after the enemy's carriers."

"What would be the best ship to do that?" Mangum asked.

"I would think something fast and maneuverable," Portnoy said. "And something with some real punch, to take out a big ship like that."

"So something like what they're designing?" Mangum asked. "A new ship class? That will take time."

Kendall looked pensive, and Mangum concentrated on him, holding up a hand to Portnoy to keep him quiet for the moment. Then Kendall stirred.

"Maybe not, Bert. What about the *Silverheel* platform?"

"*Silverheel* is a courier ship, Serp."

"As currently configured, yes. But it's a modular ship, Bert. What if you took all the VIP cabins off, and the crew spaces off, even lose the bridge, and you just had a cockpit, those monster big engines, and a bunch of missiles and point-defense guns? It does three gravities now. How fast would it be if you ripped all that unnecessary shit off, maybe shortened it a bit?"

"You still have the problem of the g forces, Serp. You could make it go faster, but nobody could fly it."

"Could we fly it remote?" Stickney asked. "A remotely piloted vehicle, like a drone?"

"Probably could," Kendall said. "Not sure it would be as effective, though."

He shrugged.

"Guess it's not so good an idea after all, Bert."

"Excuse me. If I could mention something?" Sam said.

"Sure, Sam," Mangum said. "Whatcha got?"

"Well, Bert, we've always been somewhat amused by the discomfiture of humans in high and low gravities. They don't affect us, you see. Since we don't have differentiated organs, we don't suffer the consequences that humans do."

"All right," Mangum said. "And how does that enter here?"

"We could pilot such ships, Bert."

"Yeah, but there's only two of you," Kendall said.

"That's not exactly true, Serp. We were, uh, not completely straightforward with you."

Jules looked from Serp to Sam and back to Serp.

"In fact," Jules said, "we lied."

"You want to do what?" Lieutenant Commander Gregory Upton asked.

"I want to do gravitational tolerance testing of one of my agents," Mangum said.

"That's what I thought you said. Then why do you need a ten-gravity tester, Sir?"

"Let's say I suspect him to be very good at this and leave it at that, Commander."

"All right, but even the most athletic types aren't functional much above six gravities."

"Do you have such a tester or not, Commander?"

"Yes, Sir. We have one."

"Excellent, Commander. Then we need to have an assigned slot on that machine. Oh, and I will be bringing my own chair."

What Mangum brought was not so much a chair, but a human-shaped bucket. It had arms and legs and head, like a chalk outline at a crime scene, and a sidewall around that shape several inches high. This way, Sam could assume his natural state and still extrude hands and feet where the controls were.

"But, Sir, if you put that on the acceleration couch, we won't be able to monitor the subject's autonomic responses."

"Good. I don't want you to monitor them anyway."

"But, Sir–"

Mangum gave him a hard look and he quieted.

"Yes, Sir."

The test chamber was about the size of a small powder room on the end of a hundred-foot boom, with a counterweight on the other side of the off-center pivot.

Sam, in his Jimmy Forney persona from back on Crossroads, and Jules, in his Jack Sturm persona, were there with Mangum. Sam got in the test chamber first.

"You good, Sam?"

Sam looked around.

"Yeah, I should be good, Bert."

"All right."

Mangum got out of the test chamber, closing and latching the door.

"He's going to do this in his street clothes, Sir? Not a padded flight suit?"

"Yes. Let's just see what we get."

"All right, Sir."

The boom started to rotate, swinging the test chamber around the big room. Mangum was standing with a Navy lieutenant at the panel. There was a display monitor there, showing the inside of the test chamber. Mangum shut it off.

"But, Sir–"

"Just monitor his responses in the other display, Lieutenant."

"Yes, Sir."

The other display showed the display Sam was looking at, and his responses to its questions. These had to be typed in with controls on the armrests of the acceleration couch.

Faster and faster the boom spun. A gauge on the instrument panel showed the g forces in the test chamber. As they climbed higher and higher, Sam's responses to the display did not show any deterioration of his responses.

"Nine gravities now, Sir," the lieutenant said. "His responses are still good."

In fact, Sam went all the way to ten gravities without losing his ability to respond appropriately to the display in the test chamber.

When it was his turn, Jules did the same.

The lieutenant was nonplussed.

"I never saw anything like that, Sir. They're flukes."

"They certainly are, Lieutenant."

That night, during Mangum's nightcap, they talked about the testing.

"I have to admit, Bert. Ten gravities was getting to be a bit much. But nine gravities was no big deal."

"What about you, Jules?"

"Yes, Bert. About the same for me. Nine gravities was fine.

But ten gravities was getting uncomfortable."

"Well, ten gravities would turn me into soup," Mangum said, "so nothing to be embarrassed about there."

Sam chuckled.

"So I guess we should probably set nine gravities as our operational limit, Bert."

Mangum nodded.

"OK, Sam. We'll see where we get with that."

All ten were again present at another afternoon meeting in Mangum and Dent's unit of The 909.

"Ten gees?" Kendall asked Sam. "You guys are tough as nails."

"Nine gees is better," Sam said. "There is no discomfort to nine gees."

"So that's what?" Portnoy asked. "Three times *Silverheel*'s current acceleration? Can we get engines that big?"

"Nah," Kendall said. "That ain't how you do it. Start ripping shit offa there. Get the mass down to a third, you got nine gees."

"Can we even do that?" Mangum asked.

"Sure," Kendall said. "There's all kinds o' stuff you don't need on there. For a fighter, anyway. And you'd have to add some stuff. I just don't know the masses."

"I can get that," Dent said. "Phyllis, you look up available systems. I'll look up *Silverheel* as she is now."

"Got it," Stickney said.

The two computer experts bent over their displays. They probably could have hacked their way in, but they didn't need to. Isabela Febo had seen to it that her brain trust had access to information across the Association's departments.

"OK, I've got *Silverheel*," Dent said. "What comes off, Serp?"

"The VIP cabins. The crew spaces. The bridge. Uh, lessee. The galley. The food storage units. The sick bay."

"All right. What else?"

"What else is in there, Gloria?"

"The hyperspace drive?"

"Yeah, rip that out."

"Reaction mass."

"Well, you need some, to feed those big thrusters. But cut that way back. You don't need months of reaction mass. Just like a day's worth. But it's gotta be a whole day at the rate those big thrusters use it."

"Got it. OK, Serp. Well, we're under twenty percent of the mass now. This thing'll go fifteen, sixteen gees."

"Yeah, but you gotta add stuff back, Gloria. We need a pilot's cockpit. Missiles. And some point-defense-style guns. They're gonna be shootin' at other fighters, so we gotta give 'em guns. Save the missiles for the big baddies."

"I've got those, Gloria," Stickney said. "Sending them over."

"One-man or two-man cockpit, Serp?" Dent asked.

"One man. Or alien, or whatever."

"Got it. What kind of guns?"

"Big ones. Like on the heavy cruisers. Couple of 'em."

"They're heavy, Serp."

"Yeah, but firepower is worth it."

"OK, got 'em. How many missiles?"

"The old wet-navy attack planes had like one torpedo or one bomb, but I don't care for that. Can you do like a dozen, Gloria?"

"Yeah, I think so. Again, heavy."

Dent bent over her display as she ran the calculations.

"OK, got it. We're on the high side of thirty-five percent of *Silverheel*'s current mass, though. And the ship looks kind of barren. Spread out. You know."

"They got a smaller frame for that class, Gloria? You know, something with a shorter keel?"

"I've got that, Gloria," Stickney said. "Yeah, here's one. Coming over."

"Oh, nice," Dent said. "And this one has nose thrusters, Serp."

"I love it. That'll swing her around fast. Maneuverable as hell. What's our mass now?"

"Just under thirty-two percent of *Silverheel.* Estimated acceleration with those thrusters is nine-point-four gees."

"Bingo," Kendall said. "There's your attack fighter. Now, are all those modules we got there standard parts? That new frame and all?"

"Yeah, Serp. Current production."

"OK, good. The problem with non-standard shit is you gotta test it all. You're looking at five years. You don't wanna put guys out there in shit that ain't space-certified. I was really careful about that when I bought *Ladyhawke.* No unauthorized mods. And we never had any trouble with stupid breakdowns or not being able to get proper parts during refits."

Mangum had been watching this interplay with interest. They were on a roll, and he let them go. Now he had a question.

"You said five years for certifying non-standard modules, Serp. What are we looking at with standard modules? To get ships together?"

"Shit, Bert. You could have a fleet of these in five months."

"Nice. Show us, Gloria."

Dent adjusted her roll-up display. She had brought her big display to these meetings, and she projected the resulting ship so everybody could see it.

It was small, it was compact, and it was mean-looking as hell, with two battleship-grade point-defense guns, one mounted either side of and just behind the cockpit. It had six missiles mounted above and six below. The monster thrusters on the rear were stupidly outsize for the size of the vessel, and made it look fast as hell to experienced eyes.

"Ni-i-i-ice," Kendall said.

"Now we need to think about carriers," Mangum said.

"I don't think so, Bert," Kendall said.

"What now, Serp?"

"How many berthing spots does a consortium heavy cruiser have for parasites?"

Stickney worked her display for a moment.

"Twelve, but eight of those are for small shuttles. There are only four for bigger craft."

"Yeah, and how heavy is our attack fighter?" Kendall asked.

"Huh," Stickney said. "Light enough to use the small-shuttle berthing spots."

"There you go, Bert. Ten of those on a heavy cruiser. Hell, *Ladyhawke* could mount six of them."

"*Ladyhawke* as a carrier, Serp?"

"Why not, Bert? Put a couple dozen of those point-defense guns on her as well, and she'd be hell on wings in a scrap."

That night, after his first sleep-cycle, Mangum sat with Sam and Jules in the living room of their penthouse unit in The 909.

"What did you guys think about the fighter design?" Mangum asked.

"It looks good to me, Bert. I especially like that it is all modular, and the modules are all standard production units. That will make it both very reliable and easy to build."

Mangum nodded.

"We can thank Serp for that. He knew the issue. It also means we can have them fast. So I guess we should build up two of them right away."

"Two, Bert?"

"Well, there are only two of you, so we have two pilots. Nobody else can use the full potential of those attack ships."

"Uh, Bert."

Mangum looked over at Sam. He actually looked embarrassed. That was new.

"Yeah, Sam."

"I'm afraid I haven't been completely honest with you about something."

"About what, Sam?"

"Well, you remember the ship you crashed on our planet with? The courier ship?"

"Right."

"Well, the radio still worked. That's how you called for help."

"Right, Sam. I remember. Then it was just a case of waiting several weeks for someone to get out there."

"Right. But, Bert? The radio still works. I've been in contact with home on a regular basis the last fifteen years."

"What?"

"I mean, it's within the limits of spoken English, which leaves much to be desired, but I have stayed in touch with my people. And I've just received instructions."

Mangum's head was spinning.

"Instructions?"

"Yes. Bert, I need to meet with Chairman Febo."

Febo And The Aliens

Bert Mangum put in the request for a meeting with Chairman Febo through the Agency's contact address for her. A reserved address, only Henry Grant normally used it, but Grant did not turn down Mangum's request for the address. He didn't know what was going on, but Bert Mangum was, well, Bert Mangum.

Mangum got a return mail from Febo, setting the meeting for that day, mid-afternoon. It was her normal 'nap' time, the time of day in which her appointments and calls were not on her public schedule.

Mangum and Sam had talked about the meeting, and how it would go, but, once his and Jules' bona fides as aliens were established, Sam would be on his own. He did not share with Mangum his plans for the rest of the meeting.

It was a bit of a turnabout for Mangum. He had always been in control of their missions for the Agency, and Sam had tagged along, apparently for fun, though that was now in question in Mangum's mind.

The tables had turned.

The big government car, flying the Association's flags on its fenders, pulled up in front of The 909. Mangum was waiting with Sam and Jules, in their golden doodle personas and on leashes. This got a raised eyebrow from the driver as he held the door for them, but questioning Madam Chairman's guests was not part of his job description.

The car was waved through the gates into the fenced compound of the executive building in the Association government center west of downtown. The driver pulled up under the portico, where a man was waiting.

Their guide led Mangum and the aliens into the entry lobby where the security checkpoint was. Having been briefed by Stavros, Mangum went over to the supervisor of the checkpoint and handed him his card.

ASSOCIATION OF PLANETS
Agency for Interstellar Trade

Bert Mangum
Head of Field Operations

The supervisor scanned the card on a display on a side table, and Mangum's face and a very brief and unclassified bio came up. The supervisor turned to Mangum.

"Yes, Sir?"

"I have a meeting with Chairman Febo. Take me to her."

"Yes, Sir. And the dogs?"

"They're with me."

"Yes, Sir."

The supervisor led them deeper into the building. They took an elevator to the top floor, where he led them past the more intrusive security check on this floor, then down to the end of the hall, to the outer office of the chairman's office.

"Guests for the chairman," the supervisor told the receptionist there.

He turned to Mangum and nodded.

"Sir."

The supervisor left, and the original guide, who had followed along, addressed the receptionist.

"Mr. Mangum and, er, guests to see the chairman."

"Please wait here, Mr. Mangum."

The receptionist went through the door into the inner office and came back within a minute.

"This way, Mr. Mangum."

Isabela Febo got up and came around her desk to greet Bert Mangum. She had agreed to this meeting because Bert Mangum was the most successful operative the Agency ever had. He had consistently carried out the most dangerous missions, had proposed working solutions to nearly intractable problems, had been, in fact, the go-to man for the Agency's most difficult assignments.

If Bert Mangum wanted to meet with her, she was more than willing.

The dogs were a curious addition to the agenda. She had no idea what was going on with them, but presumably Mangum would tell her.

As Mangum walked into the room, Febo had to admit they were beautiful dogs, and incredibly well-behaved. In completely strange surroundings, they looked around curiously, but remained at heel and silent.

Mangum himself Febo had never met before. He was darkly handsome and had a dangerous edge to him. She could certainly see in him the person who had pulled off such dangerous missions.

"Mr. Mangum, it's good to meet you. I've read so many of your reports, I feel I already know you."

"It's good to meet you, Madam Chairman. Thank you for taking this meeting."

Febo nodded and waved to her side seating arrangement.

"Let's have a seat."

Mangum sat down across from Febo, while Sam and Jules jumped up on the armchairs to either side and sat on the seat cushions.

"I must say, Mr. Mangum. No one has ever brought their pets to a meeting with me."

"And nobody still has, Madam Chairman. My companions here are not dogs. They are shape-shifting aliens."

"I find that very hard to believe, Mr. Mangum."

Sam changed into his persona of Carl Ikenberry, the station manager of Crossroads, and Jules changed into his persona of Jack Sturm, the head of the Abelon Intelligence Service.

"And yet it is true, Madam Chairman," Sam said.

Febo rocked back in her chair and her eyes widened. She looked back and forth between the two, then seemed to regain her balance.

"Perhaps some explanation is in order, Mr. Mangum."

"Indeed, Madam Chairman. Fifteen years ago or so, my first mission for the Agency was a courier run. The ship developed system problems, and the crew made a heroic effort to reach and land on a survivable planet. The cascade failure resulted in a crash landing on the planet. The crew was killed, but I survived in the VIP emergency survival pod.

"That planet is populated by aliens, Madam Chairman. They kept me alive during the time I waited for a rescue ship, called from the surviving ship's radio. When I was rescued from the planet, Sam here came along."

Mangum gestured to Sam.

"Ultimately, Sam had a child, Jules."

Mangum gestured to Jules.

"They have assisted me and other Agency personnel with carrying out our missions for the past fifteen years."

"If I might demonstrate, Madam Chairman," Sam said.

"Please. Go ahead, Sam."

"Thank you, ma'am. It was a simple matter for Bert

Mangum to penetrate General Spaceship of Mystik's headquarters as Jeremy Faust."

Sam flowed down to the floor and up around Mangum, turning him into the heavier Faust, even to the color of his hair.

"Heavens," Febo said.

Sam flowed back down to the floor and back into his chair as Carl Ikenberry. He stood and walked over to the ventilator grille on the side wall of Febo's office.

"It was also easy to get around on Crossroads and surveil the various locations used by the RDT organization."

Sam oozed through the ventilator grille and disappeared.

"Where did he go, Mr. Mangum?"

"Anywhere he wants, Madam Chairman."

After a minute, Sam oozed out of the ventilator grille on the other side of the office and walked back over to the seating arrangement.

"The Crossroads police and Mr. Ikenberry were impressed to think that Jack Sturm, the head of the Abelon Intelligence Service, was present on Crossroads."

Sam shifted to the persona of Jack Sturm. Febo looked back and forth between Jules and Sam, both now looking like Jack Sturm.

"I see. That is quite remarkable."

"Oh, but there is more, Madam Chairman. Bert Mangum sent me on the most recent mission to Vauxhall. I had no trouble penetrating the palace grounds as a deer."

Jules jumped down from his chair and shifted to his deer persona. He then shifted to his persona of a captain in the Vauxhall palace guard.

"Of course, an officer in the palace guard has no trouble moving around the palace. And it was Bert Mangum himself who confronted King Albert XIV in his office."

Sam shifted to his persona of Bert Mangum. Febo looked back and forth between Jules and the real Bert Mangum seated across from her.

Febo smiled at Mangum as Jules resumed his Jack Sturm persona and sat down.

"Well, now I know how you were always able to penetrate the most secure facilities, carry out the most dangerous missions, and be successful, Mr. Mangum. You cheated."

"In espionage, Madam Chairman, if it works, it's not cheating."

Febo nodded.

"I agree, Mr. Mangum."

Febo gestured to both Sam and Jules.

"The efforts of both of you gentlemen have been much to the Association's benefit over the years. I thank you both."

"You are most welcome. Madam Chairman. And having demonstrated our bona fides, we come to the substance of today's meeting."

"Please. Continue."

"Yes, Madam Chairman. Mr. Mangum and his friends in the Agency have designed an attack ship of outstanding capabilities to defend against Vauxhall's more feeble designs under way. The big problem with that is that the full capabilities of this ship are not within the performance envelope of a human pilot. They are within the performance envelope of us, however."

Febo looked to Mangum and raised an eyebrow.

"Sam and Jules have much faster reaction times than a human, ma'am. They are stronger. They are also fully functional to accelerations exceeding nine gravities."

"My word."

"Yes, Madam Chairman," Sam said. "Humanly piloted

vehicles will not be capable of fighting against the new fighters Mr. Mangum and his friends have designed. As long as they are piloted by us, that is."

"But there are only two of you."

"Madam Chairman, there is, within Association space, a planet of tens of millions of us. I have been in contact with my fellows. We will man your fighters."

"Why? Why would you do this for us?"

"I have for fifteen years observed you, Madam Chairman. You humans. I have observed your government. Your society. Your values. Your actions, even in the most trying of times. Jules and I saw the society, the government, and the values of Earth, during the mission to rescue Dr. Varley. Jules also saw the society, the government, and the values of Vauxhall, during the mission to acquire the revocation of the letters of marque against Mr. Mangum and others.

"We have reported what we have seen back to our people, and they have considered the issue. We know what our fate would be under a system such as Vauxhall, Madam Chairman, and we are not amused. So as you move toward a confrontation with the monarchies of the core worlds, we will not simply stand by and watch you vie with these perverted systems in an existential struggle.

"You are playing a game for all the marbles, Madam Chairman, and we will stand with you, and with our friends."

"And you can speak for your people, Sam?"

"I have been named Ambassador Plenipotentiary to the Association of Planets, Madam Chairman."

Mangum started at that. He'd had no idea what had gone on between Sam and his fellows back home, and this was news to him. Febo seemed less taken aback, and shifted gears effortlessly.

"Well, Mr. Ambassador. Let us talk terms then. There is always a give and take in any good relationship. You offer us a great deal. What can we offer you?"

"We wish to be a protected planet of the Association, but not an Association planet itself. Association citizens have the right of free travel among Association planets, but we wish to retain our planet as it is, and not have it be developed along the human model."

"That seems more than fair, Mr. Ambassador. Yet a protected planet, in that the Association will protect you from military adventurism. That also seems fair, since a number of you will be serving in our military. What else?"

"We would like free travel within the Association, Madam Chairman. Not to be Association citizens. To vote and the like. But to be able to travel among humans. To have jobs here. To live here, perhaps for extended periods, as Jules and I have done. We realize that arrangement is somewhat non-bilateral, but we doubt humans would want free travel on our planet anyway. Our natural habitat is, in human terms, a primordial swamp."

"So not of interest to us anyway, Mr. Ambassador. But I would have to impose a condition on this provision."

"Yes, Madam Chairman?"

"You are not to use your shape-changing abilities to impersonate real persons, or to commit fraud or other crimes in the guise of another person."

"Agreed, Madam Chairman. That is not part of our culture anyway, and we have done nothing of the kind outside of our Agency missions."

"That's different, Mr. Ambassador. Our Agency operatives often operate outside local laws, with dispensation from their own superiors. That is, therefore, not an exception to the general rule."

"Agreed, Madam Chairman."

"Then I think we have the makings of a deal, Mr. Ambassador. A formal treaty. I will have something drawn up. But what do we call you? What do we call your planet?"

"We have given that some thought, Madam Chairman. The Japanese word for alien, in English characters, is Erian. We propose that our planet be called Erias in English, and our people be called Erians. That retains the meaning, while sidestepping the connotations."

"Very well, Mr. Ambassador. I will be in touch with you when we have a treaty ready."

"Thank you, Madam Chairman. I look forward to signing it on behalf of all Erians."

Febo stood up, and so did Mangum, Sam, and Jules.

"Thank you, Mr. Ambassador."

"Thank you, Madam Chairman."

They shook hands. Then Febo shook hands with Mangum and Jules in turn.

"Thank you, Mr. Mangum, for the most interesting meeting I think I have ever had."

"Madam Chairman."

"And thank you, Jules."

"Thank you, Madam Chairman."

Mangum held the leashes up, and Sam and Jules extended a tendril through the collars and took up their golden doodle personas again.

"Remarkable," Febo said.

Called by Febo's pocket beeper, her receptionist opened the door and stood in the doorway.

"This way, Mr. Mangum."

Mangum nodded to Febo and left, the dogs perfectly

behaved as before. The receptionist closed the door behind them, and Febo went back around to sit at her desk.

"Well, that doesn't happen every day," Febo muttered. "How extraordinary."

Once back at The 909, Mangum brought it up with Sam.

"Ambassador Plenipotentiary, Sam?"

"That is the correct term, is it not, Bert?"

"Oh, yes. That's the correct term for someone with extraordinary powers to negotiate a deal. But for a whole planet? For an entire race of sentient beings?"

Sam shrugged.

"Well, someone had to do it."

A Plan Comes Together

"So where we at, Bert?" Serp Kendall asked at their next meeting.

"Things are moving along, Serp. Sam has negotiated a treaty with the Association of Planets. He and Chairman Febo will sign it soon. That treaty means the aliens – now called Erians – will assist us by piloting the attack ships and assuming other military roles for which they are most suited."

"Great. Congratulations, Sam."

"Thank you, Serp. We are most pleased by it."

"And the attack ships are in production now. Just a case of getting the right modules together. Those will be getting deployed to the heavy cruisers soon."

"What about *Ladyhawke,* Bert? I wasn't kidding that she would be a formidable opponent with some modular stuff and a few attack ships."

"There'll be enough units for that, too, Serp. We are keeping our options open for the mission."

"The mission?" Portnoy asked.

"We're going to try to get some serious opposition to the current regime going on Vauxhall."

"You sending *Ladyhawke,* Bert?" Kendall asked.

"That's the plan so far, Serp."

"Then you better let Emmet know. Isn't he coming up on the end of his two years' commitment?"

"Yep. Good point. I'll take care of it."

"Who's going to Vauxhall, Bert?"

"I was thinking you and Phyllis, Claude. Probably Jules, too."

"Will Judy Blunt be available?" Portnoy asked.

"I don't think so, Claude. She's dropped off our radar. We haven't been able to reach her."

"I'll take that assignment, Bert," Jules said.

"You, Jules?"

"Yes. I think I know where she is."

"Very well. You guys surprise me every day anymore."

"What else goes on this mission?" Portnoy asked.

"Narlaxatrophine-II. Lots of it. And some modular factories for making more."

"You know what else you need to send, Bert? Weapons. Infantry weapons. The kingdoms all control guns pretty hard. They bleat about it being a safety issue, and it is, I guess. For them. But any group of revolutionaries will have a hard time being properly armed."

"The other thing I think you should send, Bert?"

"Yes, Sam?"

"Erians. A few hundred of us. We make great shock troops. We're bulletproof. And when we kill the front lines, we can stop and eat them, which is going to make everybody else run away."

"How do we manage that on *Ladyhawke*, Sam?"

"I can check on that, Bert," Kendall said. "I think there's some standard barracks containers. Latch 'em to *Ladyhawke* and you get as much bunk space as you need."

Dent looked up from her display.

"I got 'em, Serp. One container has like eight bunk rooms, with up to six people per room. Figure forty-eight people to a container."

"You can double that number, Gloria," Sam said. "Or quadruple it. We like crowding. It makes us feel all warm and fuzzy. Secure."

"All right, Sam," Kendall said. "Figure a couple of those modules, then, Bert. Couple, three, four hundred guys like Sam would sure be useful to a revolution."

Mangum nodded.

"I feel a plan coming together."

Jules, in his Bert Mangum persona, walked out of the front door of The 909.

"Good afternoon, Mr. Mangum."

"Good afternoon, Steven."

The autocab he ordered from upstairs showed up, and Jules got in it and set it for the Ashur Zoo.

When he got out of the autocab, Jules switched to his Jack Sturm persona. The persona Judy Blunt was familiar with from the package drop she made for him on Vauxhall.

Jules headed for the big predator exhibits.

Jules had been watching Peggy Dawson work the big predator exhibits for a couple hours. He would sit on a viewing bench and watch her work, then, when she switched to a different enclosure, he would switch to a different viewing bench and watch some more.

At one point, he was sitting on a bench off the beaten path, around the back of one of the enclosures. When she finished in that enclosure, Peggy Dawson came out and sat on the other end of the same bench.

"What do you want?" Dawson asked, without looking at him.

"I'd like to get a message to Judy Blunt."

"She doesn't live here anymore."

"So I'd heard. It is important I get in touch with her, however."

"Why? What's going on?"

"There is going to be another mission to Vauxhall. The king and his son are building a navy they think will be able to come out here, defeat the cluster navy, and make the cluster part of Vauxhall."

"Oh, that would suck. How do you know that?"

"On our last trip, I placed a surveillance transmitter in the king's office. Slick little unit. BIE. Audio and video over QE radio, so no radio emissions. Untraceable. We've been monitoring the king's private conversations for two years."

"You placed it?"

"Yes, Ms. Dawson. My name is Jules. I am an Erian. A shape-shifting alien. You should be hearing about us soon. We are signing a treaty with the Association. In any case, it is easy to get around the palace as a palace guard officer."

Jules looked around, but they were out of sight of anyone else here behind the exhibit. He switched personas to his palace guard captain persona.

Dawson looked at him out of the side of her eye.

"That's a slick trick, Jules."

"Thank you, Ms. Dawson."

Jules switched back to Jack Sturm.

"So why Judy Blunt?"

"What we want to do is foment a revolution. Topple the king and the nobility. It will be helpful if certain assets on the king's side become, uh, unavailable at inconvenient times."

"I see. It sounds like this one is serious business."

"Oh, yes. The king and Chairman Febo are both playing for all the marbles on this one, Ms. Dawson. It will determine how the cluster is ruled into the foreseeable future. We have a choice. Ms. Blunt and I are in a position to select the future we want and make it happen."

Dawson nodded.

"Who else is on this mission, Jules?"

"I and a number of my fellow aliens, Mr. Portnoy, Ms. Stickney, and Ms. Blunt, if she is available."

"Very well, Jules. I will try to get in touch with Ms. Blunt. I will have her contact Mr. Mangum. Does that work?"

"Yes, Ms. Dawson. Mr. Mangum himself is planning this mission."

Dawson nodded once, got up, and went back into the exhibit.

Jules waited several minutes, then left the zoo and took an autocab back to The 909.

When Jules got back to The 909, it was toward the end of the work day. Mangum came out from the office to consider what to do about supper this evening.

When he saw Jules, he was interested.

"How did your trip go, Jules?"

"Very well, Bert. You should be hearing from Ms. Blunt."

"Really. How did you manage that?"

"I know her real identity, Bert. I had met her, of course, on Vauxhall, and I once saw her here in Ashur. I stressed to her the importance of this mission, and the dangers of Vauxhall attacking the cluster militarily."

Jules did not reveal Blunt's true identity, and Mangum did not ask. The business they were in demanded discretion at all times, and if Jules knew her identity, Mangum didn't need to.

"Well, that's excellent work, Jules. I think we should all go out to Marceau's tonight to celebrate. You can go as Sturm, and Sam can go as Ikenberry."

"That would be fun, Bert," Sam said. "We like their food a lot, since we figured out the onion problem, but it would be fun to actually eat it at the restaurant."

Mangum nodded.

"We should figure out some last names for you fellows, though. Sam and Jules won't work long term. There aren't enough first names in all human languages together to give all Erians a unique, or at least usably rare, identifier."

"Understood, Bert. I had thought of Hawker, which is similar to 'auctor,' the Latin word for someone who makes things happen. As my son – sort of; child, anyway – Jules could take the same last name."

"Sam Hawker and Jules Hawker?"

Mangum shrugged.

"That works, I think."

"We also need to think about changing our appearance, Bert. For our normal personas. It would be inappropriate under the treaty for us to continue to use the appearances of Jack Sturm and Carl Ikenberry as our personas."

"Well, you can mix and match parts from various people, Sam. You guys have enough different personas by now to create your own, I would think."

"We've been working on that, Bert. What do you think of this one?"

Sam changed persona to a new person, someone Mangum had never met. Someone who probably never existed. He was a bit on the tall side, of an appropriate weight, and with a serious but friendly demeanor. Just the sort of person one would expect to be an ambassador plenipotentiary.

"Maybe a touch older, Sam. Aim for sixty or so. A little gray at the temples and above the ears, perhaps. A few more facial creases, especially the smile lines."

Sam adjusted his appearance a little, and Mangum nodded.

"There you go. I think that works. What about you, Jules?"

"Similar, for the family resemblance, Bert."

Jules shifted persona to one that did in fact bear a family resemblance to Sam's, but with darker coloring and somewhat sharper features. His (fictional) mother must have been a beauty, to result in those facial features in combination with Sam's.

"A little younger, I think, Jules. Mid to late thirties would be right, I think."

Jules adjusted.

"There you go. I think that's perfect."

Stavros walked in from the office then.

"Hi, hon," Mangum said. "Have you met Sam and Jules Hawker?"

"Sam and Jules Hawker? Oh! Sam and Jules. Oh, those I like. These your new, unique personas, Sam?"

"Yes, Elina. We've touched them up quite a bit further from where we got with you earlier. What do you think?"

"They're excellent, Sam. Perfect."

Mangum looked over to Stavros.

"Jules managed contact with Judy Blunt. She's on board for the mission."

"Wow. Nice job, Jules."

"Thank you, Elina."

"So we're all going out to Marceau's to celebrate. You, me, the ambassador, and his son."

"Oh, what fun. Have you let them know?"

"Yes, our table will be ready at seven."

"I'll go get ready."

"Good evening, Mr. Mangum. Ms. Stavros."

"Good evening, Honoré. I'd like you to meet Ambassador Hawker and his son."

Marceau's was the premier restaurant in the capital city of the wealthiest of the six star nations of the cluster. It was not Honoré's first encounter with an ambassador by a long shot.

"Mr. Ambassador. Mr. Hawker. Welcome to Marceau's."

"Thank you, Honoré," Sam said in the measured mellifluous baritone of his ambassador persona.

"Right this way, Mr. Ambassador, everyone."

Honoré seated them at Mangum's normal table, diagonally opposite the door into the dining room, in the corner, next to the rear exit. Mangum and Stavros sat with their backs to the wall out of habit, and Sam and Jules sat with their backs to the room.

"Honoré, my son and I are both allergic to raw onions. If you could take special care on that matter, I would appreciate it."

"Of course, Mr. Ambassador. I will see to it personally."

"Thank you, Honoré."

There had been some back and forth on some of the wording, but the treaty negotiations had been straightforward. Both sides knew what they wanted from the agreement, and both sides knew just how important each item was to themselves and the other.

Mangum and Stavros had been over it, as well as Kendall and Schofield, Portnoy and Stickney, and Dent and Varley, all at Sam's request. Sam had also sent the agreement back to Erias for validation from his fellows back home.

The big day finally came, and Sam made the trip to the executive building of the Association of Planets. The big government car pulled up at The 909, and Sam, alone, got in the car for the trip to the signing ceremony.

At Mangum's suggestion, Sam had had business cards made. What to call the planet Erias was a matter of discussion.

"How about republic, Sam? It distinguishes it from any form of hereditary rule, like a kingdom or empire, but it's generic enough to leave things open beyond that."

Sam nodded.

"From the Latin 'res publica,' meaning 'public matters.' I like it, Bert. That's what I'll do."

The presentation of his business card at the security checkpoint of the executive building worked a similar magic to Mangum's and Stavros'.

Sam presented his card to the supervisor at the checkpoint as he had seen Mangum do. The supervisor glanced at the card.

REPUBLIC OF ERIAS

Sam Hawker
Ambassador Plenipotentiary

"Of course, Mr. Ambassador. Right this way, please."

The checkpoint supervisor did not lead Sam to the upper floor office of the chairman, however. Instead, he led Sam to a formal public room on the first floor. The press was there, and there were cameras and all. They went into a private room behind the dais where the chairman waited.

Sam walked up to the chairman and shook her hand.

"Good morning, Madam Chairman."

"Good morning, Mr. Ambassador. That's a particularly compelling persona you adopted for today."

"Thank you, Madam Chairman. With a lack of context, appearances can be very important. And, per the treaty, it is not a copy of any living person."

Febo nodded.

"Will this be your public persona going forward now, Mr.

Ambassador?"

"Yes, Madam Chairman. Continuity, too, is important."

"Excellent. Well, we're about set to start. Are you ready, Mr. Ambassador?"

"Yes, Madam Chairman. At your convenience."

Febo waved him forward, and the doormen opened both doors into the signing room. They entered together, and each went to a podium.

Sam had been warned there would be short public statements by the chairman and himself before the formal signing of the treaty, and he had reviewed hundreds of such speeches in the prior week. Most had been almost empty of content but high on fellowship and goodwill, so he copied that.

Sam was pleased to note the chairman followed the same formula in her own remarks.

"Ambassador Hawker, distinguished guests, people of the Association and of Erias, welcome.

"Today, the Association of Planets and the Republic of Erias will sign a treaty setting forward the relationship between our two nations. We have been cooperating on many matters over the last fifteen years, to the lasting benefit of us both. It is now time to deepen that relationship – that friendship – with a formal treaty between our nations.

"Therefore, I ask you to welcome Ambassador Hawker as he and I sign this treaty of enduring friendship between the people of the Association and Erias."

Febo stepped back from her podium and turned to Sam, applauding. The room took it up. Sam nodded to her, and, as the applause subsided, stepped forward to his own podium. He delivered his own remarks in a sonorous baritone.

"Thank you, Chairman Febo, distinguished guests.

"It is my deep pleasure this morning to act on behalf of the people of Erias in signing this treaty. Earlier today, I reflected on the relationship between the Association of Planets and the Republic of Erias as it has developed over the last fifteen years, and my own role in that development. I also considered the future, and the deepening of that relationship, with the hope that I may spend many more years watching our relationship prosper.

"Thank you, Madam Chairman, for this opportunity to best serve both our peoples."

Sam stepped back from his podium and turned to Febo, applauding. Once again, the room took it up.

Febo waved to the table, and she and Sam both walked to their spots at the center table and were seated by aides.

Two copies of the treaty were produced, in leather folders, and one laid before each of them. Febo and Sam both opened the folders, then took up pens and signed their copy. Aides then swapped the folders between them, and they each signed the other copy.

Sam and Febo stood and shook hands while the room applauded.

The first aliens humanity had found had come out into the open.

Erias

"Either Jules or I need to go to Erias, Bert."

"Actually go there?"

"Yes. We need to be able to communicate all we've learned, before Erians leave the planet to join your forces. It may affect who wishes to go and who doesn't. We can't do that in the English language over the QE link."

Mangum nodded.

"OK, Sam. I can see that. Who do you think it should be?"

"Well, it could be either of us. One of us should go to Erias, and the other can be learning to pilot the attack ships. They can communicate that knowledge to the pilots once they get here."

"Then you should probably go to Erias, Sam, and Jules learn the attack ships."

"Why that choice, Bert? I don't necessarily disagree, but why do you say so?"

"Because the Navy people are going to have real concerns about putting someone who is apparently sixty years old in an attack ship, but someone who looks a fit thirty-five probably not so much."

"Ah. I see. It will just make things simpler. For us, too, it will probably be simpler if I go to Erias. People there know and remember me, where none of them have met Jules."

Stavros looked up from her display.

"Oh, can we go, too, Bert? I think it would be fun to see Erias."

"Both of us gone at the same time, Elina? Who runs field operations while we're in hyperspace?"

"Ouch. Yeah, that's probably not a good idea. And I would

just as soon not be separated for a month."

Mangum nodded. Stavros was pregnant again, and the separation would not be welcome.

"It's not much different than the bayous down in the delta of the Ashur River, Elina. Except the whole planet is like that."

"Ooo. Could we go visit the bayous sometime, Bert? That sounds like it would be really nice. Also a good vacation spot for my fellow Erians when they get homesick."

"Sure, Sam. I should have thought of it before this. We'll go at some point."

"Thanks, Bert. That would be most pleasant."

The troop ship APN *Lester Cawley* dropped out of hyperspace at the hyperspace limit of the Erias system. She made for the planet at one gravity.

The crew had been briefed that they were picking up a thousand aliens from what had been previously considered an unpopulated planet. That was weird enough.

The food stocking for this trip was weird, too. Eggs, sausages, canned mixed fruit, hamburgers and buns with all the fixings, and frozen ham and pineapple pizzas. Tens of thousands of them.

Oh, and no onions were to be served unless they were grilled first.

The crew casually referred to the ship as the *Less Crazy* out of hearing of the captain and senior officers.

But it seemed this trip was more crazy than usual.

"Have you picked up the beacon of the crashed ship on the surface, Captain?" Sam asked.

"Yes, Mr. Ambassador," Captain Denholm Schenk said.

"Very well, Captain. There is solid ground there, just east of that position. The small shuttle will land there and drop me off. Then the shuttle can return to the ship. You are to return to that spot in five days' time to begin ferrying operations with both large transfer shuttles. It will be two round trips for both shuttles."

"Yes, Mr. Ambassador."

It had been impressed upon Schenk that Ambassador was the equivalent of full admiral for this trip, and Ambassador Hawker was getting his instructions directly from Chairman Febo, so whatever the Ambassador wanted, the Ambassador got.

The shuttle was coming down in the clearing next to the crashed courier ship. It was overgrown with vines and had clearly been there a while. Surrounding the clearing, the ground sloped away into a morass of swampy jungle growth. Alien vegetation grew in the standing murky waters, and vines hung from the trees.

"Holy crap. Look at that shit."

"Yeah. Make sure you set down on the highest dry ground you got. I don't want to end up living here."

"And we're just supposed to drop this guy off here for five days? A sixty year old ambassador guy in suit and tie and all?"

"Them's the orders."

"Damn."

The shuttle touched down and the engines spooled down to idle.

"We've landed, Mr. Ambassador. You're free to exit the shuttle now."

Sam touched the transmit stud on his seat in the small passenger compartment.

"Thank you, gentlemen."

Sam got up and went over to the cabin door. The loadmaster cycled the door and he stepped out of the shuttle. He walked away from the shuttle to clear it for takeoff, heading directly out into the standing water.

When Sam was far enough away, he waved to the shuttle. The engines spooled up and the shuttle lifted, heading back to the APN *Lester Cawley*.

"That's it? We leave him there?"

"Yeah. Hey, they told me he's one of the aliens, too. He's home now. I figure he can handle it."

"Yeah. 'There's no place like home.' In this case, at least, that's true. Criminy."

With the shuttle gone, Sam shifted into his natural state, an amorphous brownish-orange goo, and moved further out into the deep swamp. His fellows surged toward him, and he sent out tendrils to touch the dozen closest. They in turn sent out tendrils to touch others, and the neurologically interconnected mass of them grew and grew.

When over a hundred thousand of the Erians were neurologically linked, Sam began to tell his story.

The story of fifteen years of living among the humans.

It took Sam the better part of four days to communicate his story, even at the speeds the aliens could communicate neurologically. There was just so much to tell. About human society, human language, humans' way of thinking about things. The things humans did that originally seemed so crazy to Sam. The things that still did.

There followed the reactions of his listeners as they discussed everything he had told. Much of it was amazement that humans had managed to handle everyday things, like being properly fed. Their lives seemed so chaotic. Their decisions so irrational. Yet they seemed to make it all work for most things.

The human failures were cataclysmic, however. The prospect of impending war put point to that. And the implications of humans at war finding their planet were not lost on the aliens.

In the end, Sam had many more volunteers than he needed or could take. The group decided who should go as they decided everything else.

Rationally.

The big crew transfer shuttle aligned itself carefully with the landing zone as it came down. It wouldn't have to be off by much to get bogged down here.

Once down and the engines at idle, the loadmaster opened the door. They were supposed to pick up two hundred and fifty people here? From where?

And then they came, walking out of the bog. Rank upon rank of them. Young men all, of varying appearance and ethnicities. All dressed in Association of Planets Navy officer uniforms, mostly lieutenants, with a smattering of lieutenant commanders.

At their head was Ambassador Hawker. He walked up to the shuttle door, and through it, with a nod to the loadmaster.

"Thank you, Chief."

"Yes, Mr. Ambassador."

The men all took their seats, filing down the rows, and buckled up for the flight, in complete silence. Without any guidance, or direction, or hectoring. It was unnerving.

The loadmaster shrugged. Everybody's different, and aliens are differenter, he guessed.

With everybody seated and strapped in, the loadmaster gave the signal to the cockpit, the shuttle's engines spooled up, and they were away.

When they came back down for the third load, the second shuttle having taken one load in between, the scene changed somewhat. The men boarding the shuttle were now Association of Planets Marines, in Marine Combat Uniform (MCU). Most were privates, though there was the mix of NCOs and officers you would expect for that many enlisted.

Once again, they filed into their seats, sat and buckled in. This time the loadmaster just shrugged and sent the Ready signal to the cockpit.

"How are things working out with our arrivals, Jerry?"

"Good, Sir. They seem to have settled in well. We haven't had any incidents at all. And they loved the ham and pineapple pizza last night. Breakfast this morning, too."

"Sausages, eggs, fruit cups."

"Yes, Sir. They dug right in. Quiet bunch, though. They don't talk much. They do stay in contact with each other, though."

Captain Schenk nodded.

"In my briefing, they said the aliens communicate with each other neurologically if they can touch each other. They're probably talking up a storm. We just can't hear it."

"Yes, Sir. They also like the showers a great deal."

Like any troop ship, the APN *Lester Cawley* had large communal shower rooms.

"The showers?"

"Yes, Sir. They block the drains, get the water a couple inches deep and then lie in it. In their natural state. Looks a lot like a beef stew with paprika. Brown and orangeish. They take turns lying in it."

"Well, you saw what the planet looked like, Jerry. They spend their whole lives lying in shallow water. A lot like home, I guess."

"Yes, Sir."

The executive officer paused.

"Sir, is it true what they say? That these aliens can take high gee forces, and are crack shots? That they are going to fly the new attack ships?"

"That's what I was told, Jerry. For the Navy guys at least. Those ships can take nine gees, and they just fly 'em like nothing's going on."

"Wow. Are they really Navy, though, Sir?"

"The officers got their commissions like anybody else, Jerry. First guy treats one of 'em like they're something less than their rank, they're going to have the world fall on them. Those are my orders."

"Yes, Sir."

"Yeah. And those Marines? They're going to Vauxhall, where they're going to cause trouble."

"Cause trouble, Sir?"

"Yeah. Turns out these guys are bulletproof. Five hundred bulletproof Marines? Yeah, that's trouble."

"Yes, Sir. I can certainly agree with that."

It was just five days back to Mardouk for the X-3-equipped APN *Lester Cawley*.

The Navy personnel were dropped at the Association of Planets Navy facility east of Ashur, on the other side of the spaceport.

The Marines were dropped at the Association of Planets Marine Corps camp a hundred miles from the capital.

Before going back down to the planet, Sam stopped by the captain's office to say goodbye.

"I'm leaving for the planet on the last shuttle, Captain. I just wanted to take this opportunity to thank you for your performance on this mission."

"I appreciate that, Mr. Ambassador, but, truth be told, it was the least troublesome transfer I've ever handled. No fights, no complaining, no trouble. You've got some great people there, Ambassador, no doubt about it."

Sam almost choked up at this approval of his fellows.

"Thank you, Captain. And good spacing to you."

They shook hands, and Sam got on the last shuttle to the planet, the small shuttle – the admiral's launch – for the trip down to the Ashur Shuttleport.

Sam took an autocab from the shuttleport to The 909.

"Hi, everybody. I'm home."

Pilot School

The instructors at the Association of Planets Navy Pilot School did not quite know what to do about their newest student. In his late thirties, he was too old. He had never flown even an airplane before. And he was the son of the Erias Ambassador to the Association of Planets.

Some had him pegged as the pampered son of a diplomat, given special status as a gift to the ambassador by the chairman.

Others weren't so sure. He breezed through ground school, covering four weeks of material in four days.

That was not typical of even the best pilots.

Their orders were explicit. Push this candidate through the program as fast as he could go. As fast as his own pace dictated. Not to be stuck to standard schedules and timeframes.

And, whether you agree with them or not, orders is orders.

At the beginning of his second week of pilot school, Jules was training in the simulator. A full cockpit mockup, with all the displays and gauges of the actual attack ship, and programmed to respond as the attack ship, in terms of acceleration, gunnery, and fuel consumption.

It was hard to have any expectations of this student, who had no flight experience but had aced ground school in record time. The more senior instructors did not have preconceived notions of his performance, because they knew that rare talents came along once in a while.

You just had to try them and see.

Jules released the docking latches and applied just over one gee of thrust to the engines. With the latches free and the mother ship accelerating at one gee, the attack ship pulled forward and free of the docking hooks.

Jules eased the attack ship away from the mother ship, getting distance before increasing the thrust. Not a good idea to go cooking the mother ship in his wash.

Once clear, Jules slammed the throttles forward, going to nine gees, speeding toward the attacking formation. Four enemy attack ships, making for his mother ship at three gees of acceleration.

Jules kept up a random variation on the nose thrusters, aiming not to be wherever their fire at him had been aimed when it got there. His ship jinked wildly in space, but always around the attack vector.

Jules' attack ship shot through the enemy formation and continued accelerating toward the enemy carrier. Its point-defense guns fired continuously, but he kept up his jinking flight. There were two minor hits on nonessential systems. He noted them and pressed on.

At the last moment, Jules dropped three missiles, then turned his ship ninety degrees to his velocity, adding just enough side velocity to skim over the top of the carrier.

Jules knew he would miss the carrier, and was concentrating on fighting his missiles. They jinked like demons as they bored in on the carrier. Point-defense took out one missile, but, given his delayed launch, the other two survived to hit the carrier amidships, and she broke up.

END OF SIMULATION the panel read.

That had been fun.

"Well, he got the carrier, but he basically ignored the enemy attack ships."

"Oh, yeah? Take another look."

"Wait. This can't be. Two solid kill shots on all four of the enemy attackers? How the hell did he do that? He went by them with twelve gravities of closing acceleration, plus all their combined velocity."

"I don't know, but he did it. We need to see how this fellow performs under real gravities."

"You mean...?"

"Yeah. Move him to the real ships. Now. None of our experienced pilots was able to do that in the simulator, even using nine gees, which they can't withstand in the real ship anyway. This guy doesn't need simulator time. He needs ship time."

"All right. I guess I agree. I mean, if we can't put him in a real ship, we're gonna have to ground all our other pilots, because he just roasted them all."

"I'll cut the orders."

A clerical error had delayed Jules' officer's commission, but it had gone through by the time he arrived on the APN *Dark Star,* one of the heavy cruisers built by General Spaceship of Mystik for the Republic of Villacqua Navy.

Jules therefore reported aboard the *Dark Star* as Commander Jules Hawker, and his persona was in uniform.

"So what are we doing, now, Sir?"

"We put Commander Hawker in an attack ship and run him against the exercises and see how he does. Oh, and turn the gee-limiter off."

"We're gonna put this guy who's never flown anything into one of the new attack ships and turn him loose without the gee-limiter, Sir?"

"That's what my orders, say, Mark, and I'm not going to buck orders from a four-star admiral."

"Well, no, Sir. I wouldn't suggest it. But it does seem reckless. Or at least ill-advised."

"Yes, but I wasn't consulted, so we do it their way."

"Yes, Sir. As you say, Sir."

Jules crawled into the cockpit through the access tube of the docking cradle. The cockpit was the same as that in the simulator, except this one had the modified flight couch.

For such a high-gee attack ship, the flight station was not a seat but a couch, because all acceleration was in the same direction – aft, against the thrust of the engines. Even when turning, because turns were made by pointing the ship in a different direction and letting the main thrusters add side velocity.

So gravity in the cockpit was always toward the floor.

A normal flight couch would be a cushioned recliner-like couch. For the Erians, though, Sam had specified a cushion with a raised lip around the outside. This would allow the pilot to assume his natural state and lay within the raised lip in semi-fluid form.

Jules climbed into the couch and assumed his natural state, then extruded tentacles and hands to the controls.

"We're ready whenever you are, Commander."

Jules extended a short tendril with a mouth on the end.

"Hawker here. Prepare to launch."

"*Dark Star* confirms. Ready for launch."

Jules released the docking latches and applied just over one gee of thrust to the engines. With the latches free and *Dark Star* accelerating at one gee, the attack ship pulled forward and free of the docking hooks.

This time was different than the simulator, though. Jules could feel the vibrations from the thrusters, the clank of the latches releasing, and the scrape as the ship pulled clear of the docking hooks.

Jules eased the attack ship away from *Dark Star,* getting distance before increasing the thrust.

Once clear, Jules slammed the throttles forward, speeding toward the attacking formation. Where the simulator gave him nine gees at full throttle, this actual ship was making more like nine-point-four gees.

This attacking formation was a simulation, as before. The difference was that Jules was fighting in the actual attack ship. The readouts on the attacking ships were fake, generated by the computer simulation program, but Jules' ship was real, as were the maneuvers he made.

Jules actually found flying the attack ship easier than the simulator. He could feel the actual accelerations, feel the engines' response to his inputs, feel the ship strain to turn when he used the nose thrusters.

As in the simulator, Jules kept up a random variation on the nose thrusters, aiming not to be wherever their fire at him had been aimed when it got there. His ship jinked wildly in space, but always around the attack vector.

Looking at the incoming attack formation, there was another difference from the one he had fought in the simulator. These ships were spaced differently. He couldn't shoot them all as he went past, because the guns could not traverse fast enough, given his rapidly increasing velocity.

The computer had changed the simulation to thwart his prior actions.

Jules considered the angles, then started the ship spinning

with the roll thrusters to port and starboard. When he passed through the enemy formation, the traverse of the guns plus the roll velocity of the ship was enough for him to get off bursts at all four of the attacking ships.

Jules broke through the attacking formation and made for the enemy carrier. It was skewing madly now, trying to escape, but such a ponderous vessel was effectively stationary to him.

Jules released a spread of three torpedoes, then stood the attack ship up on its tail, adding enough side vector to go over the top of the carrier as it turned.

The enemy carrier's turn actually hurt its chances of survival by making it harder for its point-defense to successfully engage targets. All three missiles struck home, and the carrier broke up.

END OF SIMULATION; RETURN TO CARRIER the display read.

"And now, Mark?"

"That was the most amazing thing I ever saw, Sir. Nine-point-four gees, and in control the entire time."

"And he beat the computer's jiggered spacing of the attack force."

"Yes, Sir. I wondered what he was doing rolling the ship that hard. But the traverse on the guns wasn't fast enough without it. He had to have seen that coming right off, to have reacted that fast. I doubt anyone else would have even thought of it."

The captain nodded.

"And we have a full complement of pilots coming. Five hundred of them. Enough to man every attack ship on all fifty heavy cruisers in the consortium navy."

"But he has to be a fluke, Sir. They can't all be that good."

"Did it seem like he took a long time to get the hang of it, Mark?"

"No, Sir. He acted like he'd been flying his whole life."

"Or like, for his kind, it just wasn't that hard. If that's so, all five hundred of them could be of this caliber."

"That would be amazing, Sir. If so, no one has a prayer against us."

"They'll never know what hit them, Mark. As a man sworn to protect the Association of Planets and the cluster, I am in love with this whole thing."

Jules spent five days flying two simulated missions every day, then transferred back to the surface of Mardouk on *Dark Star*'s admiral's launch.

The captain had a word with him before he left.

"Thank you, Commander. That was fun to watch."

"You're welcome, Captain. I think it will be even more fun for you to have your own people aboard, under your command, all of whom perform at that level."

"But will they Commander? Perform at that level?"

"Assuredly, Captain. I go to Ashur now to train them."

"Well, best of luck with that, Commander. Good spacing."

"Good spacing to you, Captain."

Sam and Jules both got back to Ashur on the same day. That night, Mangum, Stavros, Sam, and Jules all went out to Marceau's.

The next day, Jules went out to the Association of Planets Navy facility east of the spaceport. The five hundred pilot candidates had spent the prior evening in barracks there.

"I need one hour with the pilot candidates before you start

on them, Commander," Jules said to the Lieutenant Commander who ran the ground school classes.

"Of course, Sir."

"And then I think you might want to give them the ground school test right away."

"Without any training, Sir?"

"No, after my one hour of training."

Jules shrugged.

"We don't learn the same way as humans, Commander."

"Yes, Sir."

Jules stood at the front of the room as four hundred fifty lieutenants and fifty lieutenant commanders filed into the room and silently took their seats. The lieutenant commanders would be wing commanders, one to each of the fifty cruisers in the consortium navy.

When they were all seated, Jules took a straightback chair from the front of the room, put it in the aisle between the two front rows and sat down. He held hands with the pilot candidates on either side. All the pilot candidates maintained some sort of contact with each other through the whole room, with one person in each row reaching forward to touch someone in the row in front of them.

When they were all connected, Jules began to train them – in ground school, simulator, and real attack ship – at the speed of their kind.

"They've just been sitting there for an hour, Sir."

"Yes, they can communicate with each other without talking. Much faster, I've heard. Let them go, Commander. When Commander Hawker is done with them, do as he suggested and give them all the final exam for ground school. Let's see what happens."

"Yes, Sir."

All five hundred pilot candidates passed the ground school exam with high marks and moved on to the simulators.

Within days, the heavy cruisers APN *Dark Star,* APN *Variable Star,* APN *Dwarf Star,* and APN *Morning Star* had their entire attack wings aboard.

The APN *Lester Cawley* took the remainder of the new pilots to their assigned ships, tracking down the consortium navy's other eleven heavy cruiser divisions wherever they were posted.

Within three months, the consortium navy was immune to anything Vauxhall could throw against it.

The Marines

The five hundred Erians who had been brought as members of the Association of Planets Marine Corps started out with Basic Infantry School, officers and enlisted alike. For now, they were all learning the basics.

One thing the instructors learned early on. If they took a group of fifty through some class or lecture, the next day all five hundred knew the material. From that evolved a new strategy.

They took the five hundred and divided them up into groups of fifty, then gave all ten groups a different portion of the training. The next day, all five hundred knew all ten parts of the previous day's training.

They made rapid progress, even given the Marines' rigid standards. It wasn't long before they were working on infantry maneuvers against other, experienced, Marines.

One thing Sam and Jules had done is go through the long catalog of human nightmares. Images from horror movies, illustrations from science fiction, paintings of mythical monsters. They practiced shape shifting to those shapes, then tried them on Mangum and Stavros.

Some of the creatures they tried on Mangum and Stavros seemed to scare them little or not at all, but some were very scary, indeed.

"Why is this one so scary, Bert?"

"I think it's the teeth, Sam."

"And the muscles," Elina said. "A creature like that is not going to be stopped by anything minor."

Mangum nodded.

"It's the combination, Sam. The size and musculature, and then those teeth. It's just terrifying."

When Sam and Jules had perfected all the personas that Mangum and Stavros – no shrinking violets, after all – found most terrifying, Sam took an autocab out to the Marine base and communicated them to the Erian Marine recruits there.

They were holding another exercise today. A live fire exercise of crawling up on an embedded position manned by current Marines.

"If you don't mind, Major," said Frank Everett, the Erian lieutenant colonel serving as battalion commander. "I think we're going to try something a little different today."

The major overseeing their training was nominally their superior during the training, despite his lower rank, but he had also been told to give these particular recruits their head in shaping their own training experience to use their additional capabilities.

"Have at it, Sir."

"Thank you, Major."

The five hundred recruits were crawling forward, staying below the live-fire rounds as they advanced on the enemy fortification.

When they were a hundred yards away, though, Everett stood up into the live fire, changed shape to a man-sized dinosaur-like creature with a huge mouth full of sharp teeth, and bellowed.

All five hundred members of the battalion followed suit, then ran – at close to twenty miles an hour – at the dug-in emplacement, bellowing and roaring.

The live rounds had no effect on them as they surged toward the emplacement.

The experienced Marines forming the opposition force dropped their weapons and ran for their lives.

"That was fun, Major."

"That was terrifying, Sir."

"Yes, well, I guess it depends on which side you were on."

Everett, now in human form and Marine uniform, chuckled and casually spat out a spent round.

"For us, it was a lot of fun."

Colonel Roger Treadway, the commanding officer of the Marine Training Regiment at the base, reviewed the video of the exercise with his executive officer.

"That was unexpected," he said drily.

"Yes, Sir. We were told that the Erians can shift shapes. I guess we mostly thought about it like disguises. You know, they could change to look like your grandmother or something. But this? This is terrifying."

"It certainly is. What a terrific ability. Put them in the front lines and let them rout the enemy. Everybody else can do cleanup later."

"Yes, Sir. There is the issue that our assigned red team abandoned their positions and ran for it. Do we need to do anything about that?"

"You mean something disciplinary?"

"Yes, Sir."

"No, Charlie. When a bunch of green recruits in a training exercise – ho-hum, day-to-day stuff – unexpectedly turn into bulletproof velociraptors and charge your position, I think abandoning the field is the wise and proper move. Better to live and fight another day."

"Yes, Sir."

"Damn," Treadway said, looking back to the display. "Put them in the front line, and you could clean up with a battalion of kindergarten teachers. That's really something."

"Yes, Sir."

"Let me write the report on this one, Charlie. There's some things I want to get in there."

"Of course, Sir."

"In the meantime, we need to reshape the training yet again. These boys don't need training on how to attack a fixed position, and they sure as hell don't need to be hardened up anymore than they already are. But we still need to work on maneuver, reconnaissance, all that sort of thing. And all the support roles and weapons systems."

"Yes, Sir. I'll get together with the trainers and work on that."

"Excellent."

Treadway looked back to the display.

"Damn. That's some nice shit right there."

Dropping things from the training meant they could include other things. Lots of other things, given that all the Erians learned whatever they taught anybody.

Each group of fifty Erians was given different courses. All together, they were given every training course the Marines had. Logistics, sniper, heavy weapons, communications, armor. It went on and on.

By the end of the month, all five hundred of them knew them all.

Sam received a call request from Chairman Febo. He shifted

from his utility persona to the Ambassador Hawker persona and accepted the call.

"Good afternoon, Madam Chairman."

"Good afternoon, Mr. Ambassador. I hope I'm not interrupting anything."

"Not at all, Madam Chairman. How can I help you?"

"I just wanted to get back to you and thank you again, Mr. Ambassador. I have received reports on your fellow Erians in our pilot training and Marine infantry programs. Their instructors speak of your people in glowing terms. They are a huge addition to our capabilities."

"Thank you, Madam Chairman. We have different capabilities than humans, and, when deployed properly, it makes a more effective fighting force to have us in the mix."

"Indeed it does, Mr. Ambassador. I believe our Navy is now incapable of being effectively attacked by Vauxhall, and our Marines are the most effective infantry force anywhere."

"Very gratifying, Madam Chairman."

"And so I have a question for you, Mr. Ambassador. Your fellows in the Marines are coming up on two weeks' leave after having completed their training. Is there anything special we can do for them to show our gratitude for their service?"

"Actually, Madam Chairman, I think there is. Give them their two weeks' leave in the bayous of the Ashur River delta."

"I don't think there's enough guest housing there to handle your five hundred Erian Marines, Mr. Ambassador."

"They don't need housing, Madam Chairman. The bayous themselves will be like a vacation at home."

"Really. Well then, Mr. Ambassador, consider it done."

"Thank you, Madam Chairman."

"Where do you want us to set you down, Colonel?" the pilot

asked.

Lieutenant Colonel Frank Everett looked out over the bayous from the observer seat in the cockpit of the first of two large crew transfer shuttles.

"Anywhere you have a dry spot, Lieutenant."

"Yes, Sir. Not many of those, but we'll find one."

The pilots set the shuttles down on a raised bit of land in the middle of the bayou.

"Here you are, Sir."

"Thank you, Lieutenant. We'll see you here in two weeks."

"Yes, Sir."

The Erians got out of the shuttles and looked around in wonder. It was like a little bit of home, here on this alien world. They walked out into the water, took on their natural state, and reveled in it.

"We just leave them here?" the co-pilot asked.

"Yup. I guess they like the water."

"No shit."

Mangum, Sam, and Jules sat in the living room, looking out over the city through the big window walls of the top-floor unit in The 909. Mangum, between sleep cycles, sipped at his nightcap.

"That all worked out with the pilots and the Marines, Sam. According to the reports I'm reading anyway."

"Yes, Bert. It is most gratifying. I was pretty confident, but one can always get surprised by the unforeseen. As it is, it has worked out even better than I had hoped."

"And now the pilots are being distributed to the heavy cruisers and the Marines are on two weeks' leave. In the bayous, as I understand."

"Yes, Bert. Chairman Febo called me to thank me for our involvement and to ask what more she could do for us. Specifically for the Erian Marines with regard to their leave. And I recalled our earlier discussion of the bayous."

"Chairman Febo called you, Sam?"

"Oh, yes. She is a remarkably good leader. I am surprised that humans have such a leader, and, more, that she was elevated to the top of government."

Mangum nodded, and they were silent for a while.

"Bert?"

"Yes, Sam."

"Will a mission to Vauxhall now be necessary?" Jules asked.

"Why do you ask, Jules?"

"Well, it seems to me that Vauxhall cannot hurt us now. If they send their navy out here, it's going to get destroyed. So do we need to take any proactive measures?"

"I don't know, Jules. That will be the chairman's decision. Her and Speaker Corliss, I suppose. I don't know all the variables they're considering."

"But why bother? They can't hurt us."

"If all the monarchies – whose leaders are interrelated, remember – join against us? It may take a very big navy and huge losses to prevail, but they might be able to do it. And even if we win, we would take losses of our own."

"I see, Bert. So it depends on her read of the situation."

"Yes, of course, Jules. As always."

Mangum turned away from the view and looked at Jules.

"The nice part is she's very good at this sort of thing."

Reconsideration

"Good morning, Michael."

"Good morning, Isabela. What can I do for you today?"

"Have you been keeping up on the reports I've copied you on, Michael."

"Yes, of course, Isabela. The reports on the Erian pilots and Marines were especially interesting. Quite capable fellows, these aliens."

"Yes, Michael. And it turns out they've been helping us for years. With various missions, including the Abelon Crisis, the Crossroads Affair, the rescue of Professor Varley, and the mission to Vauxhall."

Speaker Corliss nodded. He had picked up the subtext of the reports he had seen.

"Yes, Isabela. Amazing, looking back on it all. And now they bolster us against Vauxhall and the other monarchies."

"Yes, Michael. Exactly. And so the question arises. Do we need to take any measures now against Vauxhall? Or can we sit back and let them come at us, knowing we will prevail?"

Corliss nodded. Tough call. Do they poke the wasp nest, or leave it for now?

It was not a minor matter. Leaving Vauxhall to fester was one option. There was a danger there, though. A serious one.

"I think we would be well advised not to forget the lesson of Napoleon, Isabela."

Napoleon Bonaparte had lived more than two thousand years ago, but was a major historical figure, and political leaders – good political leaders, like Gaston's Speaker Corliss and the Association's Isabela Febo – were students of history.

"Which lesson, Michael? Not to overreach, as Napoleon did in invading Russia?"

"That's a good one, Isabela, and something to keep in mind. I was thinking of a more subtle one."

"Go on, Michael."

"By the time of Napoleon, Europe had been ruled for eight hundred years or more by a single interrelated family – something of an extended clan – who called themselves the nobility. Much like the situation we have in the core worlds now.

"The French Revolution overthrew King Louis XVI, and he was executed. Ten years later, Napoleon took power in France.

"This was something the ruling family of Europe could not tolerate. One of their own – cousin to most of them – had been overthrown, and a commoner installed in his place. They joined their forces and waged war against Napoleon for sixteen years before finally defeating him and reinstalling a family member on the throne of France, King Louis XVIII.

"Bear in mind that Napoleon was a brilliant military leader and had multiple advantages, including being very popular at home. He was able to raise and field large armies against multiple coalitions of the ruling clan, and defeated them all, until he weakened France with the Russian campaign. He lost nearly half a million men, the vast majority of the army he started with.

"That turned the advantage for the ruling family, and they ultimately defeated him. Despite monstrous losses of their own, they persisted for sixteen years until they defeated him. They simply could not countenance one of their family being ousted as king of a major European country. It set a bad precedent."

"But the monarchy in France did fall, Michael."

"Yes, Isabela, more than thirty years later, in the revolutions that swept across Europe in 1848. Most of them were brutally suppressed, but the one in France succeeded. Napoleon III took power, and, twenty years later, when he died, France became a republic once again, which survived."

"And then the ruling family of Europe fell in the Great War of the Twentieth Century."

"Yes, Isabela. The family made a huge mistake. They began an internecine conflict in 1914. Safely ensconced in their palaces, cousins fought cousins through armies of commoners. Like playing chess, but with real people. But war had changed. It was the first truly modern war, and tens of millions died.

"And get this, Isabela. The bulk of the fighting and dying and destruction was in France. Why would they care? It wasn't one of the family's countries anymore."

"That's horrific, Michael."

"Oh, yes. But by the time the second phase of the Great War was over, in 1945, all the monarchies had fallen, were deposed, or the monarch was reduced to figurehead status. The family started that war among themselves, but it destroyed, finally, the family's control over Europe. Europe became a continent largely of democracies."

"So what we really want to do is get that process started in the core worlds. Is that what you're saying, Michael?"

"And not let them gang up on us in some grand coalition and prevail against us despite our military advantages, as the European nobility did against Napoleon. Exactly, Isabela. Overturn Vauxhall, and see if we can't get the monarchies fighting each other instead of us."

"We have to make sure we don't make Napoleon's mistake, Michael. That we don't overreach."

"Oh, yes. I'm with you there, Isabela. But Napoleon was, of

necessity, waging a war. We're not at that point yet. Maybe we can get something started without fighting a war ourselves. If we take out the central government of Vauxhall, and all those worlds are up for grabs, the core-world monarchies should end up fighting each other for the spoils. And that could spell their doom."

"I see."

Febo nodded.

"Well, thank you, Michael. You've given me a great deal to think about."

"No problem. Isabela. Call me anytime."

"Good afternoon, Madam Chairman."

"Good afternoon, Mr. Grant. I have some things for your people to consider."

"Of course, Madam Chairman."

Febo brought Henry Grant, the director of the Agency, up to speed on Michael Corliss' argument, without specifying it was from Corliss.

"So what I want, Mr. Grant, is for your people to consider how we can topple the government of Vauxhall and get the core worlds squabbling over the pickings. And how the availability of Narlaxatrophine-II might figure into all that."

"Of course, ma'am."

"The goal, of course, is to get the monarchies to bring themselves down. To empower movements within their own societies that will topple them or render them toothless. Let's see if we can replicate what happened in Europe between 1848 and 1945 and put this entitled nobility out of business."

"Yes, ma'am. A worthy goal."

"I think so, Mr. Grant. See what you can come up with for me."

"Yes, Madam Chairman."

"Good day, Mr. Grant."

The problem came to the Agency's analysis section. A core group of senior analysts worked through the scenario.

"Of course, what happened in France after the revolution was the Terror. Do we want to reproduce *that*?" Betty Revell asked.

"Well, one thing the Terror did was empower the mob," Jacoba Vandervord said. "The reason Napoleon was able to rule later on was that he was popular with the mob. They let him rule. That's where his strength at home came from."

"That's right," Manu Bhatt said. "One group after another of revolutionaries and power-seekers were ousted by the mob until Napoleon came along. And after he was defeated, it was only another thirty-three years of kings before the mob ousted them as well. The last couple were pretty unpopular."

"Yes, but the other powers didn't try to divide France up between them," Vandervord said.

"That was because they installed one of their own on the throne," Bhatt said. "They tried to return to the status quo ante."

"Right," Revell said. "Do you think they'll simply try to put the Duke of Earth on the throne?"

"They may," Vandervord said. "We should try to see if there isn't a way we can disrupt that as well. If we can keep that from happening, Vauxhall should break up."

"And then it's going to be a free-for-all," Bhatt said. "The monarchies'll all dive in looking for a piece."

"Those are the two big power centers in Vauxhall, so I agree that's likely," Revell said. "OK, so we want to topple Vauxhall, but probably Earth as well."

Vandervord nodded.

"Yeah, I'm in with that. Now, how do we make it happen?"

"I think Earth is easier," Bhatt said. "At least to start chaos. Earth still has all the cultures and divisions it started with. We just need to shake that up a bit, and it will sink into sectarian conflict. Vauxhall is probably far harder."

"Well, Vauxhall is more homogeneous, but that may make it easier to turn against the throne," Vandervord said. "Flip the poor in the capital city against the elites, and it's going to come crashing down pretty fast."

"OK, so two strategies, then?" Revell asked.

"In the specific case of Earth, yes," Bhatt said. "A different strategy. Any other world, the same strategy as Vauxhall would probably work."

"All right, then," Revell said. "Let's start working on those."

"Well, that was interesting," Mangum said after they had been briefed.

"In what way?" Stavros asked.

"Two strategies, one for Earth and one for Vauxhall."

"Yes, but I'm not happy with the one for Earth, Bert."

"What's the matter with it, Elina?"

"I don't think it makes any sense. Pitting poor people against each other just to keep the nobility busy? It doesn't seem, I don't know, ethical somehow."

Mangum nodded.

"I can see that, Elina. Turning the poor against the throne on Vauxhall makes sense. Why the focus on Earth, I wonder."

"Well, they said otherwise people would just put the Duke of Earth on the throne, or move the capital to Earth, but I don't think that's likely."

"Why not?"

"First, if the king has been toppled on Vauxhall, maybe executed, what are the odds the Duke of Earth would want to go to Vauxhall? Slim to none, I would think."

"OK. I get that. And moving the capital to Earth? Having the Duke of Earth proclaiming himself King of Vauxhall in place?"

"That's more likely. I'll grant that. He probably can't make it stick, though. And I think that's preferable to pitting the poor against each other. More justifiable, too. It's Vauxhall that's plotting against us. We don't know that the Duke of Earth will do anything against us. He doesn't have any beef with us at the moment, and he'll probably be too busy consolidating his rule, if that's what he does."

"I see."

"It just seems something of an overreach to me, Bert."

"Well, let's get the group together and see what we come up with."

The team got together the next afternoon. All ten of them were there, the four couples and the two aliens, in their utility personas.

"Did everybody manage to watch the briefing?" Mangum asked.

He looked around, collecting nods and yeses from everyone.

"All right. Good. I think we need to give our superiors our best opinions on the options. So what does everybody think?"

"You already know what I think, Bert. So let me bring everybody else up to speed on that."

Stavros outlined her objections to the analysis department's plan for creating chaos on Earth. To keep the Duke of Earth from a successful takeover of Vauxhall by creating sectarian strife on humanity's home planet.

When she finished, Kendall was nodding.

"I think Elina has the right of it, Bert," he said. "There was something that bothered me about it, but I couldn't quite put my finger on it. I think she's right."

"And there's another thing," Stickney said. "It's difficult to fight a war if you don't have the bulk of the population with you. One reason Napoleon was so successful for so long is he had the crowds with him.

"But if there was sectarian strife on Earth, and, say, ten million people were killed – which is not out of the ballpark, by the way – if it ever came out that we caused it, the Duke of Earth would have the planet behind him to come after us."

"Especially without cause," Portnoy said. "Everybody knows about the letters of marque now. That's all come out. If we go and get the King of Vauxhall spanked – if we turn the lower classes against the throne – well, that's what you get for attacking someone else first. Earth, though, that's different."

"They did keep Davian locked up for eighteen years, though, Claude," Dent said. "And the whole thing with the HMS *King Alfred* came up when the Earth Planetary Police discovered Varley on *Silverheel*."

"Yes, Gloria, but none of that's public."

"Ah. Got it."

"The whole thing would make me feel dirty, Bert," Schofield said. "Sectarian strife killing millions? Whereas turning the lower classes against the throne, empowering them to throw off their oppressors, feels a lot better. It's still out of self-interest on our part, but it feels better to me."

"What about Narlaxatrophine-II?" Mangum asked. "Do we give that to people on Earth?"

"The cure for RDT?" Kendall asked. "Sure. Why wouldn't we give it to both of Vauxhall's main planets?"

"And if the loss of the anti-depressive effect gets people

annoyed with each other and that results in sectarian strife?" Mangum asked.

"Well, we wouldn't have gone out of our way to cause that, Bert," Schofield said. "If that's an unforeseen consequence of giving them the cure, that's on them, not us."

Mangum looked around at the group, and several of them were nodding.

"All right. I think that's a consensus. Thanks, everybody. I'll write it up and send it on."

Isabela Febo sighed. Henry Grant had sent her the raw reports. He would usually do that on anything important. She had read the report of the Agency analysis section, and it left a bad taste in her mouth.

Febo couldn't quite say what it was that bothered her, at least until she read Mangum's group report. She knew it was Mangum's report. After reading raw reports for so long, she recognized his style.

That was it. The thing that bothered her. Creating sectarian strife on Earth could kill millions, all for causing the nobility a little inconvenience. It seemed ill-advised to her.

And one word jumped out at her: overreach.

That did it.

Febo sent the reports on to Speaker Corliss.

She also sent orders to the Agency.

Michael Corliss liked Isabela Febo. More, he respected her. She did not make mistakes on big decisions. He thought she was right here, and he told her so in her follow-up call.

"Isabela, I concur with your decision in every respect."

"Thank you, Michael. That's important to me."

Ladyhawke

"Well, we have our orders," Mangum told the group. "We will be doing the mission to Vauxhall. We will be dropping off Narlaxatrophine-II and manufacturing modules for it on Earth. We will not, however, be fomenting sectarian conflict on Earth."

"Yay," Stavros said.

"Excellent," Kendall said.

Others around the room nodded.

"That said, we now have to gear up for the mission. Serp, where's *Ladyhawke*? Do you know?"

"She's inbound to Abelon at the moment, Bert. Just dropped out of hyperspace."

"Let's get Emmet a note to head this way. We need to get her all set up. I'm sure Paul Gammon will pay demurrage if we're delayed launching the mission."

Kendall nodded.

"Got it."

"I think we have our personnel lined up."

Mangum looked to Jules, then Portnoy, then Stickney. Each nodded in turn.

"You're not pregnant are you, Phyllis?"

"No, Bert. Why do you ask?"

"There's a lot of it going around lately. I think it's catching."

Stickney looked around a little baffled. Stavros was smiling, of course, but so was Dent, and Varley looked smug.

She turned back to Mangum.

"Ah. No, Bert. I'm not pregnant."

"Good."

"And Judy Blunt is coming?" Portnoy asked.

"Yes. She's been in touch. For this mission only, but she's on board."

"Excellent."

"Sam, will the Marines be ready?"

"Yes, Bert. They're coming back from two weeks' leave tomorrow."

"What about the attack ships for *Ladyhawke*?"

"They're ready, Bert."

"And Marine pilots for the attack ships?"

"I took care of training them before they left for two weeks' leave, Bert," Jules said.

"And do we have the barracks containers for them, Gloria?"

"Yes, Bert. Three containers. According to Sam, that should be enough."

"The infantry arms and ammo, Phyllis? Where are we on that?"

"They're standard items, Bert. Stocking levels are not a problem."

"And point-defense guns for *Ladyhawke*?"

"Same. In stock and available immediately.

"OK, let's get those ordered. And the manufacturing modules and Narlaxatrophine-II stock, Davian?"

"They're already here, Bert. We're just branching them off of those inbound for the Association."

"What am I forgetting?" Mangum asked. "We can't be good on everything. Isn't that against the rules?"

People chuckled, but Mangum had run down his checklist, and everything was in stock, in place, or incoming.

"Emmet!"

"Hi, Serp!"

The two old friends embraced there just outside the inbound security and immigration check.

"You got all your shit?"

"Yeah. Just this one bag for on planet."

"And your purser and trade master?"

"Still aboard *Ladyhawke*, squaring away getting the inbounds unloaded."

"All right. Come with me then. You gotta see this place Marge and I got. We got a guest room, too, and you're welcome to stay with us."

"Thanks, Serp. A credit saved..."

The autocab pulled up in front of The 909, and Kendall and Durst got out.

"Good evening, Mr. Kendall."

"Good evening, Steven. Mr. Durst will be our guest for a couple weeks."

"Very good, Mr. Kendall. Welcome to The 909, Mr. Durst."

"Thank you, Steven."

"Damn, Serp," Durst said, looking around. "Nice place."

"Yeah, make a bunch o' money as captain, you can live wherever you want."

They got in the elevator and Kendall pushed the button for the top floor. When they got off the elevator, Kendall jerked a thumb toward Mangum and Stavros' door.

"You remember Bert Mangum. He and Elina Stavros live right there. Me and Marge are over here."

Kendall opened the door and waved Durst in. Durst's attention was captured by the two adjacent window walls, with the top floor view out over the city, with the south view of the park and the downtown to the right and the east view out over the shuttleport to the left.

"Damn. This is incredible."

"Yeah, ain't it something? We love it."

Schofield walked in from the office then.

"Hi, Emmet."

"Hi, Marge."

The two hugged, then Durst gestured to the windows.

"Any way you slice it, that is an incredible view, Marge."

"Yes, and it's an east view. I see the sun come up every morning. And Serp can watch the shuttles coming and going."

"Hey, let's order supper. The room service here is great, Emmet."

After supper, they sat in the living room looking out over the city as the shadows lengthened.

"What's this mission about, Serp? Nobody's told me anything yet."

"OK, so let me brief you, Emmet. All of this has to be real confidential."

"Sure, Serp. Not a problem."

"All right. Well, this king of Vauxhall is being a pain in the ass. He's building a new navy, to come out here and take us on."

"How's that going to go for them, Serp?"

"Poorly. We been muscling up. But if all the monarchies got together, they could give us trouble. And they're all related. So if their cousin gets in trouble out here and we kick his navy's ass, what are they gonna do?"

"Gotcha."

"So the idea is to send a mission to Vauxhall. You take along a bunch of the cure for RDT addiction, some machines that can make more, Claude Portnoy and his team of operatives, and five hundred Marines, with enough extra guns for about ten thousand more guys. The goal is to find the opposition to the government, and help them topple the king."

"Holy shit. How dangerous is this going to be, Serp?"

"To *Ladyhawke*? Not at all."

"How do you figure?"

"Because we're gonna put a dozen battleship-grade point-defense guns and four attack ships on her. And those attack ships are piloted by those Erian guys, the aliens, and they can take over nine gees. Nothing can touch 'em."

"Wow. You're gonna make *Ladyhawke* a warship?"

"Nah. You should see our real warships now. But she'll be able to take out anything Vauxhall can throw at her."

Ladyhawke had six docking ports behind the crew cabin. She would take the crew transfer shuttle and one large cargo shuttle to Vauxhall. The other four docking ports would mount the new attack ships, with full missile loadouts.

Against the crew quarters there were twelve container positions for extra supplies on long voyages. Three of the positions would be occupied by barracks containers for the five hundred Erian Marines.

With the X-3 drive already on *Ladyhawke,* she didn't need six months' of provisions for the crossing. Feeding five hundred Erians – more than ten times *Ladyhawke*'s normal crew – for the two-month trip, though, would require spare supplies containers to be swapped forward from the actual freight container section of the big ship.

The freight container section of the long open-rack system along the spine of the ship would mount containers of Narlaxatrophine-II, manufacturing modules to make more, containers of infantry arms and ammo, and a dozen containers with battleship-grade point-defense guns. These would be under cover unless and until they were needed.

All of these modifications to *Ladyhawke* were containers, which, as a freighter, she was designed to carry. Loading and configuration of the ship would not take long. The biggest part of it would be testing that everything worked once it was all latched.

"You know, Serp. Just looking over this manifest, we've got about fifteen hundred containers of capacity unused."

"Yeah. Five hundred containers of stuff for the mission is a lot of stuff, but it's still only a quarter of *Ladyhawke*'s capacity."

"Well, I think we ought to load up with regular cargo. We come in light, it's going to attract a lot of attention. And you know the import control guys pay a lot more attention to the first fifty or so containers. Then it's just 'Oh, more of that? OK.' and you waltz through. So I think we should load her up."

"Huh. Yeah, you're probably right. All right. I'll talk to Bert about it."

In the end, Durst's new trade master loaded seven hundred additional containers for Earth and seven hundred additional containers for Vauxhall. When they got to Earth, the containers of Narlaxatrophine-II and the manufacturing modules would be lost in a sea of containers going through import control.

They would pick up seven hundred containers of cargo on Earth to take on to Vauxhall, and there would be fourteen hundred completely legal containers coming down, plus the Narlaxatrophine-II, the manufacturing modules, containers with weapons and ammo for ten thousand infantry, and even the Erian Marines themselves.

That would make it much easier to sneak things through. 'Independent shippers' like *Ladyhawke* were often called smugglers, and not without reason.

Emmet Durst knew how to do this.

An issue did come up, however.

Durst was sitting in on Mangum's group meeting the next day when Portnoy brought up an issue.

"I have a question. *Ladyhawke* is not a troop ship, with a huge galley. She's set up to feed a crew of thirty or so. How are you going to feed five hundred Marines?"

"Ouch," Kendall said.

"Indeed," Durst said. "That one slipped me by. We certainly can't cook three meals a day for five hundred and thirty-five people, which is what we're looking at right now."

"Now what do we do?" Stickney asked.

"A galley module, maybe?" Dent asked.

"Then you need galley crew for it, and more barracks space," Kendall said. "And it will take up one of the latch positions on the cabin, reducing the supplies container locations."

"If I might offer a suggestion?" Sam said.

"Sure, Sam. Go ahead," Mangum said.

"When the Erian Marines were in training, the instructors found that they could train each group of fifty in a different course and they would share it overnight. So the next day, everybody knew the material. The result was that they taught every course they had to one group of fifty or another."

"How does that apply here, Sam?" Mangum asked.

"Well, one course they offered was cooking, Bert. Part of the logistics sequence, I think. All five hundred of those Marines know how to cook and clean up in a shipboard galley. They can staff their own galley."

"That still leaves us one latching position short, but we can rotate supplies containers more often," Durst said.

"Not necessarily, Emmet. We like to be crowded. We don't sleep at night, we sit in contact with each other and talk. Very enjoyable. My suggestion is that you drop one barracks container and mount a galley module in that position instead."

"Two hundred and fifty Marines to a barracks container meant for fifty?" Dent asked.

"Sounds lovely," Sam said.

"OK," Mangum said. "There's our solution. Gloria, modify the order for the barracks containers. Two barracks containers, not three, and a galley container."

"Hey, Bert," Kendall said. "Send a second galley container. Not in one of the latching positions, but with the spare food."

"Why, Serp?"

Kendall shrugged.

"In case one breaks."

"OK, Gloria. Add a spare."

"Got it, Bert."

In orbit above Mardouk, *Ladyhawke* had been cleared of all the inbound cargo containers. The long, spindly structure of the ship was now completely exposed.

Around *Ladyhawke* floated outbound containers that had been brought up by returning cargo shuttles as the ship had been cleaned off. Cargo shuttles now started mounting those containers on the ship as other containers came up from the planet.

As always, which containers went where was a major issue. Cargo had to be loaded depending on its destination and use, especially for a multi-stop trip.

In the case of the Agency's mission to Earth and Vauxhall, that order of loading was more critical than usual, but shuttle crews had manifest maps for the placement of containers, and it was something cargo shuttle pilots were used to dealing with.

The loading of *Ladyhawke* for the mission proceeded without incident.

The loading crew on *Ladyhawke* was also experienced in unloading and loading procedures. Multiple layers of containers built up along the spine of the ship as she loaded, moving her look from spindly to bulky.

As for the barracks and galley, those containers were latched, then the crew extended the boarding tubes to them. Used for accessing stores, they nevertheless had an airlock on the ship side for each of them.

The point-defense guns were mounted around the reaction-mass containers front and rear. Rear was the normal location for reaction-mass containers, to feed the engines. Those had to be plumbed in, but that process was mechanical, done from inside the ship.

The front reaction-mass containers were fuel reloads for the attack ships that clustered behind the crew cabin with the personnel transfer shuttle and the heavy cargo shuttle. They also connected into *Ladyhawke* with airlocks.

The point-defense guns were self-contained units whose containers went on last. With their gun doors closed, they looked like normal cargo containers, and shuttle crews loaded them as such, taking care to place them per the manifest map.

Once *Ladyhawke* was loaded, the cargo crew rotated for planet leave. They were not going to miss time on planet between runs, especially on Mardouk.

Departure

Mangum had one more project meeting before *Ladyhawke*'s departure. One surprise attendee was Mary Danner, a.k.a. Sally McCormack, a.k.a. Judy Blunt, a.k.a. Peggy Dawson. She was walked up to Mangum and Dent's condo by a bellhop from the front door, just as Gloria Dent and Davian Varley were.

She had warned Mangum she was coming. All her other missions had been so deep undercover that nobody in the Agency had ever seen her. Even for the prior Vauxhall mission, she had been in her cover identity from the time the mission gathered to leave. And she had been a ship's girl, and dressed like it.

Not this time. She was dressed as a wealthy socialite, and walked down to The 909 from the Ashur Park Plaza Hotel down the block.

"Mary Danner, Mr. Mangum."

"Hello, Ms. Danner. Come on in. And call me Bert."

Danner gave him a curt nod, and walked into the living room. Everyone was just getting seated in the living room. Portnoy she recognized, of course. And Stickney, Kendall, and Schofield. The others must be Elina Stavros, Gloria Dent, and Davian Varley.

There were also two Erians present, in their utility personas. As Danner watched, Jules shifted to his Jack Sturm persona and back, so she knew which had been her previous contact.

She sat next to him.

"Everybody, this is Mary Danner. She's on Claude's team for this mission. I think she knows everyone here."

Danner nodded.

Kendall recognized her as a remake of the ship's girl on *Silverheel*, on their last trip home from Vauxhall.

"What's your role on the mission, Mary?" Kendall asked.

She turned to him with a deadpan expression.

"If Claude needs someone to die to advance the mission, he lets me know and I kill them."

Her eyes were cold and dead as she said it, and Kendall suppressed a shudder. And he had thought *Mangum* was dangerous.

"You sound like a great person to have around, Mary."

"Thanks, Serp. Mostly I came to this meeting because I want to know the mission's goals and methods. If Claude and I are not able to communicate, I need to be able to carry through on my own judgment. There's too much at stake."

"Mary came out of retirement for this mission," Mangum said.

"Thank you, Mary," Portnoy said, and Danner nodded to him.

"All right. Let's get started," Mangum said. "The purpose of this mission is to topple the monarchy of Vauxhall. Not just the current king, but to topple the system itself. To that end, we will contact the opposition to the throne, the kingdom's databases and networks will be compromised, there will be general confusion about who is who, and some people will die inconveniently, largely of apparently natural causes."

Mangum had indicated Portnoy, Stickney, Jules, and Danner in turn for those last four points.

"We have the personnel assembled to carry this out, including five hundred Erians as Marines."

"Five hundred Erian Marines?" Danner asked.

"Yes, Mary. They will be in barracks containers aboard *Ladyhawke*, to form the hard point of the opposition forces.

They will break the enemy lines."

"Is five hundred enough?"

For answer, Jules stood up and shifted to a velociraptor, with a wide mouth of very sharp teeth. He roared as Danner looked at him.

"Five hundred of *those*?"

"Yes. Oh, and they're bulletproof," Mangum said.

"Yeah, that'll break the lines. Forget I said anything."

Jules shifted back to his utility persona and nodded to her.

"Still a nice trick," Danner told him.

They talked over the mission and possible methods. How to find any opposition group. How to use the Narlaxatrophine-II RDT cure and the manufacturing modules. How to encourage and then force the confrontation. Multiple methods and possible variations for each.

It went on for several hours.

When they had exhausted the topic, Mangum took the floor.

"A couple things to keep in mind, Claude. Regardless of what was said here, you are the team leader on the scene. Make the call. You do need to contact me when you get to Vauxhall, to make sure your orders haven't changed. That said, the mission itself is your responsibility. No one else's."

"I understand, Bert."

"Any other issues?"

"There is one," Durst said. "We have two empty crew cabins on *Ladyhawke*. No VIP cabins like *Silverheel*. They're both small rooms with bunks for two. How we gonna make that work?"

"Well, we're together," Stickney said, waving a hand between her and Portnoy.

Danner turned to Jules.

"Jules, I assume you have no human gender and no interest

in sex."

"That is correct, Mary."

"Do you do girl shapes as well?"

Jules shifted to a mid-thirties female persona, one he had constructed of a mix of people he had seen.

"Like this?" Jules asked.

"Perfect. And your name in this persona?"

"Jewel. Like a ruby or sapphire. Same pronunciation."

Danner nodded. She turned to Durst.

"Jules and I will bunk together in the other open cabin."

"All right, then. We're set," Durst said.

"OK, everybody," Mangum said. "Good luck and good spacing."

There were goodbyes and good lucks back and forth across the group, from those staying to those leaving.

The shuttles to *Ladyhawke* lifted in the morning.

At the shuttleport mid-morning the next day, Portnoy and Stickney watched the others arriving for the shuttle lift. Jules was with them in his Jules Hawker persona. Captain Emmet Durst was also there early, of course.

They watched as the shuttle crew loaded the baggage for the trip up to *Ladyhawke*. Crew members had picked up their spacer trunks earlier in the day. Portnoy also recognized the two spacer trunks that belonged to Judy Blunt.

Crew members floated in from leave. Judy Blunt also showed up as Mary Danner. Her hair color, as yesterday, was different than the bright blond she had favored as Sally McCormack on their last mission. It was now brown, and she wore subtle makeup, not the face paint of the prostitute and ship's girl. She was dressed as a high-end secretary or businesswoman.

Danner did not hang out with the crew as before, but came up to Portnoy, Stickney, and Jules. The crew, if they recognized her, did not mention it, and treated her as one of the operations team.

The three ship's girls of *Ladyhawke*'s crew complement did hang out with the crew members, and there was a lot of joking around and kidding as tensions built heading into their departure.

"Good morning, everybody," Danner said as she walked up.

"Good morning, Mary. Ready for lift?"

"Yes. All set. You?"

"Oh, yes. Here we go again."

Danner nodded.

"It's good to be operational again. I had retired at the top of my game, but for this mission, well, it's just too important."

The Erian Marines were actually first aboard *Ladyhawke,* since they didn't mind zero or low gravity. The ship was accelerating at just two-tenths gee when they came aboard.

Lieutenant Colonel Frank Everett was first off the big personnel shuttle that came up from the Marine Training Base west of Ashur. A crew member was waiting for him at the airlock.

"This way, Sir," the crewman said.

He led Everett through the ship to the airlock to the first of the barracks containers, the other Marines following along in line silently. Everett stopped in front of the airlock and waved his Marines on in.

All two hundred and fifty Erian Marines from the big personnel shuttle headed on into the barracks module intended for fifty humans. They distributed themselves among the ten bunk rooms and the corridor, then settled into their natural state on the floors and bunks.

When the first big shuttle left and the second shuttle arrived, it was Lieutenant Colonel Everett who met them and guided them to the second barracks container. He followed them in and shifted to his natural state as well.

Ladyhawke was making more like half a gravity as her own, smaller, crew transfer shuttle caught up with her. The shuttle docked and the crew and operations team came aboard.

"This way, everybody."

The crewman guided Portnoy, Stickney, Danner, and Jules to two crew cabins.

"It's these two cabins here."

"Thank you, crewman," Portnoy said.

"Yes, sir."

They looked into the cabins. One had a single, wider bed, the other had a two-high bunk bed.

"I guess this one's us," Danner said, waving Jules to the cabin with the two-high bunk bed.

She went on into the cabin, with Jules following, but, when she turned around she saw that he had taken on the female persona she had seen yesterday.

"Yes. Just us girls," Jules said. "Do you want the shower first? I'm going to be a while."

With everyone aboard and her shuttle latched and stowed, *Ladyhawke* increased her acceleration to one gravity, spacing for the hyperspace limit.

Once *Ladyhawke* was under way at normal acceleration, Erians from the barracks assumed human personas and moved into the galley container. With five hundred to be fed, the galley would run twenty-four hours for the trip.

The Erians didn't really care when they ate, so they took shifts both staffing the galley and moving through the dining area. With two long tables for twenty each, they ate in shifts. They were quick eaters anyway, so it went pretty fast.

The galley crew would then clean up for the next crew, who would come in and start cooking again.

The humans aboard were served by *Ladyhawke*'s galley, which had always been pretty good. Lunch this first day was only a bit delayed by how long it took to lift to the ship.

The operations team took their meals in a small meeting room Captain Durst normally used for meetings with his department heads. Like every other space on the ship, it was multi-purpose. The table was sized for six, and they invited Lieutenant Colonel Everett to eat with them.

Everett showed up as they were all sitting down.

"Welcome aboard, Colonel," Portnoy said.

"Thank you, Sir. I've already eaten with my men, but I'll sit with you."

Portnoy nodded and waved Everett to a seat.

"How was your leave, Colonel?" asked Jules.

He was back in the Jules Hawker persona everyone else was used to, switching to his female persona when in the cabin with Danner for her comfort.

"Good. Very good. You know, alligator is pretty good eating. It would probably even taste pretty good cooked."

"Did you leave any alligators, Colonel?" Portnoy asked.

"Oh, yes. One must allow the ecosystem to replenish, Mr. Portnoy, though there are fewer alligators, snakes, and fish than before we were there. Mostly the older ones. We left the youngsters and the most active breeding generation alone. Still good eating, though."

Jules nodded. They had learned long ago on Erias how to maintain the ecosystem, and it had become cultural by now. One did not risk famine through carelessness or overbreeding. That had been a hard-learned lesson.

"I think in these high-level meetings we should go by first names, Colonel, or we will be mistering and coloneling all the way to Vauxhall and back. In front of your men, that's different. In this group, call me Claude."

"Very well, Claude."

"Phyllis," Stickney said.

"Mary," Danner said.

"And I am Jules, of course," Jules said.

Everett nodded to each in turn.

"And we all know why we're here in general terms, although I think we need to bring you up to speed on the details, Frank."

Ladyhawke reached the hyperspace limit for Mardouk. She opened a rift in spacetime in front of her and spaced into it, disappearing from reality.

They were two months' voyage to Earth, their first stop.

To Earth

Ladyhawke's crossing of the void did not have all the associated psychological stress of *Silverheel*'s crossing of the void going home from the mission to Earth to release Davian Varley.

First, the X-3 drive reduced the six-month voyage to a two-month voyage. That earlier crossing had gotten really bad in the last couple of months.

Second, *Ladyhawke* was a much larger ship than the tiny *Silverheel*. There were thirty crew, the four members of the operations team, and five hundred Erians aboard. *Silverheel* had ten crew and the ops team, and it was a tiny metal bubble of air and heat in the void. *Ladyhawke* felt much more substantial.

The crew did make regular use of the ship's girls, the same popular team they had had the last couple of years. The women reported to the captain that the men were holding up well during the trip. There were no psychological issues emerging.

Stickney and Portnoy spent all their spare time researching everything that had gone on in Vauxhall since the last time they were there. They paid particular attention to the military updates they received.

Mary Danner and Jules spent interminable hours talking. Jules was surprised to find out how well read Danner was, while she had the same surprising realization about him. They talked about human history, psychology, culture, and philosophy.

The Erians, too, were busy. They had a number of the roll-up displays with them, and spent their time huddled in groups around them, reading through *Ladyhawke*'s library. They found humans and human society – and history – fascinating. Those who couldn't see the display from their position read through the eyes of those who could, as they were all interconnected by contact.

This leg of the trip passed uneventfully. Of course, in hyperspace they were out of touch with the network and were unaware of anything happening while they were in transit, but they would catch up when they dropped out of hyperspace at Earth and again at Vauxhall.

In the meantime, it was just a long voyage.

But it was one most of the humans had done before.

Early in the trip, Jules and Danner were sitting in their cabin chatting. Jules was in his female persona.

"I have a question for you, Jules," Danner said. "How did you find me?"

"It was actually something of an accident, Mary. A couple of years ago, after returning from Vauxhall, Bert and Elina took Sam and me for a walk through the zoo. We were in our golden doodle personas. And I saw you working in the wolf exhibit."

"You recognized me?"

"Yes. We are a little more subtle than humans in seeing through disguises, I think. It was something in the way you moved. I knew you from the trip aboard *Silverheel*. Had seen you talking with Claude. And I saw you in the park that day you dropped the crawlers for me."

"Ah. I see. I was just curious. I wanted to know where I slipped up."

"I don't think you slipped up, at least as far as humans are concerned. I noticed you, and I told Sam. But he said to keep your secret. We told no one else."

"You didn't even tell Bert?"

"No, Mary. It was your secret, so not ours to share. When it became important to contact you, however, I volunteered, though I still didn't tell anyone how I contacted you."

Danner nodded.

"Well, I appreciate that, Jules."

"Of course. But I have a question to ask you as well, Mary. Just out of curiosity, as you say."

"Sure, Jules. Go ahead."

"Why did you retire, and why have you come back for this mission?"

"Ah. Well, it was the Vauxhall mission that did it, actually."

"You thought that mission too much somehow? An overreach?"

"No, the opposite, Jules. That mission was important. A foreign power was interfering in the cluster. It was necessary to get them to cut it out. A truly important mission. In comparison, everything else I had been involved in recently was small. Unnecessary."

"Unnecessary?"

"Yes. The cluster nations, for the last several years, have been at peace. The threat of war between Wilbourne and Villacqua, how close it came, shook everyone. In the resolution of that crisis, the cluster chief executives formed the mutual-defense consortium. Since then, there are no military threats within the cluster."

"Were there no other missions, Mary?"

"Oh, sure. But they all seemed like cheats somehow."

"Cheats?"

"Short-cuts, say. Here's this person causing a lot of trouble. All right, then. Arrest them. Try them and convict them. If it's not illegal, leave them alone, or change the law. Killing them is just a way to short-cut the system that should be used. After

Vauxhall, after such a truly important mission, that all seemed a cheat."

"I see."

"And it's not like those missions weren't dangerous. As on Vauxhall, I was in tremendous danger, every time. But I'm risking my life for what? So some bureaucrat doesn't have to do his job? Carry through in the proper way? Through the legal system? It just became not worth it to me. Do your damned jobs and leave me alone."

"And now? Going on this mission?"

"Once again, a foreign power threatens the cluster, Jules. Add to that the oppression of their own people, on the basis of 'I was born better than you. I'm special.' Such bullshit. To threaten the cluster militarily? To attempt to impose their 'I'm special' mentality on the cluster? No, I'm all in for that one."

"I see. Thank you for telling me."

Danner nodded. Jules thought about it for several seconds.

"After the Vauxhall mission, after I heard you tell Claude about being merely his weapon, following his orders, I thought you were likely the most rational human I had ever met."

Jules nodded, then continued.

"Now I'm sure of it."

It was later in the trip that Stickney and Portnoy were talking in their cabin.

"Oh, I don't like this," Stickney said.

"What's that?" Portnoy asked.

"I find little hints in the data, here and there, about a new ship in the Vauxhall Royal Navy. Not much. Just a bit here and a bit there. But whatever it is, it's big."

"A carrier?"

"Could be. Probably is. It's certainly big enough, based on

the materials that went into it. And in the later hits I'm picking up staffing stuff. Transfers and the like."

"So it could be operational," Portnoy said.

"Or it's getting close. Yes."

"You'd think they would have picked it up in conversations in the king's office."

"Maybe they did. They didn't necessarily tell us about it."

"That would be troubling."

Portnoy thought about it before continuing.

"Collect all of that together and send an update to Gaston and Mardouk when we drop out of hyperspace. I'd like to see what Gloria can do in terms of any new data that's come in since we left."

"Oh, absolutely. And I'll be downloading the new data, too. But this could get nasty."

Portnoy nodded.

"Yeah. Naval bombardment of the planet from orbit to put down a revolution isn't likely. Too indiscriminate and prone to poor targeting. After all, they might hit themselves. But attack ships bombing crowds is a different matter."

"As are assault shuttles. Don't forget, Richard, they already have ground-based resources."

"Maybe the Association or Gaston will send out some backup, in reserve, in case it all falls into the pot."

"Maybe," Stickney said, though she didn't sound sure.

Ladyhawke dropped out of hyperspace at the hyperspace limit for Earth. She had a day inbound to make orbit.

Emmet Durst called in his trade master, Ephraim Smith. Smith had come aboard *Ladyhawke* as crew five or six years back, and he had helped Durst with trade master duties when

Kendall sold Durst the ship. He had served his apprenticeship under Durst in the cluster the past couple years.

"Hey, Emmet."

"Come on in, Ephraim."

Smith came into Durst's office and sat in one of the guest chairs.

"How are things going with getting cargo sold on Earth?" Emmet Durst asked.

"Good, Emmet. The cluster stuff is always in high demand. I'm getting good prices for most of it. I sent you my notes."

Durst opened the file in his display. The inbounds were listed first.

"Excellent. And how are you doing on getting us cargo for Earth to Vauxhall?"

"Well, there's always lots of stuff going back and forth between Earth and Vauxhall. Most of it is consignment, though, and the shipping fees demanded are pretty low."

Durst shrugged.

"Well, get what you can. We can make do with what we can find. The big money on this trip is coming from elsewhere anyways."

Smith nodded.

"And our other inbounds?"

"Consignment warehouse for now. Chemical manufacturing equipment and chemical supplies. Specialty items. Wouldn't be unusual for them to sit there for a while."

"We're going to have storage fees. Payable in advance."

"Understood. Six months advance payment. That usually shuts them up."

"All right, Emmet. That's what I thought. Just checking."

Durst scrolled back and forth in Smith's notes on his display.

"No problem, Ephraim. You're on top of it."

Once *Ladyhawke* had maneuvered itself into orbit through Earth's crowded traffic lanes, cargo shuttles from the planet came up to begin the unloading process.

Ladyhawke would often use her own cargo shuttles for less crowded planets. On Earth, though, it was easier to use local pilots. Not only did they know the orbitals and traffic lanes better, but their companies were up to date on their bribery payments to local officials.

On a planet with several levels of government, those bribe payments could get complicated. Easier to just use the locals.

Of course, *Ladyhawke* also had a reduced number of shuttles along on this trip. Most of her docking ports were occupied with attack ships. She only had one heavy cargo shuttle along on this trip.

"Shuttle 13-R-627 to *Ladyhawke*."

"Go ahead, 627."

"Inbound for offloading."

"Understood, 627. Sending the map."

Xiulan Yang, *Ladyhawke*'s communications crewman, transmitted the unloading map with 627's containers highlighted.

"Roger, *Ladyhawke*. We see it. Coming in."

"Roger 627. Advise when ready for unlatch."

"Geez, *Ladyhawke*. Whaddya have on all your docking ports?"

"Deliveries. Racing shuttles. Some rich asshole on Vauxhall wants to get into shuttle racing."

"I didn't even know that was a thing."

"Takes all kinds. You ready for unlatch, 627?"

"Just a second, *Ladyhawke*. Coming up."

Yang felt a slight shudder go through *Ladyhawke* as the

shuttle attached to her containers.

"627 to *Ladyhawke*. Clear to unlatch."

Communications handled cargo during loading and unloading. It cut down on dangerous miscommunication and coordination issues. Yang sent the signal to the containers.

"Cleared to go, 627."

Ladyhawke shuddered again as the shuttle pulled away with the containers.

"627 away, *Ladyhawke*."

"Roger that. *Ladyhawke* out."

Yang looked over to Durst.

"Nicely done, Xiulan. Nicely done."

"Did you send those findings, Susan?" Portnoy asked.

"Yes. I already got a note from Gloria. She's on it."

"Excellent. And you have new data?"

"Yes. That is, I've requested it all. It's still coming in. I'll have it all before we go back into hyperspace."

"Good. I really wonder what that new ship is."

"Well, if Gloria and I can figure it out, you'll be the first to know."

Even with all the ground-based shuttles, it took two days for all the unloading and loading on *Ladyhawke*. Sold containers went to the cargo transfer facilities, while the containers with the RDT addiction cure and the manufacturing modules to make more of it went to consignment warehouses.

No one on the crew was granted planet leave. When doing shady business, keep your nose clean, get in, and get out.

Vauxhall was a better planet leave anyway.

With all the cargo unloading and loading completed, *Ladyhawke* headed out from Earth. One day out, at the hyperspace limit, she opened a rift in spacetime in front of her and spaced into it, disappearing from reality.

The Aurora Project

Phyllis Stickney had sent her data to the BIE, to the Agency, and directly to Gloria Dent. Dent, still officially employed by the BIE as Davian Varley's security, considered the data and Stickney's preliminary conclusion carefully.

How could the Kingdom of Vauxhall have completed an attack-ship carrier, and the Agency and the BIE not known about it?

Dent went back through the archive of video and audio surveillance of the office of King Albert XIV in his palace on Vauxhall. There were no gaps. Nothing cut out. No censoring of the data internal to the agencies. Assigned to the Vauxhall project, Dent had access to it all.

What the hell? Had the king and his son never talked about it? That seemed hard to believe.

Dent had an advantage over Stickney. Stickney had access to all the data she had downloaded, and the use of her own portable computer resources on *Ladyhawke*. But Dent had access to all the data, and access to the high-speed computing facilities of the Agency and the BIE.

In her and Varley's penthouse suite in the Ashur Park Plaza Hotel, Dent bent to the task.

Digging deeply through the data, Dent came up with the missing link. The Aurora Project. It was a reference that sort of slipped through, somehow, because it was deeply secret.

But *Aurora* was the name of the new ship.

Armed with that knowledge, Dent searched the transcripts of the conversations between King Albert XIV and Crown

Prince James for 'Aurora.'

She hit the mother lode.

"And how is the Aurora Project coming along?" the king asked.

"Good. I sent you the latest updates."

"Yes, I saw them."

The king pulled up something on the display on his desk, and he and James bent over it. James pointed out salient details.

"Here you see its current status, and here you see the schedule projections."

"And the costs?" the king asked.

"Are, uh, here," James said, pointing. "Within budget, so far, and looking good going forward."

"Excellent. This is very good progress. An early version, to be sure, but excellent progress."

Dent reviewed that video and others in their original form. Of course, the audio and video pickup Jules had planted in the king's office in the prior Vauxhall mission could not see into the display from the angle it had – at least not at the display's current settings – so there had been no answer for what the Aurora Project was.

Dent now knew what it was, however, and she went back through every conversation the king and his son had that had mentioned it, reinterpreting them in the light of *Aurora* being Vauxhall's first attempt at building an attack-ship carrier.

Dent created a log of those conversations, including the dates and the comments by James and the king, following the status of the project as it went along to the current date.

To its current *operational* status.

Dent sent that analysis to the BIE and the Agency.

She hoped that Portnoy and her other friends were not spacing into trouble.

"How did we miss this, Phil?" Henry Grant asked the Agency's head of operations, Phillip Marstock.

"When they talked about the Aurora Project, it was always in general terms as they reviewed documents in the king's desk display. The surveillance camera can't see the display from the side. We assumed the Aurora Project was something like their attempt to make carbon nanotube reinforced stainless steel or the like. We didn't imagine it was a ship."

"And now Stickney and Dent have put the pieces together for us. Do you think they're right?"

"Yes, Henry. We had no idea what the project was about – we had guesses, but no answers – and this fits all the data."

"So how capable do you think this ship is? Is *Ladyhawke* in trouble?"

"Potentially. I don't think so, but potentially. There's another troubling aspect about it, though. The plan is to encourage a revolution against the monarchy by the mob. That's all ground-based. They have some assault shuttles that could get involved, but the Marines *Ladyhawke* is carrying are equipped to handle those. Attack ships may be a tougher nut to crack."

"How so, Phil?"

"If *Aurora*'s attack ships are built with their single-layer carbon nanotube stainless steel, that and their stand-off offensive capabilities are an issue. Don't forget, an attack ship is intended for space battles at large distances compared to planetary distances. Assault shuttles are not. The Marines may have trouble bringing those attack ships down, where the assault shuttles, which have to get in close, are not a problem."

"So what do we do about it?"

"The answer to attack ships is attack ships, Henry. They're intended to go after each other. If we want to protect the mob from those attack ships, we do it with attack ships of our own."

"*Ladyhawke* is carrying attack ships, isn't she?"

"Yes, but she's not a carrier, Henry. *Ladyhawke* has four attack ships along. For going after a heavy cruiser, that's more than enough. For going after a carrier, with a squadron of attack ships aboard? She's way outgunned there. And that doesn't include protecting the mob on the ground."

"All right, Phil. I understand. It sounds like we ought to send some backup over there. Have them stand off a ways – couple light-years – but be in the neighborhood in case this starts to go badly. Otherwise, from here, they're two months away."

"That would be my recommendation, Henry."

"Good afternoon, Mr. Grant."

"Good afternoon, Chairman Febo. Thank you for taking this meeting."

It was a virtual meeting, of course. The Association of Planets Chairman of the Council Isabela Febo and Director of the Agency Henry Grant had never actually met. Her whereabouts and visitors were too well tracked to maintain the Agency's undercover status, as frayed as it had become.

"Of course, Mr. Grant. Please, go ahead."

"Thank you, ma'am."

Grant explained to Febo what Stickney and Dent had found out about the attack-ship carrier *Aurora,* the possible use of attack ships against people on the ground, and the Marines' potential ineffectiveness against them. He also noted that *Ladyhawke* only carried four attack ships as counterweight to

Aurora's attack-ship wing, however big it was.

"It sounds to me like *Ladyhawke* may need backup, and closer to the scene, to guarantee the success of this mission, Mr. Grant."

"That is our recommendation, Madam Chairman."

"Very well, Mr. Grant. I will consider it."

"Thank you, Madam Chairman."

Febo read Stickney's and Dent's reports, and concurred with the Agency's assessment that they were likely correct about the Aurora Project. They had fit the pieces of the puzzle together, and it formed a disturbing picture.

At the same time, Febo would not send consortium naval forces into a foreign power without consultation. That's the sort of thing that got alliances in trouble.

Febo placed a call request with Michael Corliss, the Speaker of the Assembly for the Gaston Alliance.

"Good afternoon, Isabela."

"Good morning, Michael."

They were in different cities, on different planets, and so in different time zones. Each deferred to the other in their greeting.

"I actually anticipated your call, Isabela. I've read our agents' reports."

"And do you, like me, believe they are correct, Michael?"

"Oh, yes. Which puts us in a bit of a corner, Isabela."

"Yes. We can either abort our mission, or send them backup. At least, that's the way I read it, Michael."

"I as well. But I do not want to abort the mission, Isabela. It is too important to the long-term security and independence of the cluster."

"Agreed. So do we send backup, Michael, so we can respond with less than a two months' delay?"

"Yes, I think so. Otherwise we risk watching the mission fail, and we are even worse off than before. If it were just a case of the mission has gotten more dangerous, and our agents are at risk, well, we have both been in that position before, Isabela. This is more than that, however. The goals of the mission are themselves at risk."

Febo nodded. She had sent people out on dangerous missions before. That is why the Agency existed, after all. But the risk to the mission here was unacceptable.

"One thing I don't understand, Michael, is how they could field an attack-ship carrier so quickly."

"Our people here think they repurposed a keel already under way in their normal build schedule. That would cut the time down by a lot, Isabela. More than in half."

"Ah. That makes sense, Michael. So what do we send as backup?"

"I would think a squadron."

"A whole squadron?"

"Yes, Isabela. For two reasons. If we are going to send cluster ships to the core worlds, it is important that they prevail. There can be no failure. That would signal weakness and invite further aggression. Second, a squadron, plus a flagship, would put a senior flag officer on the scene. I think we want the best decision-making we can have in such a scenario."

Febo nodded.

"That makes sense to me, Michael. So I have your consent to carry on along that path?"

"More than that, Isabela. You have my encouragement."

"Thank you, Michael. And please express my gratitude once again to Mr. Petrov for assigning such capable operatives to this effort. Without their expertise, we would not even have known there was a problem."

"Will do, Isabela."

"Thank you, Michael."

The consortium's combined navy had two heavy cruiser flagships, in addition to six squadrons of heavy cruisers. The current two commanding admirals – two-year positions which rotated through the six cluster star nations – were currently flag officers from Gaston and Wilbourne.

Nevertheless, Febo went through channels. Her direction, counter-signed by Corliss, went through the admiralty council. Those six admirals, one from each of the star nations, consulted with their own chief executives.

By that point, Febo and Corliss between them had contacted the other four chief executives and gotten them on board with the plan. Febo and Corliss had the most influence with their fellows because they had been right on all the big issues so far.

Ultimately, orders were cut by the admiralty council.

Henry Grant got a short note from Febo.

"Backup will consist of one squadron of heavy cruisers and a heavy cruiser flagship. Flag is Gaston Admiral Harvey Winston. He will act under direction of team leader."

Grant sat back and considered.

A squadron was what he had hoped for, but had considered unlikely. Squadron plus a flag was ninety of the nine-gee attack ships. Hard to imagine a situation they could not handle.

He knew why Febo – and probably Corliss – had done it, though. That put a Gaston full admiral on scene to make the calls. It also gave him enough firepower to prevail.

Defeat would invite adventurism.

Bert Mangum was the field operations contact for Claude Portnoy, the team leader.

Grant sent a note to Mangum.

Mangum sat with Sam that night, drinking his customary nightcap after his first sleep cycle.

"So the chairman has decided to send backup for the team, Sam."

"That's good news, Bert. Gloria's report is most troubling. What is she sending?"

"Nine heavy cruisers. A squadron plus the flag. Which includes their ninety attack ships."

"And over a thousand capital-ship missiles among them. That's a lot of backup, Bert. They could take out all the Vauxhall Royal Navy ships in the system."

"Yes. I think Henry was surprised, but it's clear that Chairman Febo and Speaker Corliss are not willing to risk failure of the mission. And they want to make sure the Vauxhall navy doesn't interfere with events on the ground."

"Who tells Claude?"

"I do. As soon as they get to Vauxhall, he'll be in touch."

"I wonder what he'll think of this?"

"Squadron in formation, Sir. We've hit the hyperspace limit. All units report ready for hyperspace on assigned vector."

"Squadron orders," Admiral Winston said. "Hyperspace on the mark. Send it."

"Yes, Sir. All units. Squadron orders. Hyperspace on the mark in five seconds. Four. Three. Two. One. Mark."

Nine heavy cruisers opened rifts in spacetime in front of themselves, spaced through them, and disappeared from reality. The flagship delayed by one second.

"All units transitioned to hyperspace on the mark, Sir. We are now in hyperspace as well."

"Excellent."

The consortium navy was spacing to war, or the potential for it, anyway, in a foreign power.

It was a voice-only call.

"We're here," Portnoy said.

"In response to reports, backup is on the way," Mangum said. "One squadron plus flagship and parasites. Commanding is Gaston Admiral Harvey Winston. He will contact on near-space arrival. Expectation is two months. Adjust mission timing accordingly."

"Parameters for use?"

"Vauxhall Royal Navy is not to interfere with events on the ground."

"Got it."

Mangum cut the connection.

Vauxhall Arrival

Ladyhawke dropped out of hyperspace in the Vauxhall system, and Portnoy immediately contacted Mangum. He reported the call to Stickney.

"An entire squadron?" Stickney asked. "That's a lot of firepower, Richard. Are you sure he didn't mean division?"

"He said a squadron and a flagship, plus parasites."

"Yeah, they wouldn't send a flagship with a division. Plus parasites is ninety attack ships. Criminy."

"Yup. They want to keep the navy from interfering on the ground."

"Well, I think that would suffice."

"Oh, yes, Susan. But maybe they won't be needed."

"What do you think the odds of that are, Richard?"

"Oh, just offhand? Slim to none."

Stickney loaded Dent's report from the cluster network and shared it with Portnoy. After reading it, they compared notes.

"The attack-ship carrier *Aurora,*" Stickney said. "I wonder how big her attack-ship wing is."

"No clue, apparently. I would think the likely number is dozens."

"Still not a problem. Not for ninety of the nine-gee ships."

"No. Not a problem. We'll have to keep an eye out to keep from being surprised, though. In this context, surprise would be bad."

Portnoy went to Durst's office to brief him on what was going on.

"Hey, Emmet."

"Hi, Claude. Have a seat."

"Thanks."

Portnoy took a seat in one of Durst's guest chairs in front of his desk.

"Couple things, Emmet. I need to keep you in the loop."

"Sure, Claude, Whatcha got?"

"First, the Vauxhall Royal Navy apparently has one attack-ship carrier operational."

"Shit. How many attack ships? Do you know?"

"No, Emmet. We don't. But back home they decided that wasn't good, and they're sending us some backup."

"What are they sending?"

"A squadron, plus a flagship. Ninety of the nine-gee attack ships."

"Oh. Nice."

"Yeah. So *Ladyhawke*'s attack ships are for defensive use only. We won't participate in any attack, but use them as combat space patrol to protect *Ladyhawke*."

"OK. Got it. Sounds good to me, Claude."

"Second thing. This new ship is called the *Aurora*. Are any ships in the Vauxhall system squawking *Aurora* right now?"

Durst pulled his display over, worked for a few seconds.

"Yeah, there is one. Way out here. Transponding that she's a heavy cruiser."

He turned the display so Portnoy could see. Yeah, she was way outside normal orbitals.

"Well, we know that's bullshit, Emmet, because all of Vauxhall's heavy cruisers are named after deceased member of the royal family. Like the HMS *Prince Alfred*."

"No, this one is squawking HMS *Aurora,* and ship type heavy cruiser."

"All right. You guys need to keep an eye on her. If she leaves the system, I want to know. But if she moves in toward the planet, we might have to do something about it."

"But what if the backup isn't here yet, Claude?"

"We're setting up the timing for the mission so that nothing should get dicey before the backup is here."

"OK. Good."

As *Ladyhawke* made her way to the planet from the hyperspace limit, trade master Ephraim Smith was working on the sale of his inbounds, both those from the cluster and those from Earth.

Of course, *Ladyhawke*'s back itinerary did not show her having come from the cluster at all, and the ship had a long history in the core worlds.

Stickney and Portnoy were also working on their aliases. The previous aliases of Richard and Susan Walker, from the Kingdom of Mansfield, wouldn't do. Among other things, Portnoy didn't want their two visits associated with each other in the records.

They settled on Richard and Susan again, though, as being easiest, if nothing else. Richard and Susan Mayfield, from the planet Bledding, in the Kingdom of Lancaster, another of the core-world kingdoms with minimal contact with Vauxhall.

That would make it difficult to track down their aliases, although real couples Richard and Susan Mayfield would be found in Bledding databases. Their actual current whereabouts would be harder.

Why were they on the freighter *Ladyhawke*? Wanderlust, pure and simple. They liked *Ladyhawke*'s most likely itinerary this trip, and found booking passage on an independent freighter to be a cheaper way to get around and sightsee.

By the time *Ladyhawke* got to Vauxhall orbit, all their paperwork was in order.

For the trip down to the planet, Judy Blunt took a different approach. She was going as her Sally McCormack alias, rather than Mary Danner, and was dressed once again as a ship's girl/prostitute. She was wearing a blond wig this time, as last time.

Portnoy was interested to see what Blunt would do to get through immigration and customs this time. He and Stickney were standing in line with Jules, who this time was once again in a dog persona, a golden doodle, but with different color and of apparent different size.

Golden doodles were one of the breeds allowed on spaceships, so they were pretty common with travelers. Jules' apparent differences in size and coloring would differentiate him from his prior trip through customs.

Once again, Blunt adjusted her position in line. When she came up to the immigration control agents, she faced the same young agent who had investigated her second spacer trunk privately on the last trip to Vauxhall.

"Hi! Remember me?"

"Oh. Uh, yes. How are you?"

"I'm good! You gonna examine my second trunk privately again? You know, like last time?"

Blunt gave him a big smile and a wink.

"Uh, no. I can't. I got married a year ago."

"Oh. You're not going to examine my second trunk?"

"No. Sorry."

"Well, I'm disappointed, but you're a sweetheart for staying true to your girl."

He stamped her papers and waved her past.

Blunt grabbed her spacer trunks and dragged them off down the hallway.

While Portnoy and Stickney were waiting for a cab to the Vauxhall Palace View Hotel, Blunt came up to the cab stand. She had stopped at a restroom along the way and changed, and was now Mary Danner, the brown-haired professional woman.

She ignored them, of course, and Portnoy and Stickney boarded the next cab for the trip downtown.

"And once again with a view of the palace," Stickney said.

"Well, we did ask for their best suite, Susan. It's the same one as it was last time."

"Yes, Richard. Of course, it is."

Jules changed to his Jules Hawker persona and walked out on the balcony, looking off toward the palace, not even a mile distant. Portnoy walked up beside him.

"All this trouble, for one man and his family," Jules said.

"Never underestimate how much trouble a single human can cause, Jules."

"Oh, I understand, Richard. This one, though, I will be glad to be done with."

Mary Danner had checked into a different hotel downtown and started checking real estate listings. She was looking for a particular kind of property, an apartment within a bus ride of the side entrance of the royal palace in Vauxhall City.

Her plan was to get a job in the palace. She thought this mission might best be accomplished by someone on the inside.

She should be able to wrangle a job as a secretary or assistant to some palace official, but it didn't really matter. Maid would probably work as well.

When it came down to the clinches, though, for this mission, she wanted to be on the inside.

In orbit, *Ladyhawke* was being unloaded even as Ephraim Smith was looking for outbounds headed for Earth.

Ladyhawke, as a freighter, couldn't just sit here in orbit for months while the operation was carried out on the planet below. The demurrage on a freighter sitting in orbit was too much for a captain-owner to simply sit there and be doing nothing. It would make them stand out.

So it had been decided that *Ladyhawke* would go back and forth to Earth as the mission progressed. They would just have to time things so that *Ladyhawke* would be here when she needed to be.

When she needed to send down the Marines and the infantry weapons she carried.

"Now that we're on Vauxhall, Susan, what's your first order of business?" Portnoy asked Stickney.

"Find the opposition, if there is one. Then you try to make contact with them."

"How you going to find them?"

"Start with people arrested by the government and follow the bunny trail."

"You're going to be able to find them when the Vauxhall government's agents can't?"

"Oh, yes. Regime security forces don't want to succeed, Richard. If they made the threat go away, there go their cushy jobs. I'll find them."

Having made a few appointments to look at apartments,

Mary Danner had also moved into the first part of her mission assignment.

She already had the family tree of the Vauxhall family, listing all current living members of the royal family.

Danner began researching them. Where they lived, where they vacationed, where they partied.

She began deciding for each where they would likely die.

Ladyhawke was in Vauxhall three days. As at Earth, they used local shuttle companies to make their cargo transfers. They completed their unloading and loading, and made for the hyperspace limit. A day later, they opened a rift in spacetime and spaced through it.

The operations team for this mission was successfully on the ground on Vauxhall.

Now, though, they were alone.

Intermezzo

The time on Vauxhall passed quietly. With *Ladyhawke* out of the system and most of two months remaining before the flagship CNS *Indomitable* and her squadron arrived, Portnoy was in no hurry to initiate events.

They had spent months preparing for this mission, and, with the stop at Earth, more than two months getting to Vauxhall, so several weeks to get everything in place did not worry him. The whole mission was a long-term play.

The biggest mistake he could make at this point was being in a hurry.

Stickney spent her days seeking and researching opposition groups. There were a lot of minor players. People who caused a bit of trouble here or there. Most of them had been infiltrated and defanged by Vauxhall security forces.

What Stickney was looking for was the group that had vision, that did not waste its time – and expose itself – with minor irritations to the regime. The ones who were deeply secret, working toward a longer-term goal.

The crafty ones. They were harder to find.

Portnoy and Jules – with Jules impersonating Stickney – went for walks in the park. They took trips to the zoo, always enjoyable to Jules and the other aliens.

Portnoy and Jules even took a tour of the Vauxhall palace, which stuck to a few common rooms and was highly guarded.

They had enjoyable meals with Stickney out on the patio in the pleasant weather.

The time passed pleasantly enough, but it was often like this on missions. Long periods of waiting once one was in place, waiting for all the pieces to come together.

Mary Danner rented an apartment that was a short bus ride from the palace. She could walk it easily if needs be.

Then she applied for a job in the palace.

Judy Blunt had chosen her alias for this trip with care. Danner was not an uncommon name on Vauxhall, as the extended Danner family on Earth had emigrated to Vauxhall together two thousand years ago. There were therefore a lot of Danners on Vauxhall, and Mary was about as common a first name as you could get.

So Mary Danner applied for a job in the palace, and submitted a carefully crafted résumé. This company for several years, this other company for several years, with internal promotions indicating satisfactory performance.

All the companies Danner chose, however, were out of business now for one reason or another, so it would be very difficult to track down references. She also chose businesses in Charlestown, Vauxhall's second-largest city, to cover her recent arrival in Vauxhall City.

Danner's methods would be unlikely to work in a modern free-market economy like Gaston or Mardouk. There was simply too much data in the network's systems to assume a false identity.

But Vauxhall was more primitive in that way. When the nobility directed spending, they preferentially directed it toward themselves. Any credit spent on other things was money they couldn't spend on their luxurious lifestyles.

That was an easy decision for them to make, but it also made it easier for Danner to falsify her background.

The interview was not conducted in the palace, but in a government building downtown. Danner had no problem looking like a serious young professional. She had perfected several different miens over the years, and that was one of them.

Some of the questions were potentially trouble, but Danner had done her homework.

"Why did you think to apply for a job in the palace?"

"Rita Campbell was a friend of my mother's, and she had suggested to my mother that I move to the capital and apply for a job in the palace. She apparently enjoyed her work there and thought it would suit me. Be a step up, too, from what I was doing. When my last company folded, and then when she passed, I remembered her advice."

Rita Campbell, a long-time palace employee, had recently died of cancer, and there were various testimonials and remembrances on the funeral site about her. She had been from Charlestown as well – one reason Danner had chosen that city – and hometown friends were hard to track down.

"You just recently took an apartment, and have it on a month-to-month lease?"

"Yes. Following Rita's advice to apply for a job in the palace, I didn't want to sign a longer lease. If I don't get a job there, then I will probably move back to Charlestown. I have more contacts there in finding a new job. So I didn't want to make a longer commitment."

Being from out of town, but having an internal reference – who was conveniently dead, and so couldn't be asked questions – covered the biggest hole in Danner's background, her recent arrival.

"Well, we will consider your application and interview, Ms. Danner, and we will let you know."

"Thank you very much, Mr. Cooper. It's been nice talking to you."

Mary Danner got the palace job, as she expected after the interview. She went to the same government office building downtown to fill out paperwork and take a week-long course on the layout of the palace and proper palace etiquette.

This course included learning the identities of a couple dozen members of the royal family one might run into while performing one's duties, and the proper form of address for each.

Lèse-majesté, it appeared, would not be tolerated.

That was alright with Danner. Her job on this mission wasn't to insult or annoy members of the royal family.

Her job was to kill them.

A month into the team's stay on Vauxhall, Mary Danner reported to the palace to begin the new job. The fellow who interviewed her met her at the exit of the employee entrance security station.

"It's good to see you again, Ms. Danner. Come with me, please."

Brent Cooper, as he had told her during the interview, was the executive assistant to the head of the office pool, Morgan Saunders. Saunders appeared to be more oriented to interfacing with other department heads within the palace, and left the day-to-day operation of the office pool, including hiring, to Cooper.

Cooper showed her to the office pool's space in one wing of the palace, and left her with Megan Brie, one of the supervisors.

"You knew Rita?" Brie asked her after Cooper had left.

"She was an old friend of my mother's, who moved out of

town before I was born. I saw her in passing once in a while when she was in town visiting family and friends, but mostly they talked on the phone. She seemed very nice."

"I see. Well, she was popular here, so that's to your credit, I suppose. Let me run down what your initial duties will be."

Danner's initial duties would be simple as she learned the palace and the job. Runner. Filer. General gofer.

It was easy work, and Danner enjoyed the sense of being useful, even as she gathered information for her mission.

"I got a short status update from Mary Danner," Portnoy told Stickney over dinner one evening.

"You haven't heard from her in a month. What's she up to?"

"She's taken a job in the office pool in the palace."

"Oh my God, Richard. They *hired* her? They let a viper into the palace every morning?"

"Yep. She's right there, every day," Portnoy said, gesturing toward the palace. "That's pretty amazing."

"I'll say. And what a tremendous place to be when it all goes down."

"Oh, yes."

"It's a very smart move," Jules said. "I wondered how she would insinuate herself."

"Yes. And she had a message for you as well, Jules."

Jules, in his Jules Hawker persona, looked at Portnoy and raised an eyebrow.

"She wants you to meet with her to talk about coordinating your activities. Two o'clock Saturday afternoon. She said you would know where to find her."

Jules thought about it for a moment.

"Yes. In fact, I do, Richard."

"Excellent. Now Danner is pretty much self-dispatching,

Jules. If she has assignments for you, that's OK with me as long as we don't conflict. That's up to you to keep track of."

"I understand, Richard."

"I wonder what Danner needs with Jules," Stickney said.

"Hard to say. Jules is a man of many talents."

Saturday afternoon, Jules was at the Vauxhall City Zoo. He walked through the zoo to the big predators area and sat on a park bench. He was a little early.

Precisely at two o'clock, Mary Danner came and sat on the other end of the park bench. She spoke softly, and without looking at him.

"I got a job in the palace."

"So I heard. Smart move."

"Thanks. One big problem is that their security screening is pretty thorough. Metal detectors and all that. When the push comes, I'll need to get things into the palace. Can you assist with that?"

"Yes. That's not a problem."

"Good. I need to show you through my things, so you can get them if I'm already in the palace and need you to bring something to me."

"That's fine."

"Here's the address and a time. Come as your female persona."

Danner took a piece of gum out of her pocket, unwrapped it, and put it in her mouth. She crumpled the wrapper and threw it on the ground, then got up and walked away.

They had never looked at each other.

Jules shook his head at his erstwhile bench mate littering in the zoo, then picked up the wrapper and put it in his pocket.

Jules dawdled for another twenty minutes before getting up

and strolling through the rest of the zoo. When he was in a private spot, he pulled the wrapper from his pocket and read the address and time there, committing them to memory, then popped the wrapper in his mouth and ate it.

At three o'clock, Jules knocked on the door of the designated apartment. The building was perfect for an operative. One of hundreds of nearly anonymous apartment buildings downtown.

Danner opened the door.

"Jewel! Come in and see my new place."

Jules entered and Danner closed the door. The moment she did, she became all business.

"All right, Jules. Let me show you what I have and what I might need."

It took an hour to go through Danner's second spacer trunk. The one with all the sex toys and equipment in front. Each item was in its own pocket. Various bombs were paired with remote detonators, each in their own place. Knives. Firearms and ammunition. Drugs. Hypodermic needles. It went on and on.

Danner replaced each item carefully after she named it and showed it to Jules.

"Can you remember all that, Jules?"

"Oh, yes."

"And you can get it to me in the palace?"

"Oh, yes. I use my deer persona."

"There are thermal checks on the deer paths. We were warned on staff not to use them."

"Yes. I know. I adjust my body's surface temperature.

"Nice. Now, this apartment has an old-fashioned lock. Do you need a key?"

"Let me see the key, Mary."

Danner handed him a metal key. Jules looked at it and pressed it against his finger. Then he got up, walked to the apartment door and opened it. Jules extruded a key shape at the end of his index finger, then stuck it in the keyhole and cycled the lock.

"No, I don't need a key. Having seen yours was enough."

Jules handed the key back to her.

"All right, then, Jules. I think we're all set."

During this period, *Ladyhawke* came back into the Vauxhall system and left, multiple times. The X-3 drive had started to leak into the core worlds, and they did not try to hide their transfer times.

Emmet Durst considered it more important not to be out of touch of the mission operatives for any longer than he had to be. Things were going to heat up soon, and he wanted *Ladyhawke* to be there to assist.

They were his friends, after all.

The Resistance

"I think I have him, Richard," Stickney said.

"The leader of a credible resistance movement?"

"Yes."

Portnoy came over, and Stickney had the picture of a man centered in her display.

"Kurt Conrad. Mid-forties. Owns a small shop downtown. Bilingual in English and German."

"Shop owner is a perfect cover. People in and out all day. Packages in, packages out. Anonymous. Bilingual is strange, though."

"Family is German. They kept the language alive inside the family."

"OK. That makes sense. So how do we contact him, Susan?"

"That's up to you, Richard. I've done my job."

Stickney turned to him.

"I found him."

Portnoy and Jules went to the small shop downtown owned by Conrad. They walked in and split up, looking around. It was mostly kitchenwares and other housewares. They were the only shoppers in the store at the moment.

Conrad came back to Portnoy.

"May I help you find something, sir?"

Portnoy did not turn to him, and spoke softly.

"We need to talk, Mr. Conrad. Über den Aufstand."

About the revolution.

Conrad drew a pistol and pointed it at Portnoy. Portnoy ignored it.

"I am not a government agent, Mr. Conrad. My name is Pendergast. I am here to assist you in your efforts."

"You don't seem greatly concerned about having a gun pointed at you, Mr. Pendergast."

Portnoy shrugged.

"It's happened before, Mr. Conrad. Besides, you have not released the safety, and you have ignored my associate."

Conrad glanced over to Jules, who was holding a Siegfried arms integrally suppressed 8mm pistol aimed at his center of mass.

"Do not release the safety on your pistol, Mr. Conrad," Jules said. "Unfortunate events would ensue."

Conrad shrugged and reholstered his pistol in his waistband holster.

"Let's go in the back where we can talk."

"And your shop door, Mr. Conrad?"

"There's a locking button on the doorway to the back."

Portnoy nodded, and Conrad gestured to the door into the back room. Jules reholstered his weapon, and Portnoy, then Jules, then Conrad walked into the back room. Conrad pushed the lock button for the front door as he passed through the doorway.

"Please," Conrad said, gesturing to chairs around a table in the first back room.

Portnoy and Jules sat down.

"Assist me? I have no clue what you're talking about, Mr. Pendergast."

"I am clearly not a government agent, Mr. Conrad. If I were, I would simply have arrested you."

"Not if you wanted to find out anything else."

"Of course. I would arrest you and drug it out of you."

"Then why are you here?"

"As I said. To assist you. The King of Vauxhall is building up his navy to attack and topple my country's government, making it part of Vauxhall. We decided to topple him first."

"The two of you? How can you help anything?"

"Well, it's not the two of us, any more than it's the one of you. We have considerable assets available."

"I won't tell you about anyone else, Mr. Pendergast."

"I have no desire to know about anyone else, Mr. Conrad. I assume you are one of the ringleaders, or can be in touch with them. Nothing more. We have a plan, and we want to coordinate our efforts with yours."

Conrad considered. They had always thought they would not be able to prevail against the monarchy without outside help. Theirs had mostly been a waiting game. Wait until some outside assistance was available. Was this finally the outside help they needed?

"And how do I know you're not just two guys who wandered in here to cause trouble?" he asked.

Portnoy pointed to Jules.

"Consider my associate here," Portnoy said. "He is a shape-shifting alien."

Conrad snorted.

"A likely story."

Jules shifted to an impersonation of Bert Mangum, then Gloria Dent, then a Vauxhall palace guard, before shifting back to Jules Hawker.

"OK. Now that's a nice trick."

"And he's bulletproof, Mr. Conrad."

Jules drew his pistol, at which Conrad tensed, but Jules put the big muzzle of the integrally suppressed firearm in his mouth and pulled the trigger. Conrad jumped at the loud pop. Jules reholstered the weapon.

Jules raised an eyebrow to Conrad, then turned his head aside and spat out the spent round.

"OK. Now that's a *really* nice trick."

"Now imagine five hundred of them, Mr. Conrad. Marines all. *Bulletproof* Marines."

"You have them along?"

"I have assets available, Mr. Conrad."

"What do you need from us, Mr. Pendergast?"

"For the final push, I need crowds around the Vauxhall palace, Mr. Conrad. Protesters. Enough of them to conceal my Marines until the assault. It also needs to look like a popular uprising, for your purposes as well as my own."

Conrad nodded. If it looked like a foreign takeover, the crowd would rally behind the throne.

"What about RDT, Mr. Pendergast? A lot of people are addicted to the government's drug, and if the government withholds it, they will die. Or worse."

"I have a cure for RDT with me, Mr. Conrad. Give it to all your people, and withholding it hurts the pro-monarchy forces, while not hurting your people at all."

"What about the navy, Mr. Pendergast?"

"Vauxhall is not the only interstellar government with a navy, Mr. Conrad. The Vauxhall Royal Navy will not be allowed to interfere with events on the ground."

"Why would your government be so interested, Mr. Pendergast?"

"As I say, Mr. Conrad. The King of Vauxhall is building a navy to militarily take over my government and others in the region. We prefer not to allow that to happen, and sooner is better than later."

"How do I know any of this is real, Mr. Pendergast?"

"Two things, Mr. Conrad. Do you remember the dustup two

years ago when the King of Vauxhall issued letters of marque against five people, then withdrew them?"

"Yes. We keep track of the news out of the palace pretty closely. Wait. You're *that* Pendergast?"

"Yes, Mr. Conrad."

"My God, you're taking a huge risk."

"I have altered my appearance, and am operating under an assumed name currently, but yes, Mr. Conrad, I am taking a risk."

"And the other thing, Mr. Pendergast?"

"This weekend, a member of the royal family will die."

"There's so many of them, that could just be coincidence, Mr. Pendergast."

"Oh, not this one, Mr. Conrad. It will be, um, splashy."

Portnoy stood up, as did Jules.

"Very well, Mr. Pendergast, we will consider it."

"I can ask no more, Mr. Conrad."

Portnoy and Jules left the back room, walked through the store and out into the street after Conrad unlocked the front door with the lock button.

Back at the hotel, Portnoy sent a short message to Danner.

"One. This weekend. Splashy."

Mary Danner considered her list of targets. That is, the entire royal family. Who would be an easy target this weekend?

By this time, she had their comings and goings pretty well mapped.

Hmm. This should be easy.

Conrad called a meeting of the council. He was a member, but not the chairman. It was a virtual meeting, of course, and all attended through anonymous echo nodes and used alias images.

Conrad told them of the confrontation with Portnoy. When he was done, the chairman spoke up.

"So what are we to do, everyone? The floor is open for discussion."

"This may be the outside assistance we've been hoping for," one said. "We haven't ever seen anything this promising."

"I worry that it's too promising," another said. "When someone offers you exactly what you want, you have to be suspicious."

"Yes, but that would apply to anyone who offered assistance," a third said. "Are we to turn them all down? Then we go nowhere."

"Wait," a fourth said. "We don't need to decide anything. There's an open commitment on the table. Let's wait and see what happens this weekend. After all this time, a few days doesn't matter."

"OK, now that makes sense to me," the second said.

"Are we agreed then?" the chairman asked. "We see what happens this weekend, then meet again on Monday when we see if they keep their commitment."

Everyone agreed, and the meeting was over.

Carl Vauxhall – Prince Carl, the king's younger brother – liked the horse races. He went every Sunday, parking his luxury sports car in a special area that was away from everyone else's car and carefully guarded.

Princess Alexia, his wife, didn't like the races and never accompanied him. That was OK with Prince Carl. He liked to concentrate on the races, and not be interrupted with jabber.

This Sunday, the races were particularly enjoyable, and he

was in good spirits when he was given a lift by electric cart from the main entrance back to his car.

Prince Carl got in the car, closed the door, and turned on the ignition.

The car exploded.

It was a big explosion, bigger than it needed to be. It flipped the car up into the air and left a hole in the pavement where it had been parked. Car parts and body parts rained down as far as a hundred feet away.

Prince Carl was killed. In fact, more like disassembled.

No one else was injured.

"Nice," Danner said from her viewpoint in the back of the stands.

"I'm very sorry, Your Majesty, but Prince Carl has died."

Albert sat back in his chair. His younger brother, originally third in line after he and Ann. Now Ann and Carl were both gone. That hurt.

"How, Chalmers? A heart attack or something?"

"No, Sire. He was murdered. A bomb in his car."

"Damn!"

Albert pounded his fist on his desk.

This was like two years ago, with those cluster bastards. But he hadn't done anything against them since revoking the letters of marque.

Not that they knew of, anyway.

"All right, Chalmers. Make sure I'm copied on all the police reports."

"Of course, Sire."

"And warn all the family to stay out of public spots again. We don't know if this was a one-off or if there will be follow-ons."

"Yes, Sire."

The Monday night meeting of the council had news to consider.

"Well, they've done what they said they were going to do," the chairman said.

"Are we sure?"

"Well, we know it wasn't a false-flag attack. Albert was close to Carl. They wouldn't have killed him just to get us to trust Pendergast."

"Are we sure he's dead? Are we sure it was Carl?"

"Oh, yes," the chairman said. "There were bits and pieces of him all over the place, one of which our people obtained. DNA match. One hundred percent."

"Well, that's that, then. And Pendergast predicted a royal family member getting offed this weekend."

"Well, he said one would die," Conrad said.

"And indeed one did," the chairman said. "We are left with a question, then. What now, gentlemen?"

"I suppose we trust them."

"To the extent of working with them. I'm not prepared to share everything with them."

"Oh, agreed, agreed. But crowds of protesters in front of the palace. Civil unrest? Those things we can do."

"And the RDT cure, gentlemen?" the chairman asked.

"Well, of course we should get that from them if we can."

"I agree. If we make our people immune, it does them no good to withhold it. It just hurts their own loyalists."

"All right, then. It sounds as if we are in agreement."

The chairman turned to Conrad's alias image.

"I assume they will contact you again. When they do, you may tell them we are on board with them, on two conditions.

One is that they work through you. No deeper penetration into our organization. The other is that, whatever comes after, it's composed of Vauxhall citizens only. No outsiders. No foreign government. No foreign interference."

"I understand," Conrad said.

Portnoy and Jules stopped by Kurt Conrad's shop on Wednesday morning.

"Ah, gentlemen. I have a product you should see. Come with me, please."

Conrad led them to the back room, and locked the shop door on his way in.

"Please be seated, Mr. Pendergast."

Portnoy and Jules sat down.

"We thought we would give your leadership some time to consider our proposal, Mr. Conrad."

"Indeed, Mr. Pendergast. Indeed. We have always known we would need outside help to prevail, but paranoia grows over time. Your prediction of Carl's unfortunate demise assisted a great deal."

Pendergast nodded. That had always been the calculation.

"So what now, Mr. Pendergast? You are driving the timing now."

"I have a shipment for you, Mr. Conrad. Four million doses of the cure for RDT. Not only does it cure the addiction, it makes the person immune to RDT in the future."

"And if a person who is not addicted to RDT takes it, Mr. Pendergast?"

"There is no harm done, Mr. Conrad, but they, too, become immune to RDT in the future."

"Indeed. Four million doses, you say?"

"To start, Mr. Conrad. Yes. There is more. This shipment is

one container, filled with one-gallon plastic bottles. The medication itself is odorless and colorless. The dose is one to two ounces, and is not very sensitive. I imagine a jigger glass would work well. Dump it in someone's drink and that's it."

"How splendid, Mr. Pendergast."

"One note, Mr. Conrad. Consignment warehouse rules say I must disclose who is buying it. I have no leeway there."

Conrad nodded.

"This store is the consignee, Mr. Pendergast. I can arrange delivery."

"Excellent."

"So what is the plan, Mr. Pendergast? How do we prevail?"

"Once our assets are all in place, Mr. Conrad, we will begin hitting members of the royal family. Here, there, the other place. But never in the royal palace."

"You want them to retreat to the palace, Mr. Pendergast?"

"Yes, Mr. Conrad. Then your protesters will take to the streets. Our people will be scattered among them, in disguise. We expect at some point for the palace to give us some event – some act of carnage – that makes the whole thing their fault."

Conrad nodded.

"Smart."

"Yes, Mr. Conrad. And then the crowd, in their righteous anger, will attack the palace. With our people in the lead."

"They will attempt to escape via shuttle. Mr. Pendergast."

Portnoy nodded.

"So I suspect. We have that covered as well, Mr. Conrad. There will be no escape short of death."

Conrad raised an eyebrow, but Portnoy did not respond.

"Now, I have been told to impose two conditions on our participation, Mr. Pendergast. One is that we expose no more of our organization to you. Not its size, or other members, or anything like that. I can commit to you that we can put thousands of people in the street, but that is all."

"I'm good with that. And I will not expose all of my assets to you either, Mr. Conrad."

Conrad nodded. Sensible.

"The other is that, whatever emerges, it must be run by the citizens of Vauxhall. No foreign power."

"I agree, and can do you one better, Mr. Conrad. When the transition is announced, I can sign a mutual defense and free trade agreement with the new government, as Ambassador to Vauxhall."

"That is extremely generous, Mr. Pendergast. We expect a certain amount of adventurism by other star kingdoms to try to fill the power gap when the royal family is gone."

"We do as well, Mr. Conrad. The other planets of the Kingdom of Vauxhall, sure. But we will allow no aggression against the free planet of Vauxhall."

"And you can enforce that, Mr. Pendergast?"

"Oh, yes. And we will, Mr. Conrad. We will."

Applying The Pressure

When Portnoy and Jules got back to the Vauxhall Palace View Hotel, Portnoy put through the sale of one of the containers of Narlaxatrophine-II with the consignment warehouse. He used Conrad's shop as the buyer.

Several hours later he got a notice it had been picked up by a shipping company and the sale completed.

"Well, they're certainly not letting any moss grow under their feet," Portnoy said. "They've already picked up the first container of the cure."

"Wow. So what's our timeframe now, Richard?" Stickney asked.

"The heavy cruisers should be in place in two weeks. *Ladyhawke* just left for Earth again, so she will be back in two weeks. Looks to me like anytime after two weeks works."

"That's about the time we figured it would take to get the royal family unnerved enough to move into the palace."

"Right. So I guess it's time to give her the go-ahead to get started."

"Sounds like it to me, Richard."

Portnoy sent a cryptic message to Danner that evening.

"Four in next two weeks. Slow, then faster."

Danner read the message and nodded. That's what they had talked about. Build the pressure, and accelerate it as they went.

Danner looked at her royal family list. Someone in the next week, for sure. It was Wednesday night, and she had just hit

Carl Vauxhall last weekend. So someone this weekend would work.

Hmm. Look for the easy target. That would increase the pressure to button up.

Here's one. Danner scanned the information.

Yes, this should work nicely.

Princess Caroline, Princess Ann's daughter and the king's niece, was the royal sponsor of the annual Vauxhall City Marathon. The course ran through the downtown and out into neighboring areas, coming back into downtown to finish down the boulevard across the front of the royal palace.

Danner knew the setup from recordings of the past few years. Caroline would fire the gun that started the race, standing on a stage at the start/finish line, then retreat into an air-conditioned trailer for the four hours of the race. She would emerge just before the lead runners arrived, watching the overall winner break through the tape at the start/finish line.

During all of this, Caroline would be well away from the crowds. But at the end of the race, she would come down off the stage to congratulate the male and female winners. She walked through a chokepoint there where she was less than five feet from one of the barriers holding back the crowd.

Danner, disguised as a variant of her Sally McCormack alias, positioned herself in the second row of people from that barrier. She saw the beginning of the race, and noted that everything was as it had been last year. The setup was the same, and Caroline's actions were the same.

At the end of the race, Caroline came down off the stage and walked through the chokepoint to meet the winners and congratulate them. She passed within just four feet of Danner, in the second row of the spectators.

The dart from Danner's gun, held waist-high between the two men in front of her, caught Princess Caroline in the left upper thigh, the needle easily penetrating her light summer skirt.

Caroline seemed to stumble, then stopped and wavered, before collapsing. She was dead before she hit the ground.

Danner screamed.

She had already hidden the small weapon.

"Your Majesty, Princess Caroline has died."

"How, Chalmers?"

"Well, they thought it might have been a heart attack, Sire."

"In her thirties?"

Chalmers shrugged.

"It does happen, Sire. But, as it turns out, she was hit by a poison dart from someone in the crowd at the marathon."

"Damn it, she should never have gone."

"She was the royal sponsor, Sire."

"Yes, I know. And now she's the dead royal sponsor. Shit. Remind people again to stay out of public areas, Chalmers. Someone is targeting us."

"Yes, Sire."

"Is there anything more on Carl's death?"

"The police say the explosive was not sourced on Vauxhall, Sire. It was a foreign explosive."

"Probably stuff those cluster bastards left behind when they were here two years ago."

"Yes, Sire."

"Well, tell people to be smart, Chalmers. Smarter than Caroline, anyway."

"Of course, Sire."

On Sunday, Danner considered her next target. Probably Wednesday or Thursday would be good, which meant it would have to be in the evening. She worked at the palace during the weekdays, and the goal was to make the palace a safe harbor. Some place the family would gather to escape the mayhem.

Hmm. This was interesting. The king's first cousin, Prince Frederick – Albert's father's sister's boy – maintained a mistress. A commoner, of course. Frederick was in his forties and single, and a notorious ladies' man, but he visited his mistress every Thursday evening, before his big weekend of partying. To take the edge off, Danner supposed.

Danner started making plans.

Danner, in the same variant of her Sally McCormack alias she had used at the marathon last Saturday, sat in the elevator lobby on the third floor of a downtown apartment building. She periodically checked her watch, clearly a prostitute waiting for an arranged assignation.

Danner had planted a surveillance camera in the lobby of the apartment building on the first floor, an apparent fertilizer stick in a potted plant. She watched the feed on a small roll-up display, pretending to be reading.

There was Prince Frederick, arriving at his normal time for the evening with his mistress, who lived – in an apartment he subsidized – on the third floor. Danner watched him get in the elevator alone, then rolled up her display and pocketed it. She sighed – clearly stood up by her client – and walked over to the elevator.

When the elevator door opened, Frederick got out and Danner got on. They smiled and nodded to each other. Danner pushed the button for the first floor, then shot Prince Frederick in the back with a poison dart from her air-powered dart gun as the elevator doors were closing.

Danner was on the first floor within seconds, and walked out of the apartment building into the night and disappeared into the city.

Judy Blunt, a.k.a. Mary Danner, a.k.a. Sally McCormack, changed back into her Mary Danner alias in an alley, with clothes she pulled out of her large bag. She also dumped the wig and the facial prosthetics she had used.

Blunt had long experience fooling facial pattern-matching software in the cluster, much more competent software than that available to the security forces in Vauxhall.

The police would match McCormack from the security recordings of the apartment building tonight with the news recordings of the marathon last Saturday, and come up with the same assassin. That was good. Portnoy wanted the family to know they were being hunted by a single organization.

There would not be a facial match to Mary Danner, an employee in the royal palace on Vauxhall, however.

Blunt was better than that.

"Your morning update, Sire."

"Very good, Chalmers. Leave me now. I will call when I am done."

"Yes, Sire. I might point out the primary item is that your cousin, Prince Frederick, died last night. Murdered."

"Damn it. What happened to him?"

"He was found dead in the elevator lobby of the apartment building where he maintained a mistress, Sire. Poison dart to the back as he got off the elevator."

"Do the police have anything yet?"

"Yes, Sire. The woman in the security recordings from the

apartment building who is the most likely suspect was also present at Princess Caroline's murder last weekend. Within feet of her when she was shot with a similar poison dart."

"A woman?"

"Yes, Sire."

"So it's one outfit. Not copy-cats piling on."

"It would appear so, Sire."

"All right, Chalmers. Keep me informed of developments."

"Of course, Sire."

"And let the family know there's plenty of room here if they want to move into the palace until this blows over."

"Yes, Sire."

Portnoy and Stickney watched the king's reaction to the death of Prince Frederick on the surveillance camera in his office, via the feed from the cluster.

"Well, Richard, there's your opening."

"Yes. He's invited everyone into the palace. That's perfect."

"What do you do now?"

"Shift the venues."

Danner saw the feed, too, and was not surprised at the message she got from Portnoy.

"Shift to their homes."

Prince William, youngest brother of the king, had a pool behind his house in Vauxhall City. The pool was in the middle of the gardens, and was big enough to swim laps.

His daughter, Princess Marie, was in her twenties. She loved the pool, and swam laps most evenings when the water was still warm but the day had cooled.

On Tuesday night, she had just finished her laps and was

floating in the deep end of the pool catching her breath when a crawler scuttled across the pool deck behind her and dropped into the water. She turned at the sound, but didn't see anything.

When the crawler was three feet below the surface, it detonated. Marie was not caught in the explosion, but the tremendous concussion of the blast, traveling through the incompressible water, killed her.

Coming out to investigate the noise, the staff found Marie floating face down in the pool.

Danner was busy at the palace the rest of the week as the office pool was brought in to help family members move into the palace. It wasn't all of them yet, but a number of them had had enough. That the pretty, young Marie was killed in the pool behind her father's house, within the walled gardens, was enough for them.

But it was going to get even worse.

The king's cousin Prince Andrew, Albert's father's brother's son, lived with his wife in the estate section of Vauxhall City not far from Prince William's home, where Princess Marie had been killed.

He and his wife Bernadette were nearly Albert's age. After dinner on Friday, they would often sit in the back living room of the big house reading. The back living room – the reading room – had a big picture window looking out over the grounds.

At night, however, and absorbed in their reading, they did not notice the crawler inching its way up the glass. When it reached the center of the big window, the crawler exploded.

Spears and shards and bullets of glass sleeted through the

room, shredding everything. The doors, which opened into the room, were shut against their stops and held long enough for the overpressure in the room to blow out the exterior wall.

The shredded bodies of Andrew and Bernadette were found outside the house, on the flagstone deck.

On Saturday morning, Danner got a call to report in to the palace for work.

When Danner got to the office pool, she asked Megan Brie, the supervisor, what was going on.

"Oh, Mary, it's terrible. Prince Andrew and his wife were blown up last night, right in their own living room."

"How awful!"

"Yes. So the king has ordered the family to take up residence in the palace until they can get on top of all this. We're going to help out housekeeping today and tomorrow getting everyone moved in."

"Well, I'm happy to help any way I can, Megan."

Which was true, after all. Claude Portnoy and Judy Blunt wanted the whole royal family in the palace. That would make it easier to kill them all.

"Oh, good. It's nice to know I can rely on you, Mary."

Convergence Of Forces

It was the beginning of the next week when Portnoy heard from Admiral Winston. The squadron was in place, just two light-years from Vauxhall. That was six minutes in hyperspace with the X-3 drive.

"You're here, Admiral Winston?"

"We have arrived, Mr. Portnoy. We are in place, two light-years from Vauxhall, and can be there in minutes. That would be at the hyperspace limit, of course, which is normally a day out, accelerating and then decelerating at one gravity. For an attack ship at nine gees, accelerating all the way, contact is more like eighty minutes from launch at the hyperspace limit."

"So if I sounded the alarm, attack ships would be at the planet in ninety minutes, Admiral?"

"Yes, sir. That's about right."

"And your orders, Admiral?"

"We are an auxiliary force attached to your mission, Mr. Portnoy. You call the shots. Now, if you told me to bomb the planet, that would run against my general orders, which are to assist you in ensuring the Vauxhall Royal Navy does not interfere with events on the ground. Within that broad charter, though, I am under your orders."

"Very well, Admiral. I will try not to give you any moral dilemmas as things unfold here."

"I appreciate that, Mr. Portnoy. What is your status at the current time?"

"*Ladyhawke* is due back from Earth shortly, Admiral. She will be in close orbit within another day. That gives me an even faster response time for some activities, as well as ground forces. We have been building the pressure up here, slowly so as not to have things boil over before you got here. With you here, though, we are going to turn up the heat."

"Very well, Mr. Portnoy. We are on alert out here, and will respond to your call with dispatch."

"Thank you, Admiral."

Ladyhawke showed up the next day, dropping out of hyperspace at the hyperspace limit and heading for the planet. Emmet Durst called in for instructions.

"Hi, Emmet."

"Hi, Claude. What's your status? What are my orders?"

"We've been building the pressure on the regime, and are going to kick that into high gear now. And the squadron has arrived. They have a response time to orbit of an hour and a half or so."

"Nice. And my orders?"

"Take a normal orbit and unload your cargo as per usual, Emmet. Ho-hum, just another day stuff. When we need something from you, though, it's gonna be on short notice."

"And that's likely to be?"

"Marines and infantry weapons to the surface. And attack ships against armored assault shuttles."

"Got it. We'll be ready to go on all that, Claude."

"Then we're good," Portnoy said.

Portnoy also called Kurt Conrad's shop.

"Everything For The Home," Conrad answered.

"Hi, Kurt. Chuck here. Are you seeing any crowds downtown?"

"No. Nothing yet."

"Huh. Someone told me crowds were forming."

"I'll check again tomorrow and let you know, Chuck."

"OK. Thanks."

"So what all is going on, Richard?" Stickney asked.

"The squadron is here. *Ladyhawke* is back. And the resistance will start demonstrating outside the palace tomorrow."

"Oh, my. After two months on planet, this is all starting to come to a head fast now, isn't it?"

"Yes. It was the squadron we were really waiting for, Susan. With them here, no reason not to get the show on the road."

"And the Marines?"

"Standing by."

"I think you should get them down here, Richard. They can augment the crowds for now. But you don't want them in orbit when things break."

"How would we do that though, Susan? We don't have any large personnel shuttles on *Ladyhawke*. Those are all with the squadron. Should I bring them down a few at a time? And how do we get them past immigration control?"

"I don't know, Richard. What were we going to do before the squadron was sent out here?"

"Bring them down once things broke. Have a few go and steal a few large personnel carriers to bring the rest down. Bringing them down early, though, is a problem."

"Claude, if I might offer a suggestion?"

"Of course, Jules."

"Bring them down as cargo. As they are. Two barracks containers, the galley container, an extra food container, and the weapons containers. Just bring it all down with *Ladyhawke*'s inbound cargo, and transfer it on consignment to the resistance."

"And if the resistance betrays us?"

"They can't hurt us, Claude. If they betray us, the revolution starts early. With them."

Portnoy thought about it. The barracks, galley, and weapons containers had all been repainted, so they were no longer in Marine colors or had any Marine markings. They had been repainted as generic cargo containers, with inventory numbers and the like, but no special markings. They would be anonymous in *Ladyhawke*'s inbound cargo.

Where to put them until crunch time was another issue, but presumably the resistance could handle that.

"That's a good idea, Jules. I think that may be the way to go."

The next morning, protesters started gathering in front of the palace, in the street before the main gate to the palace grounds. The crowd continued to grow throughout the day.

"Well, we know they are going to carry through on their part of the plan," Stickney said.

"Yes. So far, anyway."

"What are the blue flags about, Richard?"

Some of the protesters carried solid blue flags. No stripes, no central logo or crest.

"The royal flag is red and yellow, with the crown seal in red, yellow, black, and gold in the center. Of the three primary colors – red, yellow, and blue – there is no blue on the king's flag. All blue means no king."

"Ah. I see. Clever. So they will peacefully protest there?"

"We'll see how big the crowds get. If they start growing in a big way, something will happen. It won't stay peaceful."

"And what do we do now?"

"Bring down the Marines. I think Jules is right. No reason to wait."

Portnoy called Kurt Conrad's shop.

"Everything For The Home," Conrad answered.

"Hi, Kurt. Chuck here. I have a shipment for you. Six containers."

"Six containers?"

"Yes. It's all those things we talked about. You know. Five hundred of this, so much of that."

The only thing they had talked of five hundred of was Marines.

"Oh, yes. That shipment. Special handling instructions?"

"Oh, it could be almost anywhere. Warehouse. Even a farm. Just not a public place. You will need water and power."

"Understood."

"I'll make the transfer, and you'll get the consignment papers soon."

"Very good."

"Hi, Emmet."

"Hi, Claude. Whatcha got?"

"We're transferring the Marines and the weapons down now. Right in the containers. Both barracks containers, the galley container, an extra food container, and the weapons containers. Just put them in with the inbound cargo, and list them for the consignment warehouse."

"All right, Claude. You got it."

"Just have them button themselves up and ride down with the cargo."

"You gonna talk to Frank?"

"Yeah. I'll give him a call."

"Hi, Claude," said Lieutenant Colonel Frank Everett, the battalion commander of the Erian Marines aboard *Ladyhawke*.

"Hello, Frank. We're going to move you guys to the planet. Things are going to start popping here soon."

"Sounds good. How's it work?"

"We need you to button yourselves up in the barracks containers, then we're going to transfer you down to the planet as cargo, buried in all the inbounds from Earth. The barracks, the galley, an extra food container, and the weapons containers. Does that work for you?"

"Sure."

"The resistance will pick your containers up from the consignment warehouse, and transfer you to some place they have. You can monitor with the outside surveillance on the barracks containers. Your job is to get down here and stay out of sight."

"Can do, Claude."

"Then I'll start to have assignments for you. Probably first will be to swell the crowd protesting outside the palace. But I'll let you know all that once you're down here. Things are moving fast now."

"All right, Claude. We'll see you on the planet."

Emmet Durst watched as the containers were latched by shipping company shuttles and transported to the surface. He hoped everything worked out.

Ladyhawke was stripped pretty clean by the time all the inbounds and the Marines complement had been transported to the surface.

On the ground, one of the containers was searched. It was one of the barracks units, with the Marines on board.

There were advantages to be being a shape-shifter, however.

When the container door was opened, there were two

hundred and fifty identical store mannequins standing in the compartments of the container, along with twenty-five sets of bunk beds.

"'Store fittings' it says," the customs inspector said. "Looks right to me."

None of the other containers were searched.

Once the containers were on the ground, Portnoy issued a bill of sale and release to the consignment warehouse. Container trucks picked them up later that day, the overhead crane of the consignment warehouse mounting each container on a truck.

The trucks took the containers to the dock of an empty commercial building downtown and unloaded them with a container lift, leaving them in the receiving area.

After store hours, Kurt Conrad stopped by there to see what all they had.

"Well, six containers. As they said," he said to himself.

Once he had spoken, though, one of the containers opened, and a man in the uniform of a Marine lieutenant colonel walked out.

"You Kurt Conrad?" he asked.

"Yes, that's me."

"Frank Everett. Pleased to make your acquaintance."

They shook hands, and Conrad nodded to the containers.

"What do we have here, Colonel?"

"Ah. I thought you were expecting us, sir. Five hundred Marines, equipment, galley, and food."

At that, Marines started filing out of the container. The other barracks container opened, and Marines filed out of that one as well. Soon, five hundred Marines, organized by company, platoon, and rifle squad, with NCOs and officers, stood in the large space to either side of Conrad and Everett.

"My word," Conrad said. "You really are Marines."

"Yes, Sir. As promised."

"We're going to have to get you some civilian clothes so you can blend into the crowds."

Everett gave a hand signal, and all five hundred Marines shifted into an assortment of civilian clothes. They were laborers and shop keepers, book keepers and cooks, both men and women.

"We're good, sir. What we could really use is water and power connections."

"Oh. Yes. Yes, of course. Let me show you, Colonel. By the way, what is in the other containers?"

"That container is our galley, sir. We run our own shop there. One container is enough food for several weeks. And those two there are our weapons."

"Two containers of weapons?"

"Yes, sir. Enough assault rifles and ammunition for five thousand of your people, and full kit for us. We didn't bring any armor, but we brought everything else we might need."

A tear ran down Conrad's face. They finally had the outside help they needed to be rid of the monarchy once and for all. He didn't doubt any of Pendergast's promises anymore. Not after seeing this. This was extraordinary.

"The water and electric, sir?"

"Oh, yes, Colonel. This way."

Everett signaled an engineering team, and they followed Conrad to the equipment room.

Once the engineers were working on connecting the galley and barracks containers, Conrad came back over to Everett.

"You know, Colonel. I have a request for you. Something I think it would be very helpful to get seriously under way."

"Of course, Mr. Conrad. I would have to check with my superiors, but I am open to any request you might have."

"Excellent, Colonel. Here's what I was thinking...."

The Effect Of The Cure

"So the Marines are all on planet now, Richard."

"Yes, and Mr. Conrad has a request for them."

Portnoy explained, and Stickney's eyes grew wide.

"Oh, what a great idea."

"Yes. I've given Frank the go-ahead."

Around Vauxhall city, here and there in the commercial centers, tables appeared with two men attending them. On the table was a gallon bottle of a clear liquid and a stack of paper cups.

Also on the table stood a small flagpole on a base, a four-inch by six-inch blue flag sticking out from it.

They appeared first in the poorer areas, like the north side.

"Cure for RDT? Be rid of the drug forever. Take a drink and be free of it."

Passers-by stopped to talk to the men. Many of them took the cure. For each such, one man at the table would pour an ounce and a half of the clear liquid in a cup and hand it to the person, and they would drink it. That was it.

The number of people stopping by increased as the word got around, especially when people who had been cured told their friends over the next few days.

There were some incidents.

On the north side, one of the gangs came by to break up the operation in their territory and beat up the men who had such audacity to do any such thing without their permission.

"You guys need to get out of our territory," the lead tough said.

"Oh, I don't think so," one of the men said. "Why don't you boys run along now."

The lead tough pulled a small gun out from under his jacket.

"You get out of our turf or you're gonna die."

"Oh, I don't think so. Move along, you kids."

The man at the table – an NCO in the Erian Marines, but in civilian clothes – just smiled at the gang leader. The man's condescension infuriated the tough, and he shot the NCO.

"Your toys aren't going to hurt us," the NCO said, then spat out the spent round.

The NCO then pulled a large semi-automatic handgun out of seeming nowhere and pointed it at the toughs.

"Now, are you guys bulletproof, too, or am I going to make a mess on the sidewalk if I use this?"

The toughs backed away, holding their hands out to the sides in acquiescence, and the leader put his gun back in his jacket. Slowly.

"By the way," the NCO said. "You boys want the cure from RDT as long as you're here? No hard feelings. We'd be happy to give you the cure."

The gang members actually took the cure

There were no more troubles with them.

The police stopped by, too, once they started setting up tables in the downtown proper, outside of the poor areas the cops left to the gangs.

"What are you guys up to?" the senior of the two officers asked.

"Hello, officer. We have a cure for RDT addiction. Would you gentlemen care to take the cure? It even makes you immune to RDT in the future."

"You can't sell medicines on the street."

"But we're not selling it, officer. We're giving it away."

"Even so. You can't distribute medicines on the street. You can't distribute medicines at all without a license."

"Why?"

"It's against the law, is why. You have to stop or you'll be arrested."

"Oh, we're not going to stop, and you're not going to arrest us."

"The hell I'm not."

The police officer drew his weapon.

Things happened very quickly after that.

The two men at the table wrapped an incredibly long arm around each police officer, took their weapons away, then handcuffed their hands behind their backs. It took seconds, and it seemed to the police like each man at the table must have four arms.

The men then replaced the police officers' firearms in their holsters.

"Now you run along back to headquarters, officer, and forget all about us. Because if you come back with more manpower, we'll have to get nasty."

Of course, the police did come back with more manpower. Police are like bees: if you annoy one, they will swarm. An hour later, a police van pulled up and a dozen men with automatic rifles, wearing body armor, piled out of it.

"HANDS UP!"

"No."

The lead officer fired at the NCO – one round, center of mass – and the NCO smiled at him, then spat out the spent round. The PFC at the table with the NCO then produced a grenade launcher, seemingly from nowhere.

The police officer looked at the two-inch diameter muzzle of that weapon, and swallowed hard.

Two dozen men in Marine uniforms carrying SBRs and grenade launchers came running around the corner and took aim at the police tactical team.

"FREEZE!" the first sergeant of the Marines shouted.

"Are you bulletproof as well, officer?" the NCO asked. "Because if you're not, you should probably stand down. By the way, while you're here, would you like the cure for RDT? It's free, is a total cure, and will protect you from the drug into the future."

Military uniforms showing up made all the difference for the police leader. Whatever was going on here, if the Marines were involved, it clearly had the approval of someone much higher up the chain than him and his superiors.

He signaled his men to 'at ease,' and the first sergeant did as well. As men will do when violence is off the table, they all ended up chatting.

And while they were there, the police tactical squad did take the cure for RDT.

The word spread through the police that the RDT cure was some kind of approved activity, and there were no more incidents with law enforcement.

In fact, a number of police units came to the tables now spread throughout the city, and got the RDT cure.

"The damnedest thing is going on, Father," Crown Prince James said.

"What's that, James? Something new?" King Albert XIV asked.

"Yes. There are people within the city passing out what they claim is a cure for RDT addiction. More, it makes one RDT immune forever."

"Shit. We need to shut that down."

"The police have tried. They shoot the men at the tables, and they just spit out the bullets. A tactical squad showed up at one of the tables, and two squads of Marines showed up with weapons, including SBRs and grenade launchers."

"*Our* Marines?"

"They must be, Father. Who else has that many Marines on Vauxhall?"

"Oh, now that's a nasty thought. Either way. They're either our own Marines, or some foreign power has injected their own military into Vauxhall. I'm not sure which would be worse."

"We've inquired of the Marine leadership, and they say all their men are present and accounted for, except for those out on leave, and they aren't allowed to take weapons with them off-base. Not those kinds of weapons, anyway."

"Yes, James, but if they're our own Marines, the leadership could be lying to us."

"Then what do we do?"

"I don't know, James."

"We could halt the distribution of RDT, Father. That would render addicts helpless."

"But the people who are being trouble now are cured of the addiction, James. We would just be hampering our own side."

The king thought about it.

"Shit."

Kurt Conrad stopped by the empty building where the Erian Marines were based, and met with Lieutenant Colonel Everett.

"How are we doing on distributing the RDT cure, Colonel?"

"It's going really well, sir. We've distributed over two

million doses in three days."

"That's over half the container. We're going to run out."

"Oh, no, sir. That's just one of the containers we brought along. We have dozens of them."

"Dozens?"

"Yes, sir. Not enough for the whole population, but we also brought manufacturing modules to make more."

Conrad just gaped at him.

"We're good, sir."

Portnoy and Stickney had watched the meeting between the king and the crown prince.

"The king doesn't know what to do, Richard."

"Eventually, he'll resort to the military. They always do. But the longer he waits, the worse it gets for them."

"Really?"

"Oh, yes, Susan. Have you paid attention to the size of the crowds now?"

"No. The news isn't reporting it."

"No, but the network is full of recordings. Posted through anonymous servers. The crowds in front of the palace now are getting into the thousands. It'll be tens of thousands within the next couple days."

"Really?"

"Oh, yes. It's the cure, you see."

Unlike in the cluster, where RDT had been made illegal, in Vauxhall and the other core-world kingdoms, RDT use was encouraged. The interrelated noble families of the core-world kingdoms wanted the commoners addicted to an anti-depressive drug that kept them contented and docile, and which the nobility controlled access to.

That it was massively addictive, and withdrawal from the drug would cause mental decline and perhaps even death, was just icing on the cake.

When a commoner was arrested on Vauxhall, they were given RDT in jail, whether they were previously addicted or not. The same with commoners being treated in a hospital. The nobility did everything they could to get commoners addicted to the drug, even as they avoided it themselves.

The distribution of the cure for RDT broke the dependence of the people of Vauxhall City on the drug, and it made them immune to the drug going forward.

That had several immediate effects, all of them bad from the point of view of the nobility.

First, that means of control was gone. Halting the distribution of RDT would have no effect on those who took the cure. And those most likely not to take the cure were the crown loyalists. They had eschewed taking the cure from people who flew the flag of revolution right there on the distribution tables.

If the government cut off RDT now, the major impact would be felt by their own people. Worse, it would drive their own loyalists to the revolutionaries, to get the cure for the addiction they could no longer quench with RDT.

Second, government efforts to encourage the use of RDT were now defunct. Since the cure made one immune to the drug going forward, there was no longer any way to get people addicted and under the government's control.

But the third effect was the most insidious. People were no longer under the anti-depressive effects of the drug. They were no longer contented with the way things were, no longer docile about it. They looked around at their lives and saw them for what they were.

They also saw the lives of the nobility for what they were. The big houses, the fancy cars, all the little luxuries. And the natural question that arose was, Why are they special? Why are they in charge? Why do they get to tax us, when they're the ones with all the money?

They've been using us – abusing us! – for centuries. Why do we let it continue?

The people of Vauxhall City were waking up.

And they weren't happy.

As it turned out, Portnoy was wrong. The crowds got even bigger than he thought, quicker than he thought, and the mood of the crowd began to turn ugly. Blue flags began to show up everywhere, but especially in the growing throng that filled the street in front of the palace every day.

People shouted for the end of the monarchy. Vauxhall royal flags were torn down, from government buildings, from anywhere they appeared.

The monarchy still ruled, but, more and more, it ruled just the palace and the military.

Sooner or later, push would come to shove.

Countermeasures

Mary Danner was watching the situation unfold from inside the palace. It wasn't long into the demonstrations that it became too dangerous for palace staff to go in and out of the palace every day.

"We're sending the office pool and the kitchen staff home for the duration, Mary," Megan Brie told her. "It's become unsafe to let people in and out. They're going to have to seal the gates. And it's unsafe for palace people to walk home. We're afraid they'll be mugged."

"What is the royal family going to do for food? For services?" Danner asked.

"Some of us are staying in the palace. We'll sort of camp out."

"I'm up for that if you need the help, Megan."

The last thing Danner wanted was to be on the outside when the crunch came. Being on the inside in the clinches was the whole point of getting a job in the palace in the first place.

"Oh, thanks, Mary. That would be great. I knew I could count on you."

The gates of the palace compound were closed and locked, and the solid steel inner gates – usually kept retracted against the interior side of the palace compound wall – were closed. There was no ground-level in and out from the palace anymore.

The next change Danner noticed was the influx of common soldiers – well, Marines – into the palace compound. These were brought in on shuttles from the Marine base outside the capital to supplement the palace guard.

The Marines built what grew into a mini Marine base on the palace's front grounds, using supplies from containers brought in by shuttle. Mess tents, barracks tents, even a headquarters tent.

The Marines, once established, also built a parapet walk along the inside of the palace grounds wall. There were reinforcing columns part way up the wall on the inside, spaced about every ten feet. The Marines built a parapet walk from one to the next of these across the front wall of the grounds facing the street. They then manned those with Marines who kept an eye on the crowd on the other side of the wall.

The Marines also built a few raised firing platforms about twenty feet off the ground. These were on stilt legs with a little sheltered hut on the top. The side walls of the hut were metal, to absorb small arms fire.

Danner watched all this with fascination. She knew, of course, that the most likely result of the use of military forces against a large crowd would be a paroxysm of violence.

Danner also knew that the Erian Marines were experts at violence.

The outcome, if it came to that, was not in doubt.

One thing that did confuse Danner was the regime's use of the Marines, when the king and crown prince had expressed concerns that the Marines could have been compromised. She searched back through their conversations on the feed from Mardouk, to which she was patched through *Ladyhawke*.

Danner used sound localization on her roll-up display, so what she was listening to could not be overheard by others in their makeshift dormitory in the palace.

Danner found the conversation, just the day after the previous one, in the archive, and listened to it.

"Have you given any further thought to the issue we discussed yesterday, Father? The potential problem with the Marines?" Crown Prince James asked.

"Yes. I think we have to assume the Marines are loyal to the crown," King Albert XIV said.

"What about the Marines protecting the people distributing the cure for RDT addiction?"

"But are they Marines, really, James, or just pretending to be? Perhaps they are a small group within our Marines. Who knows, maybe some other government is interfering with events. But I don't think, absent any other information, that we can assume our own Marines, or the bulk of them anyway, have been subverted."

"I see."

"The other thing, James, is that, if our own Marines have been subverted, what are we to do? Without them, we have no way to defend the crown. We may as well just pack up and leave town. And I, for one, am not prepared to do that."

"And if it comes to that, Father?"

"If it does come to that – and I am not at all prepared to concede that it will – then we will decamp. I have already made plans for that eventuality if it comes about."

"Very well, Father. For what it's worth, I agree with your thinking on this matter. Thank you for sharing your thoughts on it."

Danner nodded. So the king did have an escape plan if it came to that. Probably for the whole family.

What form would that take?

Danner had some ideas. It would have to be a shuttle, and a pretty large one. Without taking any support personnel – not even Chalmers, the king's secretary – the family numbered nearly fifty individuals.

Of course, a Vauxhall shuttle would potentially be a target for the revolutionaries if air assets on both sides were involved at that point. How would they avoid being shot down?

Hmm.

Danner was therefore not surprised when, as the demonstrations started to turn ugly, one shuttle coming in to the palace grounds was apparently a medical shuttle.

Painted white, with big red crosses on both sides, the top, and the bottom, it did not land in front of the palace, in the large open grounds where the Marines were encamped. Instead, it landed behind the palace, in the open lawn between the flagstone patio and the woods behind.

The trees came up close to the wide patio – within fifty feet or so – on either end, but in the middle a lawn spread three hundred feet to the trees. The medical shuttle – so painted, anyway – landed back toward the trees, so the engine wash would not affect the palace.

And there it sat.

You bastards, Danner thought, for she knew their plan now. If it all fell apart, if the king decided to flee, he and his family would depart the palace under the universal symbol of mercy for the honorably wounded.

Oh, you fuckers. I am so going to enjoy this.

As the demonstrations built, Portnoy started to worry about what came after. He had no concerns now that they would be able to topple the monarchy. But then what?

Portnoy and Jules went to visit Kurt Conrad in his shop. They met, as before, in the back room.

"I have to ask, Mr. Conrad, what comes after the revolution. There are some particularly bad examples in history. Have you planned how to avoid them?"

"Yes, Mr. Pendergast. Without the outside assistance we thought necessary to prevail, we spent our time pondering and debating the future.

"We have prepared a charter for a democratic government to succeed the monarchy. An elected assembly, a prime minister, a cabinet. The powers of each. The rights of the citizens. We stole from some of the best documents of that type across human history, including the cluster worlds, in crafting it."

"Excellent, Mr. Conrad. And in the interim?"

"The revolutionary council will take charge for a six-month period, building to planetwide elections. The chairman of our council will act as president of this government."

"And how will he not become Robespierre or Napoleon, Mr. Conrad?"

"He will not run for the assembly, or stand for prime minister. His intent is to retire, Mr. Pendergast."

"And you believe him, Mr. Conrad? History is full of examples of people finding it impossible to fulfill those oaths when the time came."

"Understood, Mr. Pendergast. But, in this case, I believe it. He is a true believer in democracy, and says an honored retirement as a hero of the people is much to be preferred to the day-to-day scrap and tangle of politics."

"He has grown weary of heading your council, Mr. Conrad."

Conrad chuckled.

"We do have our own scraps and tangles, Mr. Pendergast, and the chairman's insistence on consensus among us has proved troublesome at times. And this is in our private meetings. Much more difficult in the open, in a publicly visible government. I do not think he relishes such a role."

"Ah. I see. Well, Mr. Conrad, remember that I do have an assassin available on planet if it comes to that."

Conrad grew wide-eyed, then nodded. Sensible, after all.

"One more question, Mr. Conrad. What of the rest of the kingdom of Vauxhall? Will you attempt to rule the entire kingdom, or just the planet?"

"Just the planet, Mr. Pendergast. The other planets are conquered territories all. We will not attempt to perpetuate that injustice."

"Every man for himself, Mr. Conrad?"

"Ruling just this one planet will be difficult enough, Mr. Pendergast. And I do not expect, for example, the Duke of Earth to take orders from our elected government here."

Portnoy nodded.

"And the Vauxhall Royal Navy, Mr. Conrad?"

"We will keep the navy assets that are already here in the Vauxhall system, to defend the planet, Mr. Pendergast. The navy assets that are currently deployed to other worlds within the kingdom can remain there as well."

"That makes sense, I think. You wouldn't want to leave them defenseless, Mr. Conrad."

"No, but in making that decision we are relying heavily on your own commitment to protect Vauxhall against the military adventurism of our neighbors, Mr. Pendergast. You have not wavered there?"

"No, Mr. Conrad. In fact, I have been empowered by my government to sign a basing agreement with the new government of Vauxhall, when it emerges, to keep a squadron of our heavy cruisers and a flagship here for as long as that government desires it."

Conrad sat back in his chair in surprise.

"That is very welcome news, Mr. Pendergast. After all you have done for us already, that is a tremendous additional boon. How can the people of Vauxhall ever repay your government – and the cluster at large, I suppose – for your efforts on our behalf?"

"We would like to sign a free-trade agreement with Vauxhall as well, Mr. Conrad. Duty-free trade between the cluster and Vauxhall. We think everybody would benefit from that."

"I agree, Mr. Pendergast. I agree. Especially as we will likely be cut off from trade with the other monarchies in an attempt to weaken us. The nobilities on the core worlds by this point are all relatives of each other. An extended ruling clan. They will not stand idle while a planet turns out their cousin for a democracy."

Conrad thought about it, then nodded.

"I will take all of this to our council, Mr. Pendergast, but I predict the news will be greeted very positively."

"Until next time, then, Mr. Conrad."

"I think we need to do something about the crowds, Father," Crown Prince James said. "We can't continue to let them grow like this. They're getting ugly."

"What do you suggest, James? We can't just have the Marines fire on them. That will explode, like throwing a match into gasoline."

"No, I have a better idea."

James explained and King Albert agreed.

The king sent the orders.

First Blood

The conversation between James and Albert was flagged to Portnoy and Stickney by the Agency monitors on Mardouk.

"Well, now we know what they're going to try," Stickney said.

"Yes," Portnoy said. "Kind of clever, actually."

"Yes. They're going to clear the crowd without firing a shot."

"But it won't work, Susan."

"It won't? Why not?"

"Because it's my job to make it not work."

Lieutenant Colonel Frank Everett got off the phone with Portnoy. Yes, that would work as a countermove. It would also escalate the situation, but so would the king's move.

Most of Everett's men were in the crowds in front of the palace every day, monitoring the situation. Prepared to intervene if things kicked off fast.

Some of them were still distributing the RDT cure on city sidewalks throughout Vauxhall City.

He even had a couple guys assigned to provide cover for Portnoy and Stickney.

But Everett had his reserves.

He also had a bunch of the Marines' Intelligent Guided Rockets, the IGR-15s. It was a fire-and-forget weapon.

Everett started giving orders.

Portnoy also called Emmet Durst on *Ladyhawke*.

"Hi, Emmet."

"Hi, Claude. Whatcha got?"

"I need you to go on the next higher alert level, Emmet. The king is going to try a move down here with Marine assault shuttles. I don't want you to interfere with that. We'll handle this one here. But, depending on what the king does in response, things could take off pretty fast."

"Gotcha, Claude. You guys safe down there?"

"Yes, we're good. We have Jules here, and a couple of other fellows took a suite across the hall in case we need help. You know, those Erian fellows. So we're good."

"All right, Claude. We'll be ready to go when you give the word."

"OK, so your orders are to hover over the street, about twenty feet off the deck, and slowly move down the street. Slow enough people can get out of your way. The goal is to get the crowd to disperse, trying to get out of the wash of your engines. Got it?"

"Yeah, we're good, Sir," one of the pilots answered.

"All right. Now, if you get light arms fire, no problem. That's not gonna hurt you. Anything heavier, lift off and get out of there. But you are not authorized to return fire. Understand?"

"Yeah, Major. No firing into the crowd. We don't want to start anything. We got it."

"All right. Off you go then."

The major left and the two pilots looked at each other. One shrugged.

"Piece o' cake."

"Yeah. Like a balloon in a parade or somethin'."

"OK. Let's go do this."

Frank Everett also had instructions for his people.

"OK, I got a squad of you at each end of the street, well back from the crowds. Now, we don't want to hit them from the front, right? The loss of thrust in the front will flip the shuttle over and toward the crowd.

"We want to let them go past and hit them from behind, in the inboard engine of each. That will flip them away from the crowd, and into each other.

"You got it?"

"Yes, Colonel. We got it."

"All right. Get going."

The Marines grabbed the IGR-15s and moved out to their staging locations.

The two big assault shuttles flew toward the city, then lined up with the broad boulevard that ran past the front of the royal palace. They started to descend to just above the deck for their side-by-side slow pass of the boulevard.

The crowds were now filling the boulevard for the three blocks directly in front of the palace. The shuttles were two blocks away from the crowd when they started their slow pass. The idea was to give the crowd the idea they were coming, so they would start to move out of the way.

The Erian Marines, though, were three blocks from the crowd. Two men ran out into the broad boulevard, raised their IGR-15 launcher, and painted the inboard rear engine on each shuttle. That is, the rear engine on the side closest to the other shuttle.

With target acquired, both of the Erian Marines hit the launch button, then dropped the launchers and ran for cover.

The attack indicator in the shuttles shrilled, and the pilots did what they were supposed to do. Attempt to lift and get out of there. They slammed the throttles to full thrust.

It was the wrong thing to do. As all the engines wound up, the rockets hit the shuttles' rear inboard engines and detonated. With the engines on the other three corners approaching maximum thrust, one rear engine on each shuttle simply disintegrated, shooting shrapnel out in all directions.

When the thrust on that corner went to zero, with the other engines at full thrust, the outside and front of both shuttles shot up in the air. The attitude control computer couldn't keep up, and both shuttles flipped over and toward each other, collided, and, upside down, accelerated into the ground.

Both shuttles broke up when they hit the ground. The nearly full fuel tanks were sundered, hot engine parts were flying everywhere, and both shuttles burned in a massive fire in the middle of the street.

From the crowd, a great cheer went up.

King Albert and Crown Prince James were looking forward to the Marines' operation to clear the street this afternoon. It had been James' idea, but the king liked it.

Now, they were going to be able to watch it live.

"This should be fun, Father."

"Yes, James. It will be nice to see those people forced to abandon the street. And without firing a shot. Brilliant."

"Thank you, father."

They were watching the feed from the surveillance camera on that corner of the wall around the palace grounds.

"Should be soon now," the king said.

"There they are."

Albert and James watched the shuttles slow their approach well short of the crowd and descend to twenty feet. They halted there for a moment before starting their slow hover down the street.

"Who are those guys?" Albert asked.

He pointed as two small figures ran out into the street behind the shuttles.

"I don't know, Father."

Both men fired rockets at the shuttles, dropped their launchers, and ran. The king and his son saw the smoke of the rocket trails shoot toward the shuttles.

"Shit," the crown prince said.

One of each shuttle's engines exploded, the shuttles flipped over backward and collided, then fell to the ground, pushed by their own inverted engines. They crashed, and a huge fireball went up, then settled down into a raging fuel fire in the middle of the boulevard.

"Oh, fuck," the king said.

"Dammit, where did they get rocket launchers?"

"I don't know, James. But this changes everything. We have to clear those crowds. I don't care if we have to shoot or bomb every fucking one of them. We have to clear the crowds."

Stickney and Portnoy were watching live as well, though they were watching a different feed, from the Marines posted behind the shuttles.

"Well, that was impressive," Portnoy said.

"Yes. It's a good thing those guys ran. The shuttles almost came down on their launch position."

"Yeah. The goal was to flip them away from the crowd. That worked."

"It sure did, Richard. We had to fire first, though."

"No, we didn't. Those shuttles were an assault against the crowd. We neutralized the threat."

"Wanna bet the king doesn't see it that way?"

"Well, we can check. I wonder if the king was watching."

Portnoy opened the feed from the king's office and adjusted the time back ten minutes.

"Oh, yes. Here we go."

They watched the king and crown prince watching the surveillance feed, and their reaction to the shuttle crash.

"He doesn't seem at all pleased, Susan."

"No, Richard. He doesn't. And it sounds like he's going to kick things up a notch or twelve."

"Let's watch for orders. What's he going to do?"

Mary Danner was watching the same surveillance feed as the king and his son. She shouldn't have access to that feed, but security on the palace surveillance system was pretty rudimentary and Phyllis Stickney had given her some nice software tools on the voyage to Earth.

Oh, that was a nice one! Take out one engine and they flip over. She hadn't known that trick.

Hmm.

Danner had picked up the inventory number of the medical shuttle parked on the palace back lawn when she went out for a walk on the patio.

Let's see here. Inventory number. Follow that. OK, there's the model type and revision. Follow that. Ah. There they were.

The plans for the shuttle parked out back.

Let's see now....

"There it is, Richard," Stickney said.

"Yes. It's smart in a way. It won't work, though."

"Why not?"

"Because by tomorrow morning, all the assault shuttles will be smoking debris."

He nodded to her.

"I need to call Emmet."

The huge crowd dissipated every night, down to a few thousand who were now camped on the lawn of the island of the boulevard that passed before the palace. In the morning, the crowd would show up again, growing every day.

The king's idea was simple. Bring in the assault shuttles before the crowd started to grow, chew up everybody there, then continue firing on people as they showed up until they stayed away rather than be killed.

It was a fair plan. It might even have worked, if Portnoy didn't do anything to counter it.

"Four o'clock tomorrow morning, Vauxhall City time, Emmet. Destroy all the assault shuttles on the ground at the Marine base. Strafing runs by the attack ships."

"You got it, Claude. What about us up here in *Ladyhawke*?"

"Admiral Winston is my next call, Emmet."

"Oh. Good. Thanks, Claude."

"And send me the current position and orbit of the *Aurora,* Emmet."

"Winston."

"Claude Portnoy, Admiral."

"Yes, Mr. Portnoy. Is it showtime?"

"No, Admiral. Not yet. Quarter past four tomorrow morning, Vauxhall City time. I need you to wait until then, in case I need to abort, and then expedite your movements to be here."

"I understand, Mr. Portnoy. What's going on?"

"The king plans to fire on the sparse early-morning crowd at six, Admiral, then fire on anyone who persists in showing up. He's planning on doing that with assault shuttles, but at four o'clock, we're going to destroy his assault shuttles on the ground. That will expose *Ladyhawke* as a combatant."

"I see. And we need to come to *Ladyhawke*'s aid."

"Yes, Admiral. The biggest threat is *Aurora,* Vauxhall's new attack-ship carrier. We need you to use your attack ships to take out the *Aurora* and any Vauxhall attack ships she's launched. I'm sending you the position and orbit of *Aurora* now."

Winston nodded and looked off to the side of his display.

"Got it, Mr. Portnoy."

"Your secondary mission, Admiral, is to warn Vauxhall Navy fleet elements in the system not to take any action, and especially not to fire on the planet. The king may decide to bomb the crowds from orbit."

"That would be a risky business, Mr. Portnoy."

"Yes, but people backed into a corner do stupid things, Admiral. You need to keep their navy from getting involved."

"And if some ship takes offensive action against us or the crowds on the ground, Mr. Portnoy?"

"You are authorized to use extreme prejudice, Admiral. Take them out. No halfway measures. Those would only encourage others."

"Understood, Mr. Portnoy. If I don't hear from you to abort before oh-four-one-five hours, that is when we will space."

"Excellent, Admiral. Good hunting."

Oh-Four-Hundred Hours

The attack-ship wings of Admiral Winston's squadron had taken all the colors for their call signs. Red, Blue, Green, Yellow, Purple, Orange, Black, White. The flagship's attack-ship wing took Gold. Each attack-ship wing was ten ships.

So *Ladyhawke*'s four attack ships called themselves Grey. Grey Leader, Grey One, Grey Two, and Grey Three. It seemed appropriate, since *Ladyhawke* carried her four attack ships sort of incognito. She was a freighter, after all, not a carrier.

The early-morning pilot briefing was no hardship for the Erian Marines who had had flight training. They had remained aboard *Ladyhawke* when the rest of the Marines went down to the surface. The Erians didn't sleep in the same way as humans did, and the hour was no burden for them.

The target was simple. The assault shuttles of the Marine base within easy flight time of Vauxhall City. Catch them on the ground, and take them out. No maneuvering, no shooting back. Should be easy. They even had satellite imagery. One shuttle was in a building being serviced, and they knew which building it was.

Oh, it was in atmosphere, and in gravity. The handling of their ships was optimized for vacuum at zero-gee, but they all knew what the accommodations needed to be.

Not burning up on entry would be good, for example.

"Grey Leader. Sound off, Grey Wing."

"Grey One. Ready."

"Grey Two. Ready."

"Grey Three. Ready."

"Grey Leader to *Ladyhawke*. Grey Wing ready."

"Roger that, Grey Leader. Stand by for launch."

Xiulan Yang watched the Vauxhall City time approach oh-four-hundred. When it hit, he looked at Emmet Durst, sitting in the captain's chair. Durst nodded.

Yang released the latches on the four attack ships.

"*Ladyhawke*. Grey Wing, you are go for launch."

"Grey Leader. Grey Wing, throttle up."

The four attack ships, located around *Ladyhawke,* accelerated out of their docking hooks and moved away from the ship.

Once they had cleared the ship, they went to nine gees, heading for the planet.

At the Marine base outside Vauxhall City – officially called 'Camp King Charles VII Vauxhall City Marine Facility' but known to Marines everywhere as Camp Charlie – the flight-line crews were working on the assault shuttles parked along the apron to the shuttlepads.

"We gotta top off and system check every one o' these, First Sergeant?"

"No, Jackson. The other two crews are doing two-thirds of 'em."

"But, I mean, between us we gotta do 'em all?"

"That's the orders, Jackson. And they all gotta be done by oh-six-hundred. That's from the big boss, so whatever else you don't do this year, don't miss that time. C'mon, you guys. Hustle it up."

"All right, First Sergeant."

Ladyhawke's launch of its parasites was noticed on *Aurora.*

"That's curious, Sir."

"What is, Lieutenant?"

"This, Sir."

The main display centered on a ship.

"This freighter just released four parasites, Sir."

"At once?"

"Yes, Sir."

"Are they cargo shuttles?"

"They're making nine gravities toward Vauxhall, Sir."

The lieutenant commander on the graveyard watch grunted. He considered, then stirred.

"Call the Captain to the bridge."

"Aye, Sir."

"And keep an eye on them."

"Aye, Sir."

Vauxhall Space Traffic Control kept trying to raise communications with the radar images on their screens, but they were not transponding, and they were not responding to queries.

And, boy, were they coming in hot.

"Grey Leader. Grey Wing, flip ship for deceleration."

The four attack ships cut their thrust and flipped over, with those big thrusters leading, and went back to nine gees of thrust against their orbital direction.

"What have you got, Rusty?" Captain Raymond Latham asked when he came onto the bridge.

"We're not sure, Sir. This freighter launched four parasites, and they headed for the planet at nine gravities."

"Nine gravities? Missiles?"

"We don't think so, Sir. They look like they're being flown."

"Drones, then. They're gonna make craters when they hit the planet."

"They're decelerating now, Sir, and dropping toward the planet. It looks like they're headed for Vauxhall City."

Lieutenant Commander 'Rusty' Fender yielded the command chair to the captain. Latham sat down.

"Scanning," Latham asked, "are they transponding?"

"No, Sir. They're going in silent."

"Combatants then. Sound general quarters. Alert to the ready wing. Prepare to launch attack ships. Alert a second wing to stand by."

"A second wing, Sir?" Fender asked.

"Yes, Rusty. That freighter's not getting away, either."

"Aye, Sir."

The general quarters alarm sounded, and, all over *Aurora,* spacers ran for their duty stations.

"That's it, Sir. Oh-four-hundred hours.

"Fleet orders. General quarters. Space on the mark. Send it."

"Aye, Sir. Fleet orders sent. Counting down one-five minutes."

Aboard those nine ships, spacers ran for their duty stations.

The attack ship pilots were already briefed and aboard their craft.

Fifteen minutes later, on the mark, Admiral Harvey Winston's flagship and its squadron opened rifts in spacetime and spaced through them.

They were six minutes to Vauxhall's hyperspace limit.

"Ready wing ready to launch, Sir."

"Launch them."

"Aye, Sir. Launch under way."

"Send them after those four ships making for the planet. Launch second wing when ready."

Twelve attack ships peeled off of *Aurora* and made their way for the planet at three gees.

"*Aurora* is launching parasites, Sir," Lara Perez said from the Navigation console.

"They after us?"

"No, Sir. Twelve attack ships heading for the planet at three gees."

"OK. Well, that's good, I guess."

"Wait one, Sir."

Durst waited. What was going on?"

"*Aurora* is launching another wave, Sir. Twelve more parasites."

"Where are they headed?"

"Plotting, Sir. It's going to take a minute for their bearing to stabilize."

Durst didn't have any option but to wait. It took as long as it took.

"Got it, Sir. Twelve attack ships headed our way. Three gees."

OK, Admiral Winston, Emmet thought. *Now would be a good time.*

"*Ladyhawke*. Grey Leader, you have twelve attack ships in pursuit. Three gees."

"Roger that, *Ladyhawke*. Grey Leader to Grey Wing. Stay on mission. Mission first, fun later."

The air raid siren sounded at Camp Charlie.

"Shit! Air raid. C'mon, you guys. Run for it!"

"Air raid, First Sergeant?"

"Yeah, Jackson," the first sergeant called over his shoulder. "And you don't wanna be standing next to a full fuel truck when it comes in."

Jackson looked to his right at the truck, full of jet fuel for the shuttles.

"Oh, shit."

Jackson took off after the first sergeant. He almost passed him on the way to the bunker.

Admiral Winston's squadron dropped out of hyperspace at the hyperspace limit for the planet Vauxhall. By design, they dropped out outside the orbit of the *Aurora,* which was in a high orbit of the planet.

"Fleet orders. Launch all wings. Send it."

"Aye Sir."

"Then let me know the situation we're looking at."

"Plots are stabilizing, Sir. *Aurora* has launched two attack ship wings of twelve ships each. One is bound for *Ladyhawke*. The other is chasing *Ladyhawke*'s four-ship wing on its attack on the planet."

"Two wings on *Ladyhawke*. Two wings on *Aurora*'s other wing. Two wings on *Aurora*. Three wings on fleet defense."

"Aye, Sir. Transmitting to wing commanders."

Aboard *Aurora,* Admiral Winston's arrival was noticed.

"Sir, we have nine ships that have dropped out of hyperspace outside of our orbit. They are not transponding. Mass measurements indicate heavy cruisers. They're not ours, Sir."

"Launch remaining attack ship wings as they report ready. Let's go get us some heavy cruisers."

"Aye, Sir. Launching as ready."

"Update, Sir. New arrivals are launching parasites. Looks like ten parasites per heavy cruiser. Making nine gees now."

"What are their targets, Scanning?"

"Two wings to the planet, two wings to *Ladyhawke,* two wings to us. The other three wings are setting up fleet defensive perimeter."

"Let's expedite those launches. We need to get our people out there."

"Aye, Sir."

Winston's arrival was also noticed aboard *Ladyhawke.*

"Admiral Winston has apparently arrived, Sir. Nine ships at the hyperspace limit, outside *Aurora*'s orbit. They're launching parasites."

"Give me courses when you have them."

"Aye, Sir."

Durst waited. Did Winston's people see what was going on? Would they be in time?

"I have courses, Sir. Two attack-ship wings are following Grey Wing, going after their attackers. Two wings are on the way here. Two are on the way to *Aurora*. And three are setting up a fleet defense."

"Will the ones on the way to us catch *Aurora*'s ships before they get here?"

"Yes, Sir. That won't even be close. They're coming in at nine-point-four gees. *Aurora*'s ships are pulling three gees. They're gonna just plain run 'em over."

Durst relaxed. It still had to play out, but it looked good.

"What I don't get, First Sergeant, is who would launch an air raid against Camp Charlie. I mean, we got the whole planet, right? Where would it even come from?"

The muffled sound of impacts and explosions began, and Jackson's eyes got wide.

"I don't know either, Jackson. Maybe somebody didn't like the plans some other somebody had for those shuttles this morning. But I'm just as glad I'm in here and not out there."

"Yes, First Sergeant. I agree with that."

The attack ships, intended for deep space use, had the very rudiments of a lifting body, to allow landing on a planet's surface. Generally speaking, though, they had the aerodynamics of a brick. Having reduced their speed to that required for atmospheric operation, they kept their down-pointing nose thruster firing to keep the nose up.

"Grey Leader. Grey Wing, prepare for your strafing run."

"Grey One. Ready, Grey Leader."

"Go ahead, Grey One."

Grey One came in on the Marine base west to east, so neither his approach nor exit would fly over Vauxhall City at close to mach two. The ship thundered across the base, the point-defense guns firing continuously at the parked assault shuttles on the ground.

Grey One pulled up at the far end of the base, aiming back toward space.

"Grey Two. Your turn."

"Grey Two going in."

One after another, the four attack ships laid into the parked assault shuttles. Grey Leader, the last of them, seeing that all the assault shuttles were burning, concentrated his fire on the service building in which one assault shuttle was parked.

That building was not intended to ward off the close-in fire of a point-defense gun that could disable missiles and attack ships across dozens of miles of space. It nearly disintegrated under that withering fire, then burst into flames as the parked assault shuttle's fuel tanks were compromised.

"Grey Leader. Grey Wing, form up and let's go get those guys chasing us."

The four attack ships got back into formation, then throttled up and headed for space.

The flight-crew left the bunker when the all-clear sounded. When they got out to survey the shuttlefield, Jackson expressed what they were all thinking.

"Holy shit."

All the shuttles up and down the flight line had been destroyed. They had holes punched in them, and all were on fire. The shuttle repair hangar was collapsed on top of the shuttle inside, which was also burning furiously. There were even holes in the epoxycrete shuttlepads.

Fire trucks were responding, racing down the tarmac to the wrecked shuttles.

"Yeah, Jackson. You said it. Well, guys. I guess we got the rest of the day off. The bulldozer and epoxycrete guys'll be busy, though."

Dogfight

The twelve attack ships of *Aurora*'s first wing had not yet hit atmosphere, coming in from *Aurora*'s high orbit. They now found themselves between a rock and a hard place.

The four attack ships they were chasing had now turned around and were coming back at them, while twenty attack ships launched by the newly arrived heavy cruiser squadron were coming in behind them.

They flipped ship, turning to meet the bigger threat.

"Red Leader. Red and Blue Wings, stand by for action. They've turned and are coming back to us. And don't hit our own fellows coming up behind."

"Grey Leader. Grey Wing, be careful not to hit our own guys. Looks like we're all going to get to the same place at same time."

The *Aurora*'s dozen attack ships, decelerating hard, were almost stopped when Grey Wing, Red Wing, and Blue Wing passed through the same volume of space. There was a flurry of fire from point-defense guns, and then the formations parted, Grey Wing upward toward *Ladyhawke,* and Red and Blue Wings toward the planet.

There were no *Aurora* attack ship survivors.

"Red Seven. Red Leader, I took a hit there. Engines are failing. I am proceeding to the planet."

"Roger that, Red Seven. Good luck."

The pilot of Red Seven didn't have any choice but to head to the planet. He was headed there right now, with quite a bit of speed, and he didn't have enough thrust to miss it.

He flipped ship and used what thrust he had to cut back his speed, trying for a close orbit. Close enough to be in the upper atmosphere and burn off more speed with drag.

The ship began to heat up when it hit the upper atmosphere, and the pilot of Red Seven watched his temperature gauges closely. He knew about what the ship could take before it broke up, and he watched the value and the rate of rise carefully.

As the temperature rose, the pilot of Red Seven filled himself with cabin air, then dilated a vent. He extruded himself through the vent, hanging on. Then he let go of the ship, pushing himself off to avoid getting hit by his own craft.

The pilot of Red Seven swelled up to his maximum size, while extruding a short tendril with a drogue chute shape on the end. Maximize drag while retaining orientation.

The air was extremely thin this high, but he was doing OK so far, and he was still falling fast. He watched as Red Seven finally overheated and disintegrated well past his position.

He continued to make himself as big as he could, the highest drag configuration he could, as he fell.

Not the best way to make planet, but it beats being stuck out there.

When the air thickened up enough, the erstwhile pilot of Red Seven changed into an airplane shape and glided toward Vauxhall City.

No sense walking.

Green Wing and Orange Wing were quickly overtaking *Aurora*'s second wing of attack ships, making for *Ladyhawke*. Again, *Aurora*'s attack ships flipped ship, to present their best firing aspect to their pursuers.

Without having to worry about avoiding friendly ships coming the other way, Green Wing and Orange Wing had a much easier time firing on the enemy ships than Red Wing and Blue Wing had.

The two formations passed through each other, but only Green Wing and Orange Wing emerged from the other side. Behind there was only debris.

The crew of *Ladyhawke* cheered.

"The attack ships coming our way are all gone, Sir," Lara Perez said from the navigation panel.

"Excellent," Durst said.

"Grey Wing is on their way back to the ship, Sir. Green Wing and Orange Wing are taking a defensive posture around us."

"Better and better."

Black Wing and White Wing were making for *Aurora*. She continued to launch attack ships.

"Black Leader. Black Wing and White Wing. We're going to dogfight this one. Wingmen, stay with your leader. Black One, go for your attack run."

"Black One. I'm on it, Black Leader. Beginning attack run."

The Black and White Wing formations broke up into pairs, except for Black One and Black Two. These pairs – leader and wing man – swept through the enemy formations, breaking them up.

Black One had bigger fish to fry. He lined up on *Aurora*, accelerating all the way. He released six missiles at the edge of the point-defense envelope, then stood Black One up on end, gaining enough side vector to miss the big ship.

Black One was going so fast when he swept past *Aurora* that her point-defense guns couldn't traverse fast enough to lock onto him. As it was, though, they were busy concentrating on the six incoming missiles.

To their credit, *Aurora*'s point-defense gun crews got four of the incoming missiles. Only two survived to impact the big ship, one targeted for her fusion bottle, one targeted for her attack ship fuel tanks.

Aurora had been sheeted with single-layer carbon nanotube reinforced stainless steel. If she hadn't been, she would have been a goner. As it was, the big ship was streaming air and debris, but she was still launching.

"Black Leader. Your turn, Black Two."

"Black Two. Beginning attack run."

Black Two lined up on *Aurora*, coming in hard. He released six missiles even later than Black One, and missed the carrier by so little he actually took out an antenna array on the big ship by colliding with it on his way past.

Aurora's point-defense gunners took out three missiles of this wave, and the other three impacted *Aurora*. One of those three was targeted on the fusion bottle, however. It hit in the previous hole and penetrated to her power room.

Aurora's fusion bottle let go.

Aurora had been launching its attack-ship wings as fast as it could. She had a total of eight attack-ship wings aboard.

Only five of them launched before *Aurora* broke up.

That still left three attack ship wings that had not yet been destroyed, and they were making for Admiral Winston's heavy cruisers.

"Gold Leader. Gold Wing, Purple Wing, Yellow Wing. Maintain defensive posture. If somebody goes running away, don't go after them. Stay on mission."

"Purple Leader. Roger that, Gold Leader."

"Yellow Leader. We understand, Gold Leader."

Thirty-six Vauxhall attack ships accelerated to the attack on the cluster navy heavy cruiser squadron, even as fifty of the nine-gee attack ships of the cluster navy opposed them.

There was a maelstrom of dogfighting between *Aurora*'s position – now marked by a spreading cloud of debris – and Admiral Winston's heavy cruisers. The cluster navy attack ships accelerated back and forth through the Vauxhall attack ships with seeming impunity.

Six of the Vauxhall attack ships did get off missiles, of which they carried just one per attack ship. These were necessarily fired from a distance, and the coordinated point-defense of nine heavy cruisers made short work of them.

Soon there were no attack ships left in space except those of the cluster navy. Three attack ship wings remained in fleet defense of the heavy cruisers, and one attack ship wing remained in defense of *Ladyhawke,* as Admiral Winston's heavy cruisers moved in from the hyperspace limit.

Admiral Winston addressed all the ships in the system on the common hailing channel used in Vauxhall.

"This is Admiral Harvey Winston of the cluster navy.

"There is no state of war between Vauxhall and the cluster, and we will not take offensive action against you. Nor will we engage in commerce raiding or anything of the kind. Commercial ships, you are free to carry on with your business unimpeded.

"Ships of the Vauxhall Royal Navy. You will not be permitted to interfere in political events on the planet's surface. Those are not a navy matter, and do not concern you.

"If you do undertake any offensive action on behalf of either side in the political events unfolding on the planet, my orders are to destroy your ship with all hands. I can and will do that with impunity, so do not test my resolve in that regard.

"Also, no offensive action will be permitted against my formation or the freighter *Ladyhawke,* one of my fleet assets. Again, do not test my resolve on this issue.

"Winston out."

Admiral Dieter Meyer had survived the death of Prince Michael under his command on Earth more than three years ago. In fact, due to his retrieval and analysis of the thruster covers *Silverheel* had left behind when she fled the system, he had been promoted. He used his newfound status to wangle a move home to Vauxhall, becoming admiral of the home fleet.

Thus it was Meyer who was the commanding officer of Vauxhall ships in orbit – except *Aurora,* which was Prince James' pet project – on the arrival of Admiral Winston's squadron of heavy cruisers. Meyer was under no illusions of his ships' abilities to fight those heavy cruisers, armored as they were with multi-layer carbon nanotube reinforced stainless steel.

Vauxhall Royal Navy missiles would probably just bounce off of them.

Meyer had been paying close attention to the growing political unrest in Vauxhall City. As chaotic as it sometimes seemed, he knew better. Someone was waving the baton behind the scenes, and someone was providing the revolutionaries with the musical instruments, as it were.

Now he knew who. It had been a mistake for the king to antagonize the cluster nations, which Meyer had advised against years ago. Now the cluster was enabling revolution against the monarchy, and Admiral Winston was here to make sure the Navy stayed out of it.

Which was fine with Meyer.

Meyer had been OK with the monarchy. Not a fan, mind you, but OK with it. It didn't seem the best system to him, but it was the system in which he lived, the system in which he had to operate. They didn't always make the right decisions, from his point of view, but at least they made decisions.

Meyer found himself open to a new system as well, however, and now he had a reason not to interfere, regardless of the orders he was given.

Meyer sent out the orders to all his ships to stand down, ignore Admiral Winston's squadron, and carry on as per prior orders. Under no circumstances was any ship to take any action with regard to the situation in the capital.

Meyer himself was planetside, two hundred miles from the capital at the big Navy base there, and it occurred to him to take one other action.

He had the head of the Navy MPs on base put in the brig on suspicion of peculation.

The MPs had an independent chain of command, and Meyer had no intention of being removed from command for refusing any orders he received to fire on the crowds in the capital from orbit.

With their leader in the brig, though, the MPs chain of command was broken, at least for a while, and things were happening quickly.

Melee

King Albert woke up at five o'clock, because he wanted to see the action this morning as his Marines worked to dispel the crowd from forming in front of the palace. As it was, by the time he got to his office at half past five, the action was almost over.

Crown Prince James was waiting for the king in his office. He was looking into the display.

"Good morning, Father."

"Good morning, James. You're up early this morning, too, I see."

"Not early enough, Father."

"Why? What's happening?"

"A freighter in orbit launched four attack ships that set off for the planet."

"A freighter?"

"Yes, Father. *Aurora* launched two wings of attack ships in response. One to go after the freighter, the other to go after its parasites."

"Good. Excellent."

"Yes, Father. But it didn't work out the way we hoped. First, the freighter's attack ships accelerated at nine gravities."

"Were they remotely piloted?"

"They must be. Or they have some way to mitigate acceleration that we don't understand. Those attack ships attacked the Marine base here, and destroyed all the assault shuttles on the ground."

"It's almost like they knew what we were planning."

"Yes, Father. Then an entire squadron of heavy cruisers

dropped out of hyperspace at the hyperspace limit. *Aurora* launched attack ship wings to go after them as well. The cruisers also launched attack ships. It looks like ten attack ships per cruiser."

"*Aurora* has what? Eight attack ship wings? Ninety-six attack ships. Isn't that right? She should have them outnumbered."

"It's close, Father. The nine heavy cruisers launched a total of ninety attack ships."

"Nine heavy cruisers?"

"Yes. It looks like a squadron and a flagship. So the attack ship complements are pretty evenly matched. That's not the problem. They aren't evenly matched at all in capabilities. The enemy sent twenty attack ships after our attack-ship wing chasing the freighter's parasites, twenty attack ships after our attack-ship wing targeting the freighter, and twenty attack ships targeting *Aurora*. They were all doing nine gravities."

"What happened?"

"So far, our attack ship wing chasing the parasites has been destroyed, and our attack ship wing attacking the freighter has been destroyed. The dogfight around *Aurora* is ongoing. That's where we are right now."

Father and son stared into the display, watching the fighting around *Aurora* from the vantage of a surveillance camera on a destroyer a thousand miles away. It left something to be desired, but they got the gist of it.

"Oh, damn. *Aurora* got hit twice."

"But she's still launching, Father. I think her new armor is holding up."

They continued to watch as the enemy's attack ships harried and destroyed their own.

Then *Aurora*'s fusion bottle let go and she broke up.

"Fuck. There goes *Aurora*."

"Let's see if her attack ships get any of those heavy cruisers, James."

"She only launched five wings, Father. And two have been destroyed. They're outnumbered, by superior ships."

"Yes, James. It turns out it's an advantage to have fewer attack ships on multiple platforms. You don't end up with them queued up to launch. They can launch them all at once. We didn't know that before."

"Oh, this is going to go badly."

They watched as the last of their attack ships were destroyed and the enemy squadron began spacing for the planet.

They waited for what would happen next. It wasn't long in coming.

"The enemy commander claims to be Admiral Harvey Winston of the cluster navy. He's ordered all our ships to stand down and take no offensive action against them or the planet, or they will be destroyed."

"Fuck that. James, order the Navy to attack. And I want munitions on that crowd. If they destroyed our assault shuttles, fine. Bomb them from orbit."

James was composing the orders on the display when the message from Admiral Dieter Meyer came in.

"Admiral Meyer has ordered the Navy to stand down."

"That traitor! I should have known. Order the MPs to arrest him for treason."

James worked on the display, then watched for a response. When it finally came, he could hardly believe it.

"MP headquarters have lost communications with the MP commander on base, Father. They say they have no idea what's going on out there, but they have no communications."

"Traitors! Traitors one and all."

"What would you have me do, Father?"

"We still command the Marines here at the palace. Have them fire some warning shots over the crowd. Let them know we mean business."

"The crowd is starting to grow already, Father. The word got out somehow about the destruction of the assault shuttles."

"Do it anyway, James. We need to get things under control."

"Yes, Father."

The orders may have been to fire over a small unarmed crowd to disperse them, but that's not how it worked out.

First, it took a while for the orders to filter down the chain of command, be verified, and then acted upon. Sensing something was up as the news of the destruction of the assault shuttles quickly spread, people showed up early. The crowd grew rapidly.

Second, the crowd was not unarmed. Kurt Conrad and his associates had distributed those five thousand assault rifles. The Erian Marines in disguise in the crowd were also armed with a variety of weapons, especially SBRs and grenade launchers.

Finding itself under fire from the parapet and the raised firing platforms on the palace grounds, the crowd fired back. A few at first, and then they really opened up on them.

In return, the Marines in the palace compound opened up on the crowd. Where the Marines were under at least partial cover, the crowd was out in the open. A groan went up from the crowd as people started to die.

Lieutenant Colonel Frank Everett shifted to his velociraptor persona and let out a roar. The five hundred Erian Marines in the crowd all shifted persona to match and rushed the wall. In a scripted move, the first to get there turned around and hupped the followers up onto the wall.

Those with grenade launchers, once reaching the top of the wall, targeted the firing platforms. Those with SBRs worked on clearing the parapet walk.

The Vauxhall Marines fired back, but their bullets had no effect on the terrifying creatures now targeting them. They were starting to waver when an officer below started shouting to hold the line.

Everett jumped down from the wall and ran up to that officer. He grabbed him in a clawed hand and bit his head off. He then started swinging the body by the heels like a scythe, knocking down Vauxhall Marines while he chewed on the head of the Marine commander.

Outside the wall, two large bulldozers approached the wall, the crowd spreading out to let them through. On the front blade of each was an RDM-50, a Remotely Detonated Munition – Fifty Pounds. Vauxhall Marines on the wall fired at the drivers, but both were Erians.

They ran the blades up to the wall between the reinforcing columns on the back side, then dismounted the bulldozers and set off the charges. The bulldozers got shoved back almost twenty feet by the explosions, but the wall was breached.

Shoving the bulldozers back was a beneficial effect of the explosions, as it cleared a way to the wall breaches, and the crowd surged through the openings onto the palace grounds.

Then the fighting got really nasty.

The Marines on the palace grounds numbered over five thousand, and, no matter how outgunned they were, it still takes a while to kill five thousand people.

And it's not like you don't lose people of your own.

Denouement

"Shit. We have to get out of here. Get the family to the shuttle. Fast!"

"Yes, Father."

The word went through the palace, and the family started to flee toward the shuttle.

Jules was sitting on the balcony of the Palace View Hotel with Portnoy and Stickney, his roll-up display open on his lap. They were watching what they could see of the goings-on at the palace.

Then the message came.

'Jules, I need an RDM-5 at the palace RIGHT NOW. Meet me at the white shuttle. Mary.'

"Mary calls," Jules said.

Jules tossed the display aside and leapt off the balcony. He shifted to a large eagle and flew directly to Danner's apartment. Rather than fuss with elevators and doors, he simply crashed through the living room window.

Jules knew the RDM-5, knew where it was. He shifted to human form, grabbed the device and the detonator from Danner's second spacer trunk, enclosed them within his persona, then ran for the window, leaping out and shifting back to an eagle.

He made for the palace.

Flying over the palace, he could see the white shuttle on the back lawn. And there was Danner, on the patio. Jules let out a cry and saw Danner look up at him, then dropped to the ground behind the white shuttle and, out of sight of the palace, he shifted to a palace guard captain persona, but with Jack Sturm's face.

He walked around the back of the shuttle to find Danner running up to him. She was carrying a box, and opened it.

"Do you have it?"

"Yes."

"In here."

Jules put the RDM-5 and the detonator in the box. Danner took the detonator and put it in her pocket, then closed the box.

They walked around to the side of the shuttle toward the palace, to the open door, and up the loading ramp. A palace guardsman there stopped them.

"His Majesty's things," Danner said with a curtsey.

The guardsman looked to Jules, as a captain of the guard, and Jules nodded.

"Yes, ma'am," the guardsman said, waving her in.

Danner went on into the shuttle. Yeah, she had been right. Medical shuttle, my ass. It was a personnel transfer shuttle, recently painted.

Danner went to the back of the compartment and stowed the box while removing the RDM-5. She placed it carefully, against the most armored point of the exterior hull, and above the point where the fuel lines that fed the big engines in that corner passed.

Having done that, she hurried back forward and down the ramp to find the royal family coming across the lawn to the shuttle. She stood to one side there, with Jules. He saluted, and she stood with eyes down as the king, the queen, the crown prince, and all the rest of the royals hurriedly embarked.

They could hear the battle in the front of the palace intensifying.

"Hurry up," the king shouted as he got aboard. "Take off as soon as everybody's in. Don't wait for seat belts and all that shit."

"Yes, Sire."

They all got on board and the load master shut the door. The engines were already spooling up.

"RUN!" Danner yelled to Jules as she ran for the patio and the safety of the stone balustrade there.

The shuttle leapt into the air, and Danner stole glances behind her to look as she ran.

Damn, he was climbing fast. And the RDM-5 detonator had a limited range. It would have to be soon, but the parapet was still ahead of her.

Too close! *TOO CLOSE!*

Fuck it.

When Danner pushed the detonator, the RDM-5 – five pounds of remotely detonated munition – exploded. It did not split the armored exterior hull there. Instead, it overpressured the compartment, by a lot. Most of the nobility aboard were killed by that compression wave alone. Even the pilots in the cockpit were knocked out by it.

The munition also severed the fuel lines to the port rear engine of the shuttle. The thrust on that engine went to zero, even as the ruptured fuel lines sprayed fuel into the passenger compartment.

The shuttle flipped over and started to tumble. The flight computer tried desperately to restore attitude control, but couldn't keep up. The out-of-control shuttle fell to the ground two hundred feet below, hitting with a huge crash. The passenger compartment was broken open, and flying hot debris from the disintegrating engines set off the fuel-air bomb the passenger compartment had become from the spraying jet fuel.

The terrific explosion of the shuttle behind him caught Jules in the open, running for the palace. As he was thrown forward, he relaxed his royal guard persona and took his natural shape. He hit the palace wall and bounced back out into the yard.

Damn, that hurt. Mary!

Jules got up into his palace guard persona and went looking for Danner. He found her, crumpled up against the palace wall. She did not look good.

Jules shifted to his Jewel persona.

"Mary? Mary? Can you hear me?"

Danner opened her eyes. It took them a while to focus, then she saw Jules.

"I couldn't let them get away."

"I understand, Mary. I have to get you to medical help."

Danner coughed up blood, then shook her head.

"No, Jules. It's beyond that. I can tell."

Jules nodded. Between the concussion and the impact, she must have ruptured some of her internal structures.

"I understand."

"Jules. Did we win?"

"Yes, Mary. We won."

Danner coughed up blood again. She spat it out.

"It was worth it."

Mary Danner looked at Jules and smiled, then closed her eyes and died.

The huge explosion behind the palace had the combatants on the front palace grounds wondering what the hell had happened. Then Jules, in his Association Space Navy uniform, rank of Captain, walked out of the front doors of the palace carrying the broken body of Peggy Dawson in his arms.

Lieutenant Colonel Frank Everett was there on the steps, watching the battle proceed below him, in human form and Marine uniform. He turned to Jules as he came out of the door.

"What happened, Mr. Hawker?"

"She blew up the king's shuttle, Colonel. The king is dead. The entire royal family is dead."

Everett nodded. He thought about it, then turned to look out across the palace grounds, where fighting still continued. He formed what looked like a bullhorn in his hand, but, in truth, he could be louder than any bullhorn. His voice was heard throughout the front palace grounds.

"Hey, everybody. The king is dead. The whole royal family is dead. We're all just commoners now. There's no sense killing each other over some asshole who's dead."

For the Vauxhall Royal Marines, their orders came down from the commander in chief, which is to say, the king. Those orders were now null and void.

For the crowd of armed revolutionaries who had entered the grounds, the goal of ending the monarchy had been achieved. There was literally nothing left to fight for.

For the Erian Marines, their commander had spoken.

The belligerents all looked at each other and shrugged.

As the fighting stopped, Everett had another announcement.

"It's all over. Everybody go home now. We'll figure it all out tomorrow. Medical personnel, attend to the wounded."

The revolutionaries on the palace grounds exited through the breaches in the wall. The Vauxhall Marines and the Erian Marines sought out and attended to the wounded.

Everett turned to Jules and saluted. Not him, Jules realized, but Peggy Dawson.

"She finished it," Everett said. "She won the revolution."

Reconstruction

The whole thing was over by noon that memorable day, then the cleanup began. Even though the fighting and destruction was limited to the palace and the palace grounds, the cleanup seemed to take forever.

First job was to attend to the wounded. To facilitate that, Vauxhall Marine engineers opened the solid-steel inner gates and the wrought-iron outer gates of the palace grounds. A solid stream of ambulances and other vehicles came through to carry the wounded to area hospitals.

The two thousand surviving, unwounded Royal Marines and the five hundred Erian Marines walked the battlefield. The job went faster because the Erian Marines, by looking at the body temperature, could generally tell if someone was alive or dead.

With the wounded seen to, it was time to pick up the dead. They were all checked to make sure they weren't wounded who had been missed in the first pass. The bodies were collected in a makeshift morgue, one of the mess tents that was now surplus to need.

Peggy Dawson, though, Jules lay on a table in the palace foyer.

The palace staff was allowed to go home finally. Most exited the palace by the staff entrance they had always used.

Megan Brie, however, decided to use the front entrance for once. When she did, she came upon the body of her friend Mary Danner, laid out on the table in the foyer, and guarded by an Erian Marine.

"Oh, Mary! Oh, no!"

Brie fell to her knees by the body and cried for her friend.

With the dead and wounded taken care of, the palace was next on the agenda. There was a lot of broken glass on the palace, especially on the back side. They put plastic over all the windows to keep the rain out until glass could be installed. The palace was now a public property, an asset that should not simply be damaged by circumstance.

They also mounted a guard on the palace. Erian Marines guarded the palace around the clock.

In any chaotic situation, there are assholes who will loot or pillage anything not nailed down. The Erian Marines guarding the palace had orders to shoot to kill any attempted looters. After a few such, the problem faded.

That afternoon, a pre-recorded message was sent out over the network on Vauxhall. In the recording, a man in his sixties addressed the population.

"People of Vauxhall, my fellow citizens, my name is Donald Nelson. I am the chairman of the revolutionary committee. We are the people who distributed the free cure for RDT addiction. We are the people who distributed rifles to members of the militia.

"The King of Vauxhall is dead. The entire royal family is dead. There is no successor to the throne, which will remain empty. We will instead seek to rule ourselves for a change.

"In six months we will hold elections to a planetary parliament. That parliament will elect a prime minster, who will name a cabinet. Everyone living on Vauxhall will be allowed to vote, and on the same terms.

"We are all commoners now.

"In the meantime, as chairman of the revolutionary council, I will rule Vauxhall as interim president. You may not agree with everything I do, but I ask you to go along with the transition process, and work your issues through the parliament. That is only six months away.

"I also ask you to refrain from taking vengeance on each other for some wrong committed during the prior regime. We all dealt with living under the hereditary monarchy in the way we thought best. That is all behind us.

"We are all commoners now.

"As for me, after this six-month period as interim president of Vauxhall, I will retire. You will have no Robespierre or Napoleon. I am beyond such ambitions now, having achieved my life's work.

"So carry on, my fellow citizens. Open your store tomorrow. Go in to work. Carry on, and we will build a better Vauxhall for us all."

Portnoy and Jules met openly with Kurt Conrad now. He came to their suite in the Palace View Hotel in downtown Vauxhall City late in the afternoon of the conclusion of the revolution.

And he brought a friend.

Portnoy opened the door and Kurt Conrad entered, followed by a tall man in his sixties.

"Oh my gosh," Stickney said. "Mr. President."

Nelson chuckled and held up a restraining hand.

"Don will do nicely, Ms. Stickney. I'm not much for protocol."

"Well, it's good to meet you, Don," Portnoy said. "Call me Claude."

"And please call me Phyllis, Don."

"And I am called Jules, Don."

Portnoy waved the other two men to seats. When all five were seated, Nelson spoke to Portnoy.

"It's good to finally meet you as well, Claude. We owe you, and your government, a great deal."

"We were happy to help, Don. We were on the same side, after all."

"And still are, I hope. I find your offer of a basing agreement here very compelling, as well as the mutual-defense and free-trade agreements, as I don't expect the king's relatives in the other star kingdoms of the core worlds to be happy about his demise. I'm sure they could find some distant relative to offer in his stead. The Duke of Earth, for example."

Portnoy nodded.

"They will find, however, that we are not amenable to such an arrangement, Don, and we will maintain a squadron here."

"Welcome news indeed."

Nelson nodded, then sighed and continued.

"I have so much to do right now, Claude, I hope you will be amenable to working through Kurt here for most of what you need. Of course, if you need to speak to me directly, feel free to contact me. I wanted to stop by today to see you quickly. I have already spoken with the commanders of the Marines and the Navy, to ensure they are with me. You were next on the list. I have three more meetings still today before I can go to bed."

"Of course, Don. You've got a ton of things on your plate, and we have no problem working with Kurt."

"Good. Thanks, Claude. I appreciate it."

Nelson's view shifted out the window, to the palace on the hill outside of downtown.

"And what are we to do with that?" he asked.

"Make it a museum?" Stickney asked.

"That's a good idea," Nelson said. "Perhaps we shall."

"And I have a suggestion as well, if I might, Sir," Jules said.

"Sure, Jules. What is it?"

Jules told him his idea, and the reason behind it, and Nelson nodded.

"That's a good idea, Jules. A nation needs its heroes. As a new nation, it's good to start with one right off. Consider it done."

"Thank you, Don."

The next day, for the most part, went smoothly. Most people went about their jobs. Life in Vauxhall City returned to normal.

On the palace grounds, Royal Marines and Erian Marines continued to clean up. Fixing the lawns. Repairing the breaches in the wall. removing the wreckage of the raised firing platforms. They also took down all the tents, and the Marines started commuting in to the palace from Camp Charlie outside of town.

Gradually, the palace and its grounds got back into shape.

The body of Peggy Dawson had been removed to a mortuary and embalmed overnight, then it lay in state the next day in the lobby of the major government building there. The building in which she had had her interview for a job in the palace.

There was an announcement of the state funeral on the network, and curious people stopped by to view the body throughout the day.

Megan Brie was shocked to find out her palace friend had in fact been with the revolution. In the manner of some people, she didn't feel so much betrayed as curious. Why had she helped those people? As life improved in Vauxhall over the next several months, she would answer her own question.

After laying in state that day, the coffin containing the body of Peggy Dawson was removed back to the palace, where it was set on a raised platform in the middle of the foyer.

In the end, Megan Brie would be hired as assistant curator of the Palace Museum.

The government published a charter for the new Republic of Vauxhall. It also published election maps, marking all the precincts for the new legislature.

Don Nelson was pragmatic about it all in addresses to the people of Vauxhall.

"We need to start with something, so we'll use this. If your elected legislature wants to amend any of it later, they can. In the meantime, let's get this election campaign under way."

The other thing Don Nelson did was issue an executive order that listed a large number of regulations that were now null and void. He had the same pragmatic view.

"If your elected legislature wants to reinstate any of these regulations later, that's up to them."

Corporations on Vauxhall began looking through the regulations that no longer bound them. They concluded that they had been carefully chosen.

The economy shifted gears.

Toward the end of the first month after the revolution, when Portnoy and Stickney were getting ready for the trip home, Jules asked them if they could go for a short trip with him.

"There's something I want to see."

"Of course, Jules. And you want us to go along?"

"Oh, yes."

Jules would say nothing more about it.

One of the Erian Marines drove them to the royal palace. There was a guard at the gates, but there were also signs up announcing the grand opening of the Palace Museum next week. There would be electric cart service to the front door from the bus stop at the front gate.

For now, though, their car was permitted to drive directly up to the front door. Portnoy nodded.

"This is about your idea, isn't it, Jules?"

"Yes, Claude. Don called me to say it was done."

"Don Nelson called you?" Stickney asked.

"Oh, yes."

They got out of the car and walked up the steps and through the front door into the palace foyer.

There, in the middle of the foyer, was a simple marble sarcophagus. Carved on the side facing the door the inscription read:

PEGGY DAWSON
HERO OF THE REVOLUTION

On the wall behind the monument, there was an heroic painting on the wall where the king's coat of arms once hung. It was an epic painting modeled after "Liberty Leading The People," the famous painting of the July Revolution of 1830 in France.

In this one though, Liberty had the face and likeness Peggy Dawson had used as her Mary Danner alias, the flag was solid blue, and the revolutionaries following her were velociraptors carrying assault rifles.

Portnoy walked around the sarcophagus to stand under the painting. The brass plaque there said "Peggy Dawson Leading The Troops." Which she hadn't done, except in a metaphorical sense.

Jules walked up beside him.

"It's not a bad likeness, I don't think," Jules said.

"No, anybody who knew her would recognize her immediately."

Portnoy looked around the foyer.

"This was a good idea, Jules."

"Thanks, Claude. It means a great deal to me."

"What do you think Mary Danner would say if she saw it?"

"She'd laugh."

Preparing For Departure

A couple of days before they planned to leave, Lieutenant Colonel Frank Everett came to see Portnoy, as team leader.

"Yes, Colonel. Come on in."

"Thank you, Mr. Portnoy."

"Have a seat."

"Thank you."

Everett sat. He nodded to Jules and Stickney.

"How can I help you, Colonel?"

Everett looked at Stickney and Jules, then shrugged.

"Well, it's a bit hard to explain, Sir. Some of my men would like to stay here. There's a lot going on. Getting those manufacturing modules up and running. Getting the rest of the population on the RDT cure. Getting some police corruption cleaned up. Cleaning out the gangs on the north side. Much more interesting than Mardouk. No offense, Sir."

"None taken, Colonel. Mardouk is a much better place to live as a human, however."

"No doubt, Sir. That's the point, in a way. There's so many ways they can help here."

"Then would you be going back to Mardouk, Colonel?"

"Actually, some of my men and I were wondering if *Ladyhawke* could drop us at Earth, Sir. They have a similar problem as the people here did."

That caught Portnoy by surprise. Of course, the Erians were free to go on about their business anywhere they wanted. Not as Association of Planets Marines, necessarily, but as free citizens, they had the right of free travel.

And then there were the weapons.

"Would we leave the weapons containers with you, Colonel?"

"That would be nice, Sir, but isn't required if it's a problem. We'll figure out a way around it if we have to."

"I think I'd rather leave you the weapons, as well, Colonel. That I will need permission for. As for your right to travel to Earth if you want, well, that's up to you. Not wearing Association shoulder patches, though."

"I understand, Sir. Thank you, Sir."

When Everett had left, Portnoy sat back down with Stickney and Jules.

"Well, that's a surprise," Portnoy said.

"Not to me, Claude. I'm sorry. I should have mentioned it."

"You knew about this, Jules?"

"No, but it doesn't surprise me. We like to be useful. We were very useful here, and we enjoyed it tremendously."

"So would you go to Earth with them, Jules?"

"No, Claude. I am already useful where I am."

Portnoy nodded.

"Do we need permission for this, Claude?"

"Well, I'm at least going to ask Bert about it. Whether he bounces it up the line or not, I don't know, but that's up to him."

"Hi, Bert."

"Hi, Claude. What's going on?"

"Did you get our reports OK and all? Do they look complete?"

"Yes. I was sorry to read about Judy Blunt. Completion of the mission is always more important than survival, but that was an extreme case."

"Yeah. It kind of got to Jules, I think. They were close. And he was there when she died."

Mangum nodded. Theirs was a dangerous business, and sometimes reality drove that point home. That was always hard.

"And the agreements have been distributed to the chief executives. That should be proceeding."

"Oh, good. They really want the agreements here."

"We want them here, too, Claude. Or so I understand. So you're getting ready to come home now, if I understood your report?"

"Yes, but something's come up. Some of the Erian Marines want to stay here on Vauxhall. They say there's a lot that needs doing, and they can be most helpful here."

"That sounds like them."

"Right, Bert. But some of them want us to drop them on Earth on the way home. They think they could be very helpful there as well."

"Oh, now that's interesting."

"That's what I thought."

Mangum nodded. They had already dropped millions of doses of the RDT cure and several of the manufacturing modules on Earth. If they dropped a bunch of the Erian Marines on Earth on the way back through, Mangum didn't give the Earth regime three months before the Duke of Earth was out of business.

Which sounded like a good outcome to him.

Now, did he need to go to higher for it? Officially no. As long as the Erians did not wear Association insignia, they would not be an Association force. They would be a bunch of citizens of the Republic of Erias, with the right of free travel.

Unofficially, he probably should work through channels.

That meant it would go to analysis, and they would generate a report and a recommendation – all of that. Which would make it sort of official and generate paperwork.

Not good.

Then again, Sam did know Chairman Febo and was the ambassador for the Erians. Direct contact with her was working through channels.

"Let me think about it, Claude. I'll let you know tomorrow."

"All right. Thanks, Bert."

Mangum cut the connection, then walked from the office out to the living room.

"Hey, Sam. we need to talk for a second."

Sam looked up from his display.

"Sure, Bert. What's going on?"

"Good afternoon, Mr. Ambassador."

"Good afternoon, Madam Chairman. Something has come up I think I should talk to you about."

"Of course, Mr. Ambassador."

"I think you have seen the reports by now of what transpired on Vauxhall in the past month."

"Indeed I have, Mr. Ambassador. Your people were a great help in obtaining a satisfactory outcome for the people of Vauxhall, both in space and on the ground."

"Yes, Madam Chairman. And our people were happy to do it. We enjoy being useful. And now a proposal has come to me from my people on Vauxhall about how they might be more useful going forward than simply returning to Mardouk...."

"Hi, Bert."

"Hi, Claude. You're a go."

"Really?"

"Oh, yes. Drop them on Earth, with the weapons, access to the RDT cure and the manufacturing modules, the whole shebang. But no Association emblems or patches."

"Got it. Bert, are you sure this is going to be OK?"

"Oh, yes. Chairman Febo told Ambassador Hawker she thought it was a wonderful idea when he brought it to her."

"No shit."

"No shit."

The time finally came for *Ladyhawke* to head home – via Earth – with Portnoy, Stickney, and Jules. They had been on Vauxhall for four months, though it didn't seem like it.

Don Nelson and Kurt Conrad joined them for dinner their last night on Vauxhall. The five of them sat out on the balcony of their suite at the Palace View Hotel.

Jules was wearing his Association Space Navy uniform, with the rank of captain.

Nelson looked out over the palace grounds to where the palace gleamed in the floodlights.

"It looks nice, actually, although I like it a lot better now that there's no one there in residence who thinks he was born with the right to lord it over me."

"The memorial to Peggy Dawson looks very nice, too, Don. Thank you so much for that. It was important to me."

"Important to me, too, Jules. The surveillance tapes backed up what you said. She knew she was too close, and she detonated the bomb anyway. She willingly gave her life for the people of Vauxhall. A nation needs its heroes, and now we have one."

Jules nodded. There wasn't much more to say. Nelson had a question, though.

"Looking through the surveillance and the palace records,

though, someone pointed out that her name, as far as they were concerned, was Mary Danner."

"An alias," Jules said. "Her real name was Peggy Dawson. Back on Mardouk she worked at the zoo, as a large predator specialist."

Nelson chuckled.

"Well, I doubt she ever took on as big a predator as King Albert XIV. She succeeded, however."

"Yes," Jules said. "Peggy Dawson was the deadliest predator of them all. I think that's why they understood each other. She and the zoo animals. They had so much in common."

Unused to the frankness and insight of the Erians, Nelson raised an eyebrow, but made no comment.

"Thank you, too, for signing the basing agreement and the mutual-defense and free-trade agreement, Don."

"You're very welcome, Claude, though I think it's I who owe you, and Chairman Febo, Speaker Corliss, and the other cluster chief executives. Those agreements are very important to a free Vauxhall going forward."

"Everyone will have to execute them at the other end, of course, but I've sent the digital versions you signed to them."

"I've already received the executed copies, Claude. They're a done deal. And Admiral Winston and his squadron will be staying here for the next eight months or so. Until another squadron comes to replace them. The cluster is going to permanently base a squadron here."

"That's good news, Don. I wonder how the crews will take the news."

"Very well, I think. All of your people are very popular here right now. I suspect it's the best damn planet leave any of them ever had. And the cheapest. Nobody will charge them for their drinking. And I don't even want to think about the girls. The

Erian Marines aren't interested, but I think that won't be a problem for several tens of thousands of human spacers."

Portnoy and Stickney laughed.

The meal was very pleasant.

After Nelson had left, there was nothing to do but pack for the lift to *Ladyhawke* tomorrow.

There were four spacer trunks now, as before. Portnoy and Stickney each had the one they arrived with, and Jules had retrieved the two spacer trunks from Mary Danner's apartment.

"We can't leave any of that behind, Claude. You would not believe what she traveled with. Having it fall into the wrong hands would be a big problem."

"Yes, I suppose taking it along is the easiest thing," Portnoy had said.

So Jules had walked to the apartment – the window repaired now – and retrieved Judy Blunt's kit of sex toys, costumes, wigs, makeup, firearms, knives, poisons, needles, dart guns, and explosives.

Jules took a cab back to the hotel, as it was late and Vauxhall City was still settling down from the regime change.

The next morning saw them all at the Vauxhall City shuttleport for the lift to *Ladyhawke*. They watched while all the baggage was loaded, including Mary Danner's two spacer trunks.

Jules seemed distracted watching the trunks being loaded. He finally spoke up.

"Claude, would it be OK with you and Phyllis if I stayed in your cabin on the way back to Mardouk?"

Portnoy looked at Stickney, and she gave him a slight nod.

"Sure, Jules. That would be fine."

"Thanks, Claude. I think sitting alone in the other cabin with her trunks, and knowing she was gone, would be very disturbing for me."

"I understand, Jules. It's not a problem."

Some one hundred and fifty Erian Marines were staying on Vauxhall. Of the rest, two hundred and fifty would be dropped at Earth. Only one hundred would be going back to Mardouk.

All of the attack-ship pilots, though, were staying on Admiral Winston's heavy cruisers.

"Why are the attack-ship pilots all staying where they are, Jules?" Portnoy asked.

"They believe Vauxhall will be targeted by the other core-world kingdoms, Claude."

"They want to be here for that?"

"Oh, yes. They love to pilot the attack ships, and they love combat most of all."

Three hundred and fifty Erian Marines – with their two barracks containers, the galley container, the food container, and two weapons containers – had already been lifted to *Ladyhawke*, so when *Ladyhawke*'s small personnel shuttle lifted to the ship, she was ready to space.

For the last month, *Ladyhawke*'s crew had rotated planet leaves on Vauxhall.

Epic planet leaves.

To Earth, Again

Ladyhawke had done the Vauxhall to Earth run several times in the preceding four months. Having a freighter sitting in space accruing demurrage without spacing would have been suspicious, so she had been shuttling back and forth, making money on every trip, at least up until the demonstrations on Vauxhall had started.

Her trade master, Ephraim Smith, thus knew the run and had no trouble picking up consignment shipping to Earth from Vauxhall in the days before departure.

Ladyhawke spaced from Vauxhall with a full two thousand containers destined for Earth, among which two hundred and fifty Erian Marines and their supplies would be only five containers.

With the X-3 drive, Earth was barely a week away.

Of course, the news out of Vauxhall had made it to Earth immediately over the QE radio network. The Duke of Earth had immediately declared himself King of Earth and started consolidating power over what planets of the former Kingdom of Vauxhall he could grab.

This was actually simplified by Vauxhall Royal Navy headquarters on Vauxhall declaring itself the Republic of Vauxhall Navy and retaining only those navy resources currently in the Vauxhall system. All of a sudden there were a lot of Vauxhall Royal Navy ships in Earth orbit and elsewhere without a navy to belong to.

Without paychecks or pensions.

Navy assets in the Earth system were quick to offer their

allegiance to the King of Earth once he guaranteed navy wages and pensions. They were now the Earth Royal Navy.

Leaders of some of the other planets in the erstwhile Kingdom of Vauxhall – mostly the stronger ones – also declared themselves king of their planets and tried to gobble up whatever other planets they could. Navy assets in those systems were quick to offer allegiance to their local kings as well.

Most planetary leaders, however, afraid to go it alone, potentially against other core-world kingdoms, were happy to swear fealty to the King of Earth or one of the other strong systems. The navy assets in their systems followed the lead of the local nobility, and offered their allegiance to the acknowledged political leader.

The big worry was that no one knew what naval forces of other core-world powers were already in transit in hyperspace, or what would happen when they got there.

By the time *Ladyhawke* reached Earth, the balkanization of the former Kingdom of Vauxhall was well under way.

Ladyhawke dropped out of hyperspace at the hyperspace limit for Earth, and started for the planet.

In their cabin, Portnoy, Stickney, and Jules were hurriedly scanning the network to try and figure out what had gone on since they left Vauxhall. In the current environment, a week was potentially a long time.

"Here's something interesting," Jules said. "Ships returning to Earth – who have made trips to Earth in the recent past – are getting a pass as the customs people are concentrating on ships new to the system. Apparently, they're wary of contraband being brought in by troublemakers. Other core-world kingdoms. That's their focus."

"Even ships from Vauxhall, Jules?" Stickney asked.

"Yes. Even those from Vauxhall. We get a pass."

"We caught a break," Portnoy said.

"Looks like it, Richard."

"I'll let Emmet know."

They had a meeting in the captain's conference room. Emmet Durst, Claude Portnoy, Phyllis Stickney, Jules Hawker, and Lieutenant Colonel Frank Everett.

Portnoy brought everybody up to speed on Earth's concentration of their customs inspectors on new-ship inbounds, and giving ships with prior records in the Earth system lighter coverage.

"So we're clean past customs?" Durst asked.

"Looks like," Portnoy said. "Oh, another visit from *Ladyhawke*. Ho-hum. Nothing to see here."

"Excellent."

"That's very good news," Everett said. "My one worry was getting onto the planet clean. The rest we can handle."

"How are you going to get the containers out of consignment?" Durst asked.

Everett shifted persona to a sixty-ish businessman.

"Why, you're going to sell them to me, Captain. I need them for my business. All those whatever the hell they are."

Everybody chuckled at Everett's portrayal.

"OK, so we have one barracks container and the weapons containers," Durst said. "What else?"

"The spare galley container and one food supplies container," Everett said. "Plus one container of the RDT cure. That's already on-planet, right?"

"Yes, in a consignment warehouse at the Vienna shuttleport."

"Perfect," Everett said. "That's exactly where we need it, Emmet."

"What about more RDT cure and the manufacturing modules?" Portnoy asked. "They're already on the planet, but we're going to be in hyperspace for two months."

"I can put him on the preferred-customer list for those containers, with a price. He can pick them up any time."

"That works," Everett said. "What about the money part of it?"

"That's just shifting things back and forth, Frank," Portnoy said. "We'll take care of it. See to it you have funds."

Everett nodded.

"I can have the purser set up the accounts. So I think we have a plan, gentlemen," Durst said.

"There's just one more thing," Jules said.

He turned to Everett.

"I have something I think you could use, Frank."

"Excellent. More help is always good."

After the meeting, Jules and Everett went to what had been his and Mary Danner's cabin, and Jules walked him through all of her materials.

Jules and Everett then transferred Danner's spacer trunks to the barracks container.

On the way to Earth orbit, Ephraim Smith started buying up loads for the trip to Mardouk, though he did not specify a destination. That wasn't required for purchased loads, though consignment loads had the destination specified by the shipper.

The unloading and loading of *Ladyhawke* went without incident. She was familiar to the transfer company's shuttle crews by now, and it was just another job.

The inbounds were transferred to the planet. The inbound consignment loads went to the consignment warehouse for pickup by the receivers.

Also to the consignment warehouse went the six containers with the Erian Marines and their equipment, including galley, food container, and two containers of infantry weapons.

None of the containers were inspected, the customs inspectors being busy with the inbound loads of other ships, newcomers to Earth space. They actually did find things being shipped into Earth by foreign adversaries to cause trouble, which reinforced their decision to concentrate their available inspectors on those ships.

But they missed the most dangerous inbound shipment of them all.

The Erians watched workers moving about the consignment warehouse through the surveillance cameras hidden on the outside of the barracks container.

When the coast was clear, the door of the barracks container opened just a bit, and Frank Everett and five other Erian Marines oozed out of the door. They took the persona of warehouse workers. When the shift ended, they walked out of the building without impediment.

It was later that same day that six men in civilian work clothes walked into the office of a truck leasing company near the Vienna shuttleport.

"Can I help you?" the clerk asked.

"Yeah. Danforth Freightways. The boss said you got six trucks for us."

"Yes, of course. I'll just need to see your commercial licenses."

"Here's mine," Everett said, handing the clerk a thousand-Earth-credit note.

"Ah. That seems to be in order. And you gentlemen?"

The other five Erian Marines each also produced a thousand-Earth-credit note.

"Everything seems to be in order. Let me show you your vehicles."

The Erian Marine standing by with one of Mary Danner's dart guns concealed in his body relaxed. No need.

They went out into the yard and the clerk watched as the six started up the container trucks and pulled out of the facility. He relaxed when it was clear they were competent at handling the big rigs.

Of course, all of the Erian Marines were competent at driving the big commercial trucks. It was part of the Marines logistics training sequence.

The six trucks stopped at the gate of the consignment warehouse. Everett was in the lead vehicle.

"Six-container pick-up for Danforth Freightways."

The clerk checked his display.

"Pull-through number seventeen," he said. "Why don't you go ahead, and I'll tell each of the other guys as they come through."

"Got it."

The six containers had been transferred to Danforth Freightways by the purser of the *Ladyhawke*. They had been moved and were ready near the loading area when the big rigs pulled up.

The trucks all lined up for pull-through number seventeen. One at a time, a container was placed on a truck from the side by a container loader and it pulled forward, six times in all.

Then the trucks left the consignment warehouse, heading for a small commercial facility Everett had rented in the industrial outskirts of Vienna. The commercial facility had been chosen with care.

It was half a block from a commuter train station.

They would ride the train to the revolution.

They unloaded their containers with an overhead crane in the rented facility, then drove the rigs back to the rental outfit. It was a one-day lease, but one day was all they needed.

Ladyhawke was approaching the hyperspace limit when Durst stopped by their cabin to talk to Portnoy.

"The purser tells me Everett has already picked up all six containers."

"That was quick," Stickney said.

"Yeah," Portnoy said. "Like two days."

"We don't like to sit around and wait for things," Jules said.

"Well, Everett didn't wait," Durst said. "He and his men are already out of the consignment warehouse and set up somewhere."

"I wonder what the news will be from the Kingdom of Earth when we come out of hyperspace," Stickney said.

"You mean the Republic of Earth, don't you?" Portnoy asked.

At the hyperspace limit, *Ladyhawke* opened a rift in spacetime before her, then spaced through it and disappeared from reality. Navigator Lara Perez set course for Mardouk, and Helmsman Halim Ahmed engaged the X-3 drive.

A week later, in Vienna, Earth Planetary Police Inspector Matthew Gray was happy to be able to take his wife down to the Graben to get the free cure for RDT. She had been given the drug during a hospital stay and, of course, become addicted. The government-supplied cure was way too expensive, even on the Inspector's salary he received since moving to Vienna from Southern California.

The fellows handing out the free cure were very nice. Gray took the cure himself, to make himself immune to addiction should he end up in the hospital for some reason.

After taking the cure, Gray and his wife took a train upriver along the southern shore of the Danube to the Vienna Woods and had a pleasant walk.

The train they rode passed by the headquarters of the Erian Marines.

To Mardouk

On the trip to Mardouk, Jules initially stayed with Portnoy and Stickney. The small cabin was crowded, which was not a problem for Jules. Erians were naturally gregarious and liked crowding. He worried he was a burden on Portnoy and Stickney, however.

He began hanging out in the other cabin. The one he had shared with Mary Danner on the way to Earth, then Vauxhall. Her spacer trunks were not there.

It was just an empty cabin.

Portnoy and Stickney often came over to visit. They sat in the cabin together and talked or read together, and when they left it was all right. Jules wasn't troubled by memories of Danner.

He remembered her, of course. He just wasn't troubled by it. She had been the most rational human he had ever met. Almost Erian in the way she approached the world. And he had been there when she died, had felt her loss dearly.

But it was all right, finally. He could mourn her loss, be glad she existed, be glad he had met her, and remember her fondly, without being so troubled.

Now in his own cabin, he could lay in the shower in his natural state for hours without being in the way of the others.

Sometimes he visited or ate with the Erian Marines aboard, the hundred of them going back to Mardouk, in their barracks or galley. Sometimes he visited with the four Erian attack-ship pilots, in a single crew cabin down the hall.

The weeks of crossing the void wore on. By now it was old

hat for the crew. Two months, after all, was not bad. That six-month crossing before the X-3 drive had been another matter entirely.

Two days out from Mardouk, *Ladyhawke* dropped out of hyperspace to get her location. She corrected her navigation, and reentered hyperspace for the last bit to Mardouk.

Portnoy, Stickney, and Jules pulled all the news they could of Earth during the hour *Ladyhawke* was in normal space.

The last two days spacing was spent reading everything they could from Earth.

Stickney had to admit it. Portnoy had made the call.

"Republic of Earth. Wow," she said.

"Yes. Quite a coup, you'll pardon the expression," Portnoy said.

"That was quick."

"Not that quick, Phyllis," Jules said. "Vauxhall was only weeks once Admiral Winston's ships were in place and we got the go-ahead."

"You're right, Jules," Portnoy said. I guess it just seems longer because we were there two months waiting for them to get in position."

"And the navy didn't budge," Stickney said. "They didn't interfere."

"I think it was the announcement by Admiral Winston that turned the trick there. Was that Everett impersonating Winston, Jules?"

"It could have been, Claude. Or one of the others. Any of them, really."

"Well, it did the trick. The navy didn't fire on the crowds."

"Yes, but don't forget, Richard," Stickney said. "The navy

people had seen what happened to *Aurora*. As in Vauxhall, they weren't willing to chance it."

"I think that's it, Susan. Winston *could* have been there, his ships minutes away in hyperspace, and they knew how that would end."

"But what happened to the king, Richard. Good God."

"Yes. Dragged out of the palace and beaten to death by the crowd."

"And then his body hung from a light pole in the Graben. What's the Graben?"

It was Jules who answered.

"The Graben is the major public square in the middle of downtown Vienna. It is perhaps a block wide and several blocks long."

"Ah. That answers that. A major public display of the body, to make sure everyone knew he was gone."

"The Earl of Europe got strung up, too. And the royal family was hunted down."

"Hunted down and killed, Richard. All of them."

"Yes, Susan. They wanted to ensure there was no heir to the throne. Some of that was pretty grisly. But the other earls and the barons stepped down. When the crowds let them, that is."

"And how often was that, Richard?"

"Actually, Phyllis," Jules said, "about eighty-three percent of the time. More than four in five retired peacefully."

"And how many people were killed, Jules?"

"On both sides? Fifteen thousand is the estimate, Phyllis."

"What about on Vauxhall, Jules?" Portnoy asked.

"As of the time we left, Claude, it was about twelve thousand."

"So Earth was worse than Vauxhall?" Stickney asked.

"Oh yes," Jules said. "There was no singular event that

killed the royal family and prompted an end to the fighting, as the crash and explosion of the king's escape shuttle did on Vauxhall. The battle had to be ground out to the end. One countervailing issue is the destruction of *Aurora* and her four-thousand-man crew. Nothing of that kind happened on Earth."

"Still not a large count, Susan. Not to free a planet of billions."

"I suppose, Richard. It all just seems such a waste."

"I am reminded of an old quote, Phyllis," Jules said. "'Freedom is bought with the blood of patriots. Only a price so dear could purchase something so precious.'"

When *Ladyhawke* dropped out of Mardouk space, there was more news from Earth. The new government had signed mutual-defense and free-trade agreements with Vauxhall and the cluster.

"What is Chairman Febo going to do now, Richard? She can't send more navy out to protect them, can she?"

"I don't know, Susan. Maybe. She does have to worry about the monarchies striking at the cluster, however. That's got to be her first priority. Earth and Vauxhall are only two planets, and the cluster is more like a hundred."

"I think she'll send half the Vauxhall squadron on maneuvers to Earth," Jules said.

"Four ships, or five, to guard the whole planet, Jules?"

"No, Claude. Forty or fifty attack ships to guard the planet. The enemy will not have attack ships, I think. The change in doctrine has not had time to propagate."

"Oh, that could do it," Stickney said.

"Based on what we saw in Vauxhall, yes," Portnoy said. "I wonder if she sees it."

"Hello, Michael."

"Hello, Isabela. It's good to hear from you."

"I wanted to catch you up, Michael. And tell you what I've done while there's time to alter our course if you don't concur."

Speaker Corliss of the Gaston Alliance thought that was unlikely. Chairman Febo of the Association of Planets rarely made big mistakes.

"Well, I appreciate being consulted, Isabela, but you've been right so far. A free Vauxhall and a free Earth attest to the quality of your decision making."

"Thank you, Michael. That's very kind. The successful revolutions on both planets leave us with something of a conundrum, however. I would like to protect Earth as well as Vauxhall from the depredations of the nobility clan that rules the core worlds. They will not be pleased about their cousins being so, um, thoroughly removed from power."

"Yes. I see the problem, Isabela. We also have a hundred planets to protect in the cluster. When the ruling clan strikes out in anger, which way do they turn?"

"Exactly, Michael. Now, have you had a chance to review the battle footage from the Battle of Vauxhall?"

"Yes, Isabela. The attack ships proved remarkably effective."

"Yes, Michael. And we don't think the other navies of the core worlds have caught up with the change in naval doctrine. They won't have any attack ships. Not yet."

"And not as capable as ours in any case. Not without Erian pilots."

"Correct. So I've ordered Admiral Winston to send one of his divisions on maneuvers to Earth. I don't need the admiralty council to do that, since Winston and his squadron are already deployed to the core worlds."

"Is this OK with President Nelson on Vauxhall, Isabela?"

"Yes. I checked with him first. Made sure he knew they were not being abandoned. And Winston's second division is already en route to the hyperspace limit. I could, however, order them back if you have another recommendation."

"No, Isabela, I think you have it right. And I will so advise Ferdinand and Randall. Are you going to contact Jacques and Catherine?"

Corliss had always been closer to King Ferdinand of Wilbourne and President Randall Paxton of Villacqua, while Febo was closer to President Jacques Martin of Abelon and Queen Catherine of Lyons. Together, they were the chief executives of the six star nations of the cluster.

"That would be lovely, Michael. Thank you."

"No problem, Isabela. You're on a roll, and I'll back you."

Admiral Harvey Winston briefed his second division commander, Rear Admiral Jorge Alvarez, as the four heavy cruisers of the second division spaced for the hyperspace limit of Vauxhall. The second division had spaced immediately that Winston received orders to send them to Earth on maneuvers, so the briefing was by virtual meeting as they spaced.

"All right, Jorge. I think one of us is going to get very busy over the next couple weeks. Maybe both of us. And I've said so to Chairman Febo."

"I understand, Harvey."

"Good. So here's what we need to do. We can't let any of their platforms get away. Sure, if somebody surrenders, that's fine. Commandeer a liner and get all their people off and down to the planet, then destroy their ship. We want to reduce the forces against us, and a bunch of guys on the planet aren't a threat to us."

"Commandeer a liner, Harvey?"

"Right. A liner or a troopship. The planetary president will help with that. Let him do the commandeering part. You should contact him immediately you drop from hyperspace. Chairman Febo has already talked to him, so I think we're good there."

"All right. That works."

"Now, as far as strategy, you're out there on your own, Jorge. You're the commander on the scene and I won't second-guess you from here. But the best strategy is likely to be to keep your ships in pretty close orbits to the planet. Make them come in after you. When they're four or five hours in from the hyperspace limit, send the attack ships after them. Those damn things are so fast, they won't be able to get back over the hyperspace limit, and they'll be sitting ducks for the Erian space jocks."

"You don't think they have attack ships, Harvey?"

"We don't think so, Jorge. Now, if they deploy attack ships against you, they won't hold a candle to the Erians. Human pilots means three gees. But your strategy might shift around at that point. You'll have to maintain some fleet defensive cover, for instance. You can't send all your attack ships after the big boys. But if they don't have attack ships, just send them all."

"Got it, Harvey. I think that's smart. I was thinking along these lines myself."

"One more thing, Jorge. The Erians have worked out some sort of rescue setup. If one of their attack ships gets hit, there's a way to recover the pilot. We had one guy literally do a naked reentry during the Battle of Vauxhall, but your guys will be heading out-planet during any action. So we need to act just like it's a human pilot out there and go rescue them. We don't leave our men on the field, human or Erian."

"I'm with you there, Harvey."

"All right, Jorge. Good spacing, and good luck."

"Well, you called it, Jules. I just got a private message from Bert. Admiral Winston has sent his second division to Earth."

"Excellent," Stickney said.

"I agree with you, Phyllis," Jules said. "I piloted those ships first, and I know what they can do. If someone comes in looking to stir up trouble on Earth or Vauxhall, they're going to have their hands full."

Ladyhawke arrived in Mardouk orbit, and the majority of the crew transferred down to the planet in the small personnel shuttle. The Marines and the four attack-ship pilots were transported to the planet with *Ladyhawke*'s cargo shuttle taking the barracks chamber down to the Marine base a hundred miles west of Ashur.

That night, Bert Mangum and Elina Stavros hosted a small party in their top-floor unit at The 909. The food was from room service.

Present were Mangum and Stavros, Portnoy and Stickney, Kendall and Schofield, Sam and Jules, and Emmet Durst.

After ooing and ahing over the new baby, Harriet Mangum Stavros, they all settled down to conversation.

"Where are Gloria and Davian?" Stickney asked.

"Out at the beach house they bought. With new baby Mary Lou Varley. You have been gone nine months, you know. It was too much to ask them to come into town with a newborn."

Schofield was about seven months pregnant by this time herself.

"We didn't get started until you guys got to Vauxhall," Kendall said. "I was always a slow learner."

Everybody laughed, and then the conversation turned serious.

"That was some good work you guys did on Vauxhall," Mangum said.

Portnoy, as team leader, responded to his superior.

"Thanks, Bert. It was all the help we had. The Marines, Admiral Winston's ships, the attack ships, Mary Danner. It was hard to fail with that kind of line-up."

"I was sorry to hear about Mary Danner," Stavros said.

"Judy Blunt," Mangum corrected.

"Peggy Dawson," Jules said. "That was her real name, Bert. She was a big predator specialist at the Ashur City Zoo. That's how I knew how to get a hold of her. I recognized her on a walk through the zoo."

"That's why you stopped at the wolves exhibit," Stavros said. "That time we walked in the zoo."

"Yes. Sam told me not to tell anyone. It could compromise her identity."

Mangum nodded.

"Good call," he said.

"But when this mission came up," Jules said, "I knew how to contact her. I went to see her at the zoo. She decided to come out of retirement for this mission. Because of its importance."

"And died in the doing," Stavros said.

"Yes, Elina," Jules said. "But it was her decision, and she had no regrets. Her last words, after I told her we won, were 'It was worth it.' She smiled at me, then she died."

"I think she was right," Portnoy said. "It was worth it. Life on Vauxhall was improving rapidly even by the time we left."

"They built her a beautiful monument, too," Stickney said. "Right in the foyer of the palace. 'Hero of the Revolution' it says."

"That's nice," Stavros said.

"And now we need to see that the other core worlds can't do anything to overturn those events," Mangum said.

"Do you think they'll try, Bert?" Portnoy asked.

"Almost surely. It's a precedent they can't allow to stand. They will try to recapture the planets for their family. Prove that it won't work. That they won't let it."

"Can Admiral Winston prevail against them, though, Bert?"

"On the short-term, yes."

"And on the long-term?"

"There are twelve more squadrons building, Claude. Keels have been laid on six of them."

"Who can even do that many?" Stickney asked. "Nobody has enough yard space."

"No one company does, Phyllis," Mangum said. "But together, they all do."

Naval Construction And Destruction

New ships under construction for the cluster consortium navy were different than the heavy cruisers General Spaceship of Mystik had built for Wilbourne and Villacqua. Naval architects had been informed by the Battle of Vauxhall.

At the same time, they weren't too different. The powers that be didn't want a redesign, which could take years to pull off. They wanted more firepower sooner, not later.

As a consequence, the differences were more subtle. The keel, the ships' length and beam, the hyperspace drive, the thrusters were all unchanged.

But the missile launchers and missile feed queues were gone. In their place was hangar space for twenty attack ships. These were spares. Extras.

The main complement of attack ships latched to the outside of the big ships was increased from ten to twenty by adding another ten small docking ports.

Together with their internal second wave, which could be launched within an hour of the first wave, these new ships carried a complement of forty attack ships.

A squadron could field three hundred and twenty attack ships, carrying a total of thirty-eight hundred and forty missiles.

There were financial incentives for early completion, and shipyards across the cluster were racing to finish these new ships and collect not just the price but the bonuses.

There were objections to all this new construction, of course, the biggest being, 'How can we afford so many ships?'

Isabela Febo had a simple answer.

"We're going to sell most of them, at a profit."

"We're going to sell such capable ships?"

"Oh, yes. To Vauxhall, to Earth, to any other planet that bucks the monarchies and becomes a democracy."

"And what if those planets turn against us? Turn authoritarian? What if they turn those ships against us?"

"It won't do them any good."

"Why not?"

"Because the Erian pilots won't fight against the cluster democracies, especially on behalf of an authoritarian state."

"But with human pilots, they could still do three gravities."

"Yes, and that is not enough to prevail against us."

Such considerations were far in the future for Admiral Winston and Rear Admiral Alvarez. They were much more concerned about the here and now. With what happened if and when a core-world navy dropped out of hyperspace in their system.

Vauxhall was first.

"We have a hyperspace down-transition, Sir. Right on the limit. Making it seventeen ships. Looks like two squadrons and a flagship."

John Kirtland, captain of the CNS *Indomitable* waited for more information to come in.

"Masses showing now, Sir. Confirm seventeen battleships. They're actually squawking. Flag is SNS *Crown*. SNS is Sondheim Navy Ship. All ships squawking Sondheim."

Kirtland raised an eyebrow. Sondheim was a big kingdom, sure, but sixteen battleships was a lot to have off gallivanting about.

Kirtland turned to his display with Admiral Winston. As Winston's flag captain, Kirtland talked with the admiral a lot.

"What do you think, John?" Winston asked.

"Isn't that a lot of firepower to have off running about, Harvey? Are they not afraid of their neighbors?"

"Oh, I suspect the family is united against Vauxhall, John. They probably gave assurances they wouldn't mess around with Sondheim while the navy was off to deal with Vauxhall."

Kirtland nodded. That made sense.

"And us, Sir? What are we going to do?"

"I'll warn them off."

"And if they don't leave, Sir."

"Then we'll be forced to destroy them"

On the flag bridge, Winston turned to his comm officer.

"Fleet orders. Be prepared to launch attack ships in four hours."

"Four hours. Aye, Sir. Transmitted."

"Let's transmit to the *Crown*. Is she squawking a contact channel?"

"On the core-world network, yes, Sir."

"Record message. This is Admiral Harvey Winston of the CNS *Indomitable* to the Sondheim battleship formation. You are unwelcome in Vauxhall space. As such you are required to leave now. I am prepared to allow you to leave now with impunity. If you do not leave, you will be destroyed. Winston out. End Message. Send it."

It was a few minutes before they got a message back. While they waited, they got an early answer.

"They're under thrust now, Sir. One gravity. Making for the planet."

Winston looked down to the image of Kirtland.

"Well, I guess there's our answer, John."

"Yes, Harvey. You didn't expect them to just leave, did you?"

"Well, I had to give them an out. Them's the rules."

Winston's comm officer interrupted.

"Message from the *Crown*, Sir."

"Admiral Winston. This is Admiral Thomas Beltan, of the Sondheim Royal Navy. We are here to restore the throne of Vauxhall and install a rightful heir, and there's nothing you can do to stop us. Ship for ship, we outmass you and outgun you, and we outnumber you by more than three to one. Extending the same courtesy, Admiral, I will allow you to leave the system unharmed. There's no sense dying for a ragtag bunch of revolutionaries when you can't do anything about it anyway. Beltan out."

Winston nodded. What he expected. What he himself would have done, say, two years ago.

"What do we do now, Harvey?" Kirtland's image asked at his elbow.

"Let them come, John. Trap them in the system. In four hours, we launch."

The Agency and the BIE had been busy coming up with as much detail on core-world warships as they could find. They had pretty good data on the Sondheim battleships.

In the four hours they had until launch, the Erian attack-ship pilots studied those battleships, especially their weak points.

"Coming up on four hours now, Sir."

"Fleet orders," Winston said. "Report wing status."

"Gold Wing ready."

"Black Wing ready."

"White Wing ready."

"Red Wing ready."

"Blue Wing ready."

"Fleet Orders. On the mark, launch all wings."

Winston turned to his comm officer.

"Send the mark. Four hours."

"Aye, Sir."

The attack ship pilots knew what they were up against. Their reaction would have shocked Admiral Beltan and his officers, however.

"OK, there's only seventeen of them. We're going to have to share."

On the mark, Admiral Winston's flagship and his first division launched its attack ships.

"Gold Wing away."

"Black Wing away."

"White Wing away."

"Red Wing away."

"Blue Wing away."

"They've launched parasites, Sir."

"What? Shuttles?" Beltan asked. "Are they abandoning ship?"

"No, Sir. They're heading for us. I show them making nine-point-three gravities."

"*Nine* gravities? Are they missiles?" Beltan asked.

"No, Sir. Ships. Much bigger than missiles, but still very small. We have a total of fifty incoming."

"Fleet orders. Stand by point defense."

"Aye, Sir. Fleet orders transmitted."

"How long until missile range on those heavy cruisers?"

"Still twelve hours, Sir."

"And these incoming?"

"Will be here in about an hour, Sir."

The attack-ship wings spread out, and the ships in each wing spread out. They would come in on the enemy from multiple directions, denying the point defense easy targets and spreading out the defensive fire.

As they drew within point defense distance, the attack ships engaged their on-board ECM and started corkscrewing madly.

They had been accelerating for an hour, and they were coming in very fast.

The attack ship wings passed through the enemy formation, making their initial attack run and then firing at targets of opportunity on their way through. The first four wings, totaling forty attack ships, launched a total of two hundred and fifty missiles at the seventeen battleships.

A third of the ECM-equipped missiles avoided all the point-defense fire to score hits on their targets. Most of those hits were at weak spots the Erian pilots had identified in their study of the plans the intelligence services had provided.

Missile explosions rippled across the Sondheim formation, punctuated by the brighter flashes of failing fusion bottles.

Gold Wing held back, and went in last. Only four of the Sondheim battleships were anything other than gutted and broken hulks by then, and Gold Wing put twenty-four more missiles into those four targets.

As the attack ship wings began accelerating the other way to head back to their mother ships, there was nothing left of Sondheim's attacking force but debris.

Sondheim lost seventeen battleships and over sixty thousand spacers in less than an hour.

Even at over nine gees, it took over an hour for the attack ships to decelerate relative to the planet, and another three hours to accelerate, then decelerate, toward their mother ships and dock.

All the attack ships made it back to their mother ships save two. Even the pilot of Red Seven, who was now flying one of the spare attack ships each heavy cruiser carried latched to its supplies containers, made it back intact.

The two who did not make it back took hits that took out their engines. The ships did not explode, and the hits were not cockpit hits. On the modular ships, the cockpit was an independent module, and didn't even lose pressure.

One of their companion ships maneuvered alongside each of them. Both pilots involved in each pick-up took big breaths of air, then vented their cabins. The pilot of the stricken ship extruded himself out of the vent diaphragm of his ship, propelled himself to the other ship with air, then extruded himself into the rescue ship's cockpit through its vent diaphragm.

The rescue pilot refilled his cabin with compressed air, and both pilots rode back to the rendezvous with the mother ship together.

With those pilots picked up, all of the pilots made it back to their mother ships.

Earth was next.

"Ma'am, we have a hyperspace down-transition. On the hyperspace limit. I make it twenty-four ships. Looks like three squadrons."

Janice Jenks, captain of the CNS *Illustrious* waited for more information to come in.

"Masses showing now, Ma'am. Confirm twenty-four heavy cruisers. They're squawking Persh, Norton, and Bergheim ship IDs by squadron."

"Not being subtle, are they?"

"No, Ma'am. They're thrusting now. Making for the planet."

Jenks looked down at her link to Admiral Jorge Alvarez on the flag bridge.

"Looks like we have visitors, Janice."

"Yes, Jorge. And they didn't call ahead first. How impolite."

"Why do I feel like Napoleon?" Alvarez muttered.

"Excuse me, Sir?" Jenks asked.

"Sorry, Janice. Meandering thought. History doesn't repeat, but it does rhyme."

"So I've heard, Jorge."

Alvarez nodded.

"I think we should set launch time for three hours, Janice. Not wait four."

"That makes sense to me, Jorge. That actually gives us a higher closing velocity at intercept, and that will help against their point-defense fire."

Alvarez nodded.

"Exactly. All right, Janice. I'll send fleet orders. Then I'll warn them off."

"You think they're going to leave, Jorge?"

"No chance. They outnumber us six to one. They think."

Jenks nodded.

Alvarez turned to his comm officer.

"Fleet orders. Launch all wings in three hours on the mark. Message ends. Start the timer, Bill."

"Fleet orders transmitted, Sir. Timer running."

"Have you identified the flags?"

"Yes, Sir. The *Xerxes*, the *King Henry II*, and the *Monitor*."

"And you have channels?"

"Yes, Sir. They're squawking contact channels."

"Message to the flags. This is Admiral Jorge Alvarez to the Persh, Norton, and Bergheim formations in Republic of Earth space. Your unannounced presence here is an act of war. You are to leave the system immediately or be destroyed. Alvarez out. Send it."

"Message transmitted, Sir."

"Well, let's see what they have to say."

The reply came five minutes later.

"Admiral Brendan Doyle to Admiral Alvarez. Negative to your request. We outnumber you six to one, Admiral. I suggest you take a vacation somewhere else. Earth space is ours. Doyle out."

"Short and sweet, Janice."

Jenks' image in his armrest display nodded.

"Any change of plan, Jorge?"

"No, Janice. Let them come."

In addition to the information from the Agency and the BIE, the pilots of Green, Orange, Yellow, and Purple Wings had the attack ship recordings of the Second Battle of Vauxhall. They had been studying these for three days, since the battle, and were ready to go.

"Coming up on three hours, Sir."

"Fleet Orders. Attack-ship wings. Report status."

"Green Wing ready."

"Orange Wing ready."

"Yellow Wing ready."

"Purple Wing ready."

"Fleet Orders. Launch on the mark."

The flagship's timer ticked down to zero, and all four heavy cruisers of Admiral Alvarez's division launched attack ships.

"Green Wing away."

"Orange Wing away."

"Yellow Wing away."

"Purple Wing away."

"They've launched some sort of parasites, Sir."

"Parasites? Shuttles?"

"I don't think so, Sir. Heading our way at nine-point-three gravities. We have forty incoming."

"Nine-point-three gravities? Are they missiles?"

"No sir. Much bigger. Smaller than a cargo shuttle, though."

"Curious. Fleet orders. Stand by point defense."

"Transmitted, Sir."

"Hey, we got twenty-four of 'em. They only had seventeen on Earth."

"Great. More for everybody."

"Green Leader. Cut the chatter, everybody. Start setting up your attack vectors. Look for multi-target opportunities. Coordinate those with the flag's battle simulator so we don't all run into each other. You don't want to have to do a Red Seven."

The three enemy squadrons, from three separate navies, were spacing semi-independently, in a vee formation. The attack-ship pilots selected vectors that passed through two of the enemy squadrons, ECM engaged, dropping missiles as they went.

Orange, Yellow, and Purple wings dropped more than two hundred missiles on their way through the enemy squadrons. None of the lead squadron's heavy cruisers survived that terrific onslaught. Of the two following divisions, a total of five ships survived, though none of them were undamaged.

Green Wing, the flagship's wing, had held back, as Gold Wing had done in the Second Battle of Vauxhall. They now split up and swept through the remaining ships, dropping over eighty missiles. None of the attacking ships survived.

Only one attack ship took a hit from the less-coordinated point-defense of three independent squadrons. Two attack ships were also disabled by running into debris during the attack. All three pilots were rescued.

Persh, Norton, and Bergheim each lost eight heavy cruisers and over twenty thousand spacers.

The Battle of Earth was over.

"Well, that was decisive, Jorge," Jenks said to Alvarez's image.

"Yeah, I love those guys," Alvarez said to Jenks' image on his armrest.

Jenks nodded.

"Say what you want about the Erians, Jorge, they really know how to pilot a ship."

"Damn right. We'd all be dead without them."

That night, the Green Wing pilots celebrated by filling their shower room on CNS *Illustrious* with six inches of water and sinking into their natural state.

The galley cooks of *Illustrious* threw ten raw steaks and half a dozen ham and pineapple pizzas, followed up with several liters of soda, into the orange-brown mass of Erians.

It was a great party.

Isabela Febo

Mangum and Stavros had reviewed the recordings of the Second Battle of Vauxhall and the First Battle of Earth that morning.

It hadn't taken long.

"Well, that was decisive," Stavros said at lunch.

"Yes, you might say that," Mangum said. "If you were prone to understatement. It was brutal."

"So do they leave us alone now?"

"No. Not if history is any guide. The family that ruled Europe for almost a millennium went after Napoleon for fifteen years. Despite massive losses, they persisted until they finally beat him. They succeeded in putting their cousins on the throne of France for another thirty-three years. It took a second French revolution to oust them permanently."

"So they persist, Bert?"

"Yes. As I say, if history is any guide. May not be, but in this case I'd bet on it. The monarchs of the core worlds, if Albert is a model, are stubborn and entitled."

"Stupid."

"You have to understand, Elina. They don't understand losing. It's never happened to them before."

After lunch they were back in the office. A meeting request came in. They both got it, then Sam walked in from the living room.

"I just got a meeting request, Bert," he said.

"So did we," Mangum answered.

"From Chairman Febo," Sam said.

"Yes. So did we. How extraordinary."

"How are we going do this, Bert?" Elina asked. "The big display is in here."

"An extra chair for Sam. From the living room."

"I'll get it," Sam said.

Mangum had thought one of the side chairs, but Sam came back with one of the big armchairs. Mangum raised an eyebrow.

"It has to be bigger than yours, Bert. For the ambassador, you know."

"Ah. You're right. OK, so we all ready?"

"For this?" Elina asked. "I'm not sure I'll ever be ready."

Sam shifted into his ambassador persona.

"I'm ready, Bert."

Mangum put through the meeting acceptance.

"Good afternoon, Mr. Ambassador, Mr. Mangum, Ms. Stavros," Febo said when she appeared in the display. "Thank you for taking this meeting."

Sam, as senior, replied for them all.

"Of course, Madam Chairman. How may we help you today?"

"It strikes me that you three have been involved in all of this from the beginning. The Abelon Crisis, the Crossroads Affair, the rescue of Professor Varley, the letters of marque issue. All of it. It seems to me that you three know more about what is going on than anyone else."

"That's probably true, Madam Chairman," Sam said.

Febo nodded.

"So I would like to cut through the analysis and the overview reports and executive summaries and just talk to you three. Is that all right, Mr. Ambassador?"

"Of course, Madam Chairman."

"As for you, Mr. Mangum and Ms. Stavros, I have not informed your superiors I am speaking directly to you. So let's leave it that I spoke to the ambassador, and you happened to be in the room. Does that work for you?"

"Yes, Madam Chairman," Mangum said.

"All right. Good. Now let's get down to specifics."

Febo consulted some handwritten notes on her desk.

"The First and Second Battles of Vauxhall and the Battle of Earth were certainly decisive. Do you think they will put off the other core-world monarchies? Cause them to leave Earth and Vauxhall alone?"

"I don't think so, Madam Chairman," Sam said. "When the French Revolution accomplished a similar thing on Earth, the other monarchies in Europe – like those in the core worlds, linked by marriage and alliance – did not let it go. They fought for twenty-six years, through horrific losses, until they finally defeated Napoleon in 1815. They installed their cousin, Louis XVIII on the throne of France, restoring the Bourbon kings. It took a second French Revolution, thirty-three years later, to end the French monarchy for good."

"And you think this lot will go the same way, Mr. Ambassador, trying to restore the monarchy on Vauxhall, with Earth as part of Vauxhall?"

"Yes, Madam Chairman. I'm afraid so."

"I think I agree with you, Mr. Ambassador. Which naturally brings me to my second question. They certainly cannot defeat us now, even at wildly disparate odds. How will they persist, given that?"

Mangum looked to Sam, who nodded.

"They will design new navies, Madam Chairman," Mangum said. "Need drives advancement, and war drives advancement in military technology. Having decided they must pursue war, they will work to build new navies, design new ships, to defeat us and reclaim Vauxhall and Earth for the family."

"Will they be successful at that, Mr. Mangum? Can they, working together, overtake us?"

"No, Madam Chairman. We already have new warships in the docks, enhanced versions of the ones that defeated them already. Ships with four times the throw weight as the ones you deployed at Vauxhall and Earth."

"But they learned a great deal in those battles, Mr. Mangum. About what we have. About how we deploy it."

"Yes, Madam Chairman. But first they must now come up with a strategic doctrine. Then they must design new warships to carry that doctrine forward. Those designs will be full of committee decisions. Every senior flag officer will want their little wrinkle in the design. And then the king will have his say as well. We are looking at a minimum of three or four years before any of their new ships are available. And they will be compromised by the process."

"Whereas we will have new ships available within the year, Mr. Mangum?"

"Yes, Madam Chairman. And they still won't have nine-gee attack ships."

"I see. I hope you are right, Mr. Mangum. Another question, Mr. Ambassador."

Sam nodded.

"There are large companies on Earth and Vauxhall that are owned and run, in large part, by the nobilities and the elite. The rulers of both Earth and Vauxhall have asked me what to do about that. Should they nationalize those companies, Mr. Ambassador?"

"I would think not, Madam Chairman, for two good reasons. One is that it promotes on the part of the government a disregard for private property. Not the sort of thing we want to encourage, and the sort of thing that, once it takes root, is hard to weed out. It's certainly not the direction we hope these new governments take."

Febo nodded.

"The other reason, Madam Chairman, is that, if the nobility and elites in the other core-world kingdoms have significant property holdings on Vauxhall and Earth, it encourages a certain finesse in their operations against the planets. They would be unlikely, say, to transition ships very far out, accelerate toward the planet until they are at a velocity that is hard to intercept, and then drop nuclear or kinetic weapons indiscriminately on the planet as they pass."

"Because they would be destroying their own holdings."

"Even so, Madam Chairman."

"What are Earth and Vauxhall to do then, Mr. Ambassador? These companies, owned by the nobility and the elites, work against their own governments."

"But they cannot break the law, Madam Chairman. Make sure to enforce against those companies the laws that apply, even for infractions committed before the revolutions. And craft new laws so that they cannot actively work against the new regimes."

"Are you proposing ex post facto laws, Mr. Ambassador?"

"Not at all, Madam Chairman. The nobility and the elite in the core worlds always consider the law to apply to commoners, and not to them. Do you think that an investigation of the actions of these companies before the revolutions would turn up no violations of then-extant law?"

"That's brilliant, Mr. Ambassador. Of course they broke the law. That was and is their modus operandi."

"I suspect the damages and fines will likely be ruinous,

Madam Chairman. Perhaps even leading to the bankruptcy of some of them. A wise choice of trustee by the bankruptcy court would then resolve many problems."

"And the incentive not to bomb their own holdings, Mr. Ambassador? Have we weakened that too much with such an action?"

"I suspect the court cases would go on for some time, Madam Chairman. Several years, at least. Well beyond the current crisis."

Febo nodded and made some notes on the sheets on her desk.

"Another question, Mr. Ambassador. There are demonstrations and revolutionary attempts under way on some other planets now. It's spreading."

"Yes, Madam Chairman. The chaos will spread. The core-world monarchies are in a great deal of trouble. That is why they cannot let the precedent of Vauxhall stand."

"But I worry about the bloodshed, Mr. Ambassador. What can we do to hold that down?"

"Fan the flames, Madam Chairman."

"Truly?"

"Oh, yes. The natural reaction of the core-world kingdoms to unrest is to clamp down harder. That will not work anymore, because people know overthrowing the regime can work, like it worked on Vauxhall. The way to minimize the violence is to accelerate the process, so that it's over sooner."

"I see. What would be the best way to do that, Mr. Ambassador?"

"Ship the cure for RDT, Madam Chairman. Ship lots of it."

"Yes, that certainly seemed to accelerate things on Vauxhall. And I have the opportunity, Mr. Ambassador. With the shipping embargo the other core-world kingdoms have placed on Earth and Vauxhall, the big shipping lines there have been sending ships in this direction. We're talking about the big six-thousand-container ships. They will be here in a few months now."

"Fit them with the X-3 drive, Madam Chairman, then send them back full of the cure for RDT."

"If I could interrupt, Madam Chairman," Mangum said. "Do we have that much cure for RDT available to ship? Thousands of containers?"

"Oh yes, Mr. Mangum. It's remarkable how fast the manufacturing modules produce the stuff. And those modules themselves are mass-produced. I think the bigger problem is distributing it among the core worlds. They all have an embargo in place against shipments from Earth or Vauxhall."

"You know, Madam Chairman," Elina Stavros said, "we have a couple of independent shipper captains here on Mardouk. They must be hooked into a network of independent shippers. And the independents are not terribly careful about accuracy when specifying their planet of origin."

"You're thinking of Mr. Durst and Mr. Kendall, Ms. Stavros?"

"Yes, ma'am. Let them spread the word. Send thousands of containers to Earth and Vauxhall, and put consignment shipping fees on them. The independents pick them up and deliver them we-don't-care-where. As long as it's a core world other than Earth or Vauxhall. Put large shipping fees on them. They deliver them to wherever they have the best contacts, and collect the shipping fees. Let Serp Kendall and Emmet Durst get the word out to the independents."

"Excellent, Ms. Stavros."

Febo made a note, then turned to Sam.

"I still worry about the violence, Mr. Ambassador."

Sam nodded.

"You could send ambassadors out to the core-world kingdoms, Madam Chairman. Facilitators is perhaps a better word. Try to convince the nobility to step down from power, and continue in more of a figurehead role, while letting an elected parliament and prime minister rule."

"A dangerous assignment, Mr. Ambassador."

Mangum started suddenly.

"Perhaps not, Madam Chairman. Send Erians as the facilitators. They can't jail them. They can't shoot them or hang them. I don't even know that you can blow them up. There's at least one who survived an explosion that a human did not. And there's a bunch of Erians around who already have experience with humans."

Febo's eyes widened. She turned to Sam.

"Mr. Ambassador?"

"Yes, Madam Chairman. That would work. We would be honored to take that assignment."

"Excellent. Thank you, Mr. Ambassador. I will let you know."

Febo looked down at her notes, then looked back up.

"Thank you, everyone. This has been most helpful."

"Any time, Madam Chairman," Sam said.

Febo cut the connection.

After his first sleep cycle, Mangum was sitting with a nightcap in the living room, watching the lights of the city below him. Sam and Jules, in their utility personas, sat with him.

"That was an interesting call with Chairman Febo this afternoon," Sam said.

"Indeed it was. Where did you get all that about

bankruptcies and enforcing the law and everything?"

Sam shrugged.

"I listen. I read. Hanging around with you and your friends has been a great education, Bert. And don't forget I work all night while you sleep. Reading about the things I've heard."

They sat for a while.

"Do you think I was wrong, Bert?" Sam asked at last.

"No. No, not at all. I thought it was all correct, Sam. I was just surprised is all."

"And you surprised me with using Erians as facilitators, Bert."

"Do you think that was a bad idea?"

"No, I like it. A lot, actually. A place we can help, where someone else probably could not. It does mean sending Erians far and wide across human space, though."

"Yes, Sam, it does. I encourage you to do that."

"Why, Bert?"

Mangum took a sip of his drink and thought about it. He felt very strongly about this, and he was trying to get at the why. To find a way to put it in words.

"Because I trust you," Mangum finally said.

"Why, thank you, Bert. But how does that apply here?"

"Not just you, Sam. Erians generally. Look, there are a lot of things that need doing. Things you guys can do that we can't. Take the attack ships as a case in point. You changed the balance of power. Allowed us to stand up to a coalition of no less than four core-world kingdoms with nine heavy cruisers. That changes everything.

"Same with this facilitator business. It needs doing. It's too dangerous for anyone else. But you can do it.

"At the same time, I don't worry about Erians being taken in. Being coerced or suborned by evil. I don't for example worry about you piloting attack ships against us on behalf of the star kingdoms. It's just not in you. I think it's the way you communicate. I suppose it's pretty hard to hide one's intentions when you communicate directly. Neurologically."

"Oh, yes. Impossible, in fact."

"And you value independence. Have an instinctive mistrust of authoritarianism. Can't see how someone can maintain it's their right to decide for others. I suppose that's the flip side of the same coin."

"Yes, Bert. I think that's right. We know each other inside out. We know none of us is superior to another. Not in that way. So how can one pretend to decide for the group? The group decides. It is democracy of a form, I suppose, though more direct than yours."

"Yes. That's it. And taken all together, that's why I think you need to spread through the human race. We can get ourselves into some serious cul-de-sacs, Sam. Humans can. Like the core-world monarchies. You can see through that instantly. And you can help. Help humanity move forward without these dead-ends."

"I see. Interesting. Thank you, Bert. That's a very interesting perspective."

"Not at all, Sam. Not at all."

They sat quietly for a while, then Mangum heard Sam speak softly, as if to himself.

"Very interesting indeed."

Earth Planetary Police

Matthew Gray and his wife had moved to Vienna a year ago, after the last of their kids went off to college. Empty-nesters, they could live anywhere they wanted. Grey had been to Vienna and liked it a good deal, so they vacationed there first. Martha liked it as well, so, when they had the option, he had called Gebhard Lang.

Lang had been an Inspector with the Earth Planetary Police when they investigated Davian Varley's disappearance after the *Prince Alfred* Disaster. He had since been promoted to Supervisor of Investigations. He was encouraging of Gray's move, and offered him a position as Inspector with the Earth Planetary Police.

Gray and his wife moved to Vienna. Where they had a suburban house in Southern California – the better to raise the boys in – in Vienna they had taken a condo unit in a building in the city center.

Gray's commute from the condo was simplicity itself. Take the escalator down to the U-Bahn – the subway – and ride it to the government center east of the old city.

Living downtown had its advantages for a couple without children, though. You took the elevator to the street level, then walked a block to the Graben. Turn left, and you walked to the bakery. All sorts of cakes and treats – Schwarzwaldtorte, Sachertorte, Esterházy Torte; it went on and on – and wonderful coffee to go with it.

Turn right, and you walked to the ice cream store. The menu had pages and pages of delightful constructions, with multiple flavors of ice cream, whipped cream, nuts, chocolate sauce, and wafer cookies, and, again, wonderful coffee to go with it.

In between there were literally a dozen places to eat dinner, and, on the much higher EPP Inspector's salary, none of them were financially out of reach, even for frequent eating out.

Being downtown so close to the Graben gave them another interesting experience, however. The revolutionary crowd carried the bodies of the King of Earth and the Earl of Europe past their condo building on the way to the Graben.

Enjoining Martha to stay in the unit, Gray went down to the Graben to watch. The EPP wore no uniforms, and he was not performing any official duties, he was just watching. He was an investigator, after all. He did not stop crime, he figured it out after the fact.

Gray saw the crowd string up the bodies from lamp poles in the Graben, where they were left hanging. The crowd mocked them by curtseying and saluting. Clearly they wouldn't be doing that anymore to any living ruler.

That evening, Gray and his wife watched a speech by the new self-installed interim president of Earth. He followed the prototype of Donald Nelson on Vauxhall, and promised elections in six months. He also assured everyone he himself would not run for office in the new government. He would simply step down and hand power to the new government.

He also encouraged everyone to carry on as normal, to go to work, even government employees.

"Whatever you were doing, we probably need you to keep doing that," he said. "Show up for work. You are in no danger, though we may have new directions for your efforts."

After it was over, Martha was curious.

"So what do you do tomorrow, Matthew? Go in to work?"

"Well, that's what he said to do."

"Will it be safe, though?"

"We'll see. I'll get off a stop early and walk in. I won't go forward if it doesn't look safe."

"All right. But you take care. I don't want you hanging in the Graben."

"I will, Martha. Trust me. The street-level view of the Graben is just fine with me."

Gray did go into the office in the morning. There were no crowds or trouble, just a lot of men working on cleaning up from the day before, especially down by the palace. The crowds had concentrated their anger on the ruler, and the other government buildings were mostly undamaged.

Gray went up to his office and wondered what to do next. Well, he was an investigator, so he decided to investigate what had gone on yesterday. He had been out on an investigation, and had missed it all.

His Inspector's permissions gave him access to the surveillance videos from the day before, and he spent the morning going through those, piecing together what had happened.

All in all, it was pretty remarkable.

His boss, Gebhard Lang, called him into his office that afternoon.

"Hello, Matthew."

"Hello, Gebhard."

"Have a seat."

"Thanks."

Gray took a seat in front of Lang's desk. Lang ran his hand through his hair and sighed.

"Well, when I told you life in Vienna would be exciting, I didn't have this in mind, but you can't claim I broke my promise."

"Not at all, Gebhard. In fact, I had a ring-side seat to the activities in the Graben last night."

"Remarkable. Absolutely remarkable."

"And we were right when we included our speculations about shape-shifting aliens in our reports years ago, though no one believed us at the time."

"You're right, Matthew. You're absolutely right. Which means the cluster nations were probably behind all of this. Admiral Meyer was right when he told the king to let sleeping dogs lie, as well."

Lang shrugged.

"They didn't listen."

Gray nodded. They sure hadn't. And now what?

"So what do we do now, Gebhard? What is our mission, if you will?"

"The president's new head of security, in his cabinet, has sent out orders. He is now the superior to the head of the EPP. Very quickly named, too. This whole thing is very well organized.

"We are to continue our jobs, investigating crimes. But he made this distinction from our past duties. Crimes are actual harms – physical or financial – committed against individuals, whether commoner or nobility.

"What are not crimes are slights against nobility which would not be a crime if committed against a commoner."

"That's a big difference, Gebhard. Much of what we investigated before amounted to lèse-majesté, no more. Actual crimes against commoners didn't concern them."

"Exactly, Matthew. Exactly. And now it is the opposite.

Actual harms. And the nobility and the elites are to be treated no more or no less than a commoner, either as victim or perpetrator. No differently at all."

"Ho! Now that is a big difference, Gebhard. Before, when the trail led to a nobleman, that was it. The end of the investigation."

"Yes, but not anymore. We will track the trail to the evil-doer, whoever he is. But only if someone is actually harmed, be it nobleman or commoner."

Gray thought about it.

"Huh. You know, Gebhard, I kind of like this new regime."

Lang nodded.

"Yes, Matthew. Me, too."

"Treating everybody the same. Revolutionary concept."

"In more than one sense, Matthew. In more than one sense."

Over the next several weeks, Lang and Gray went through their list of cases. The EPP had jurisdiction over planetary crimes – that is, violations of planetary law – as well as cases in the capital environs, the greater Vienna area.

First up was to strike off all the cases of commoners violating the sensitivities of the nobility. If there was no actual harm, there was no case under the law as modified by the new regime. All of those laws had been struck off the books by executive order of the new president.

Second was to not consider any case against anyone in the crowds that broke into the palace grounds, then the palace, and killed the King of Earth, the Earl of Europe and the members of their families. The interim president, Stephan Kurtz, had issued a blanket pardon for those actions, saying, 'We cannot prosecute a hundred thousand people for the killing of flagrant criminals and the accessories to their crimes.' That was all off the table.

Third was to reinstate those cases worldwide that had been dropped when the evidence trail led to a member of the nobility. That was a huge bunch of 'cold cases' that were once again active.

It was a good thing the first two categories were moot, because the third category gave them plenty of work to do.

Triaging those cases put them in two large categories: organizations as defendant and individuals as defendant.

They went after the corporations first. They generally caused the greater harm.

Several months in, they got new guidance from the administration. They had stopped calling the new government a regime, saving that word for the prior government.

"We need to be careful that we are always prosecuting people for breaking the then-current law, Matthew, not applying current law retroactively," Lang said.

"That's not a problem, Gebhard. The nobility never considered the law to apply to them, though there were no statutory exceptions for them."

"That's all fine. They pretended like the law applied to everyone equally, and we will pursue them on those grounds. Hold them to their own laws. But we will not go after violations of current law prior to the dates of those laws being active."

"There are plenty of violations of current law after the applicable dates, too, though, Gebhard."

"And that's fine, Matthew. Actually, those are perhaps more important, because it is ongoing crime. Let's concentrate on those as our first priority."

Gray nodded. That was his judgment as well. Stopping the

ongoing criminal activity had to be first.

There were plenty of candidates.

Evidence was gathered, charges were framed, grand juries were seated.

Then the indictments started coming down.

Gray had been worried about the new administration's attitude toward the Earth Planetary Police. Would they be viewed as accomplices in what had gone before?

But as the new administration's recently appointed prosecutors started bringing charges against criminal organizations, the EPP became downright popular in the halls of power.

Stephan Kurtz was having his weekly meeting with his Minister of Justice, Gwendolyn Merker. The department had previously been called the Ministry of Security, and Merker herself had proposed the name change.

The head of the Earth Planetary Police reported directly to her.

"I tell you, Gwen, I was worried about the EPP, but those guys are doing great. Just look at the indictments."

The most recent indictment had been against Consolidated Pharma, the pharmaceutical giant based on Earth. The general manager, JuanCarlos Serrano, was an individually named defendant. JuanCarlos Serrano was also the second cousin of the erstwhile King of Earth, Miguel Serrano.

Merker nodded.

"Yes, Stephan. The EPP were not stooges of the prior regime. They operated within the guidelines they were given, whether they liked them or not. I will tell you that, from what I am hearing, they like the direction we are going. Quite a bit, actually."

"Well, I like the direction they're going, too, Gwen. Please let them know that I approve of and appreciate their efforts. This is all great. JuanCarlos escaped the mob, but he won't escape the law."

"I'll let them know, Stephan."

"You know, this was always my greatest worry. The administration of justice. Real justice. That's why I put you in charge of it, Gwen, right from the start. If we can have sensible laws, and apply them uniformly, the people will always be with us. If we go down the path of politically motivated prosecutions, however, we're no better than the last bunch. Just the new gang of thugs in charge."

Kurtz tapped the printout on his desk.

"This is the exact direction we need to be going. Real crimes. Real criminals. Prosecuted without regard to standing or wealth or influence, under the laws that applied at the time."

Kurtz nodded, then smiled at Merker.

"Chairman Febo was right. This is exactly the course we need to be following. You had told me the same thing, and then you made it happen. Congratulations, Gwen."

"Thanks, Stephan."

Gray was in Lang's office going over the latest evidence when Lang got a priority message. He glanced at it, then smiled.

"Well, that's nice."

"What is it Gebhard?"

"Priority message from the Minister of Justice to all EPP personnel. 'President Kurtz asked me to send on his regards and appreciation for your efforts toward the administration of true justice in the name of the people of Earth. Continue your efforts in this regard, that all may stand equal before the law.

With warmest regards, Gwendolyn Merker, Minister of Justice.'"

"Well, it's nice to know we're appreciated," Gray said.

"Indeed, Matthew. Indeed."

Lang grew thoughtful, then continued.

"We may actually be able to do it, you know. Have a legal system that makes sense. That administers true justice."

"What a concept, Gebhard. The mind boggles."

"Yes, Matthew. But maybe, just maybe, this time...."

Gearing Up

In addition to their home world of Erias, Erians now lived on three planets, Mardouk, Vauxhall, and Earth.

Those on Vauxhall were the one hundred and fifty who stayed behind to assist with rebuilding from the damage of the revolution. That was over, but they continued to manufacture and distribute the cure for RDT to local government health boards who provided it to the billions of people across the planet.

Those on Earth were the two hundred and fifty who went to Earth to precipitate the revolution there, primarily by distributing the cure for RDT in the capital environs, the greater Vienna area. They had helped clean up and rebuild the damage from the revolution and were now manufacturing and distributing the cure for RDT to health clinics across the planet.

Those on Mardouk were the hundred who returned from Vauxhall on *Ladyhawke* with Portnoy, Stickney, and Sam. They were sort of at loose ends, though they did teach classes to human Marines at the Marine base a hundred miles west of Ashur about their experiences on Vauxhall.

There were also the five hundred attack ship pilots spread across the fifty heavy cruisers of the cluster consortium navy. They were brought up to date on the experiences of the attack ship pilots in the battles of Vauxhall and Earth by a dozen Erian Marines who had met with the attack ship pilots in orbit, in order to transfer their experiences by direct contact.

Most of those Marines now visited the heavy cruiser squadrons, passing on those experiences to the attack ship pilots in the other five squadrons.

Two of those Marines, however, with direct experience of the revolution in Vauxhall and the transferred experience of the attack ship battles, went back to Erias. They transferred those experiences to the great bulk of Erians who still lived on the home planet.

They went to Erias in an empty passenger liner. They brought back with them another five thousand Erians who wanted to get in on the fun.

They crowded aboard the small passenger liner, a dozen or more to a cabin, as was their preference.

The food requirements were the only issue, and the galley of the liner ran twenty-four hours. New Erians manned the galley together with the otherwise overwhelmed human staff.

They had, however indirectly, complete galley training from the Marines logistics training sequence.

The new emigrants from Erias were sorely needed. There would be nearly four thousand attack ship pilots required to staff the twelve new squadrons of attack ship carriers that would soon be shoving out of space docks all across the cluster. Each of those ninety-six carriers could launch forty attack ships.

The other thousand, together with the five hundred on Mardouk, Vauxhall, and Earth, were part of Sam Hawker's and Isabela Febo's grand plan:

Distribution of the cure for RDT across human space, and sending out facilitators to try to ease the human nobility out of power without violence.

The Erians had already heard Sam's incredible story of his time with the humans from when Sam returned to Erias for the first one thousand Erian emigrants.

Those thousand new emigrants, in human persona, now

filled an auditorium at the Marine base to hear Sam's instructions about the plan, and the further things he and Jules had learned about dealing with the humans.

As before, they all made contact with each other, as did Sam, and the entire training session was held neurologically. From the point of view of the humans observing, they all sat in silence, unmoving.

They ran twenty-four hours a day for three days, breaking only for meals.

It was a bit over six months after the Vauxhall revolution when the first of the big Earth and Vauxhall freighters came to Mardouk and the other cluster capitals.

The other core-world monarchies had slapped an immediate trade embargo on the former Kingdom of Vauxhall when they got news of the revolution on Vauxhall and the death of the king and royal family. These freighters, all loaded to space, had nowhere else to go, and had spent the last six months in hyperspace to the cluster.

Their trade masters were happy to learn of the free-trade agreement between all six of the cluster nations and both Vauxhall and Earth. Their captains and crews were even happier to learn of the X-3 drive modification that the cluster would make to their engines, allowing their return in only two months.

Of course, there were financial considerations, too. The X-3 drive modifications were not, after all, free. Those charges were balanced off against the cluster's shipping charges for cargo headed to Earth and Vauxhall.

The cluster was shipping thousands of container of the cure for RDT, and the manufacturing modules to make more, to Earth and Vauxhall.

They had a small fire started in the core worlds, and Isabela Febo was shipping gasoline to throw on the blaze.

Ladyhawke was back in business as a freighter, plying its trade among the cluster worlds. She retained the four attack ships and their Erian pilots. Together with the point-defense guns she mounted, she was effectively a pocket carrier.

Those resources were kept in place against the potential of needing *Ladyhawke* for another Agency mission.

And, of course, the head of field operations for the Agency remained Bert Mangum, with Elina Stavros as assistant head.

At one point, when *Ladyhawke* was in the Mardouk system, Bert Mangum and Elina Stavros invited Emmet Durst, Serp Kendall, and Marge Schofield to dinner at their top-floor unit in The 909. Durst picked up Kendall and Schofield at their top-floor unit of The 909, and the trio walked across the elevator lobby to Mangum and Stavros' unit.

Steven Milton Kendall was just two months old at this point, and had just been nursed. He was asleep in Schofield's arms when they went over to Mangum and Stavros' unit. One thing Mangum and Stavros' unit had plenty of at this point was baby equipment, and Schofield would put little Stevie down in the crib in the living room.

"Hey, everybody. Come on in," Mangum said when he opened the door.

Schofield walked past him, and Mangum commented.

"I see Stevie's out for the evening already. Right into the crib with him."

"Thanks, Bert."

With the babies all down for the moment, including Mangum and Stavros' two, Franklin and Harriet, the five human adults settled down with drinks. Sam and Jules were bartending, and knew everyone's preferences.

"So what's this all about, Bert?" Serp asked.

Mangum shook his head.

"After dinner. Let's order."

They ordered from room service in The 909. It wasn't Marceau's, but it was very good, and it was easier, especially on short notice.

Until the food showed up, they sat and chatted over drinks, mostly about kids and the weather and *Ladyhawke*'s travels.

The food came and was up to The 909's usual standards. After dinner, they refreshed their drinks and sat in the living room.

"All right, Bert," Kendall said. "Out with it. What's going on?"

"One thing, with two parts, actually. As to the first part, Emmet, have you seen the core-world freighters showing up in the cluster?"

"Oh, yeah. They're hard to miss, Bert."

He turned to Kendall.

"You should see 'em, Serp. Six thousand containers. Incredible."

Kendall shrugged.

"Seen 'em before. In the core worlds. What about 'em, Bert?"

"They're going back to the core with the cure for RDT. Lots of it. Thousands of containers of it."

"Thousands?"

"Thousands. They're going to offload them at Earth and Vauxhall, which is only part of their trip, as far as we're concerned. We need to get them out to the other core worlds."

"Past the embargo?" Durst asked.

"Yes. Past the embargo."

Mangum turned to look at Kendall. He was lost in thought.

"Is that a problem, Serp? Surely you've gone through an embargo or two in your time."

"Yeah, I done it. Most of the independents have. Not necessarily easy, but we got some tricks. So you want *Ladyhawke* to be a blockade runner, Bert?"

"No, we have something else for *Ladyhawke*. We want to put the word out to the independents that we have cargoes for consignment shipping out of Earth and Vauxhall. Premium fees, too."

"That'll help," Kendall said.

"Yes, and not only that, we don't really care which core world they deliver them to. Initially, anyway. Wherever they have contacts and can do it easily. Once that world's taken care of, though, we take it off the list."

Kendall nodded.

"The only thing they have to do is tell us which core world they delivered it to, so we can mark that planet off," Mangum said.

"And *Ladyhawke*, Bert?" Durst asked.

"We want you to go to the core worlds – with a barracks container and galley container, plus extra food supplies – and deliver a team of Erians to the same planets where the independents are delivering the cure for RDT. Drop 'em off and get out."

"That's going to be harder, Bert. Harder than running the embargo with cargo. We have all the immigration issues to deal with."

"No, Emmet. You do a standard approach to the planet, then deviate to a very low orbit, drop the Erians, and get out."

"Drop them, Bert?'

"Yes, Emmet. Airlock 'em, and you're outta there."

"No shit," Kendall said.

He looked over to Sam, who nodded.

"They're going to Red Seven it," Sam said. "I'm told it's a lot of fun, actually."

"Damn."

"And how do we get out of the system, Bert?" Durst asked. "It's a day to the hyperspace limit."

"You still have four attack ships, Emmet, and twelve point-defense gun containers. Those are what? Two guns to a container? So two dozen point-defense guns and four attack ships. Nothing in any of these systems can stop you. You just break whatever you have to in order to get out. There's no worry about doing it clean. We simply don't care anymore."

Durst nodded.

"OK. That helps. We can certainly get out, assuming we got in clean. But we're gonna get a reputation, Bert."

"Aliases, Emmet. Squawk a different one at every planet. Never use the same alias twice."

Durst nodded.

"OK, Bert. This all makes sense. When does all this kick off?"

"It already has, Emmet. The first freighters with several hundred containers of RDT left a month ago, and they now have the X-3 drive. They'll be at Earth and Vauxhall in a month."

"Damn," Kendall said.

"Yeah. Febo's done screwing with these people, Serp. She's going to kick over the whole damn thing. The whole core. So you need to let the independents know they have consignment shipments incoming. And, Emmet?"

Durst looked a little dazed.

"Yeah, Bert?"

"You need to start packing."

Fanning The Flames

When the big freighters arrived back at Earth or Vauxhall, they had no trouble selling their cluster imports. They also had no trouble unloading several hundred containers of the cure for RDT and manufacturing modules to make more.

Now, eight months after the revolution on Earth, both planets had new, elected governments. The interim presidents had done a pretty good job in the six-month interregnum, and their parties swept the parliamentary elections. The fascists, the socialists, and the crown loyalists hadn't had a chance.

Isabela Febo had called to congratulate the new prime minister after both sets of elections. She and they got along well, and both governments knew what the huge shipments of the cure for RDT were for.

There weren't even any customs inspections. It was all an Association of Planets government shipment, and all of it came down to consignment warehouses without bureaucratic impediment.

The shipments were blocked as six containers of the cure for RDT – twenty-four million doses – plus two manufacturing modules to make more. Independent shippers were permitted one block apiece, and they had to specify the destination.

The consignment shipping fees were generous, and independent shippers thronged to Earth and Vauxhall to grab a block and deliver it.

Of course, the generous fees weren't paid unless they actually delivered the block, so there was a check on their behavior.

They were independents, after all.

Ladyhawke took a full load to Earth from Mardouk. The embargo was impacting things on the ground in both Vauxhall and Earth, and there was a lot of container traffic from the cluster to both planets to make up the shortages.

Ladyhawke did not load cargo on Earth, however. She loaded all two hundred and fifty of Lieutenant Colonel Frank Everett's Marines and set off for her first drop.

On the way, the Erian attack-ship pilots, who had met with Sam before *Ladyhawke* set out on this trip, brought the Erian Marines up to speed.

"Is it true? We get to just jump out? Like Red Seven?"

"Yeah."

"I love it."

"All right, Lara. Let's map the resources here, and plot ourselves a clean way out if we can," Durst said as they were inbound to Burton from the hyperspace limit.

"Yes, Sir. Working on it."

Durst waited. They were a day coming in on Burton. Running so light, they could go faster, but he didn't want to disclose that capability.

"I have it, Sir. A way in, the drop point, the exit, the whole thing."

"And their assets will be out of place?"

"With their current orbits, yes, Sir."

"All right. Lay it in, then keep an eye on those orbits."

"Yes, Sir."

Ladyhawke, squawking as *Grey Falcon,* approached her assigned orbit. She was running thrusters first, braking into her orbit velocity, when she cut her thrusters. She continued deeper into the planet's gravity well, penetrating all the way to the upper atmosphere, before the thrusters came on again.

Ladyhawke virtually stopped there.

The airlock door cycled open.

"Go, go, go."

Of course, that command was neurological, there being insufficient air to carry the sound.

Fifteen Erians jumped out of *Ladyhawke* and started to fall to the planet below.

"They're gone, Sir."

"All right. Full thrusters, Halim. Get us out of here."

"Aye, Sir."

"*Grey Falcon,* what the hell are you up to?"

Durst signaled his comm tech, Xiulan Yang, who touched a control and nodded back.

"Sorry, Burton Control. We lost thrusters there. We way overshot."

"I should say, *Grey Falcon,* You're in the atmosphere."

"Yeah, I know, Burton Control. I think we lost some pieces back there. We have thruster control back now. Establishing orbit."

But *Ladyhawke* was doing no such thing. Running so light, she was pulling two-point-two gravities now, and headed directly to the hyperspace limit, ten and a half hours away at this acceleration.

I think they're wise to us now, Sir," Lara Perez said from the navigation station. "They're trying to get assets in place."

"Are they going to make it? Will they be able to stop us?"

"No, Sir. They may get off a missile or two, but we will be way outside their powered envelope."

"Target practice."

"Yes, Sir."

"Everybody else has fallen behind, Sir. There's that one destroyer left. That's it. And we'll outhaul her."

"When is her closest approach?" Durst asked.

"Another five minutes, Sir."

"Watch for missile launch. That's when she'll do it if she's gonna do it."

"Yes, Sir."

The minutes ticked by.

"Missile launch. Two incoming, Sir."

"Stand by starboard point-defense."

Six containers on *Ladyhawke*'s starboard side, three forward and three aft, opened their full-length doors. Two battleship-grade point-defense guns ran out from each.

"Point-defense ready, Sir. Tracking two incoming."

"Time to point-defense envelope?"

"Five minutes, Sir. They're still under power. Oop. There we are. Flame-out. They're ballistic now."

"Point-defense. Cleared to fire when you have the range."

Tense minutes passed, as *Ladyhawke* sped for the hyperspace limit and the two missiles coasted toward where she would be ahead.

"Point-defense has the range. Hard contacts. Firing twelve. Firing twelve. Targets destroyed, Sir."

"Excellent. Helm, cut thrust to one gravity."

"Aye, Sir. Cutting thrust to one gravity."

"Sir, that destroyer is still in pursuit."

"Understood, Lara, but I want that debris to pass in front of us. No sense getting taken out by pieces of a missile you already blew up."

"Aye, Sir. Then why shoot at all, Sir?"

"I didn't want them to detonate them in front of us. Expanding cloud of debris right in our path? Harder to miss."

"I see, Sir. Debris is passing across our bows now. That destroyer is starting to make some velocity up on us. Still falling behind, though, just not as fast."

"Understood. Go to full thrust again when the debris is past."

"Mapping debris. Almost clear. There we are. Debris clear."

"Full throttle, Halim."

"Aye, Sir. Full throttle."

Ladyhawke went back to two-point-two gravities and remained there to the hyperspace limit.

"What the hell kind of ship was that?" the destroyer captain asked.

"I don't know, Sir. But those were battleship-grade point-defense guns that took out our missiles. A dozen of them."

"Well, package all the sensor data up and send it off. Maybe someone else can make heads or tails of it."

"Aye, sir."

"Hey, Greg. I was tracking some things that fell off *Grey Falcon* when she finally stopped."

"OK, so she lost some parts. That deep in the atmosphere isn't good for spaceships, you know."

"This is more than that, though. They didn't just fall."

"They didn't?"

"No. Look at this."

The Burton Space Traffic Controller ran the tracking display back, then let it run in real time. The debris from Grey Falcon looked to slow down as it got into deeper atmosphere, then glide toward the capital.

"No shit. Yeah, I don't know what kind of debris does that either. Better let Security know. They like this kind o' stuff."

"All right."

"Wow. That was great. Can we do it again?"

"On another planet, maybe," the sergeant said. "All right. Let's get into disguise, everybody. We don't know that we weren't tracked."

The fifteen Erians shifted into human personas, teenagers and twenty-somethings in work clothes. Like they had just finished working the fields. They trudged down the farm road toward the city.

About fifteen minutes later, an assault shuttle came out from the city and passed over the group. Some of them waved, some looked too tired.

The assault shuttle circled around the area, then headed back into the city.

"Didja see anything out there?"

"Nah. Some farm workers, two tractors, and a buncha cows. That's it."

"All right. False alarm. Thanks for checking it out."

"Sure. Nice flying on a pretty day."

The Erians rented a small commercial building with funds in an account set up for them. They had a shipping company claim their eight containers from the consignment warehouse and deliver them to the facility.

"OK, now here's the fun part," the sergeant said as he

opened a manufacturing module.

Inside was a cache of arms. Full Marine kit for a squad of twelve, including IGM launchers and some RDMs in various sizes.

"Excellent."

"Yeah. Bert Mangum knew we couldn't carry weapons down. We'd fall too fast for a Red Seven. So he had them here waitin' for us."

Two of the Erians held back as the others claimed their weapons, then moved in to grab a small package of their own.

"All right. We're heading into town," one of them told the sergeant.

"All right, Facilitator. If you need anything, let me know."

The Erian facilitator and his aide headed toward the downtown. They put distance between themselves and the rented facility on foot, then took a bus.

After a stop at a downtown store to buy suitcases and some clothes just for show, the facilitator and his aide checked into a nice hotel in downtown Burton City.

As in Vauxhall, everything here was named after the ruling family.

The facilitator reported back to Mardouk, using the core-world network to hit the Mardouk bridge to the cluster network.

"We're in on Burton."

The next day on Burton, some fellows were giving away what they claimed to be a cure for RDT, right on the street in the poor districts. The local gangbangers tried to stop them, and they just plain disappeared.

"It's great that the troublemakers keep coming up to us."

"Yeah. It's like the trash takin' itself out."

The other nodded.

"And they're pretty good eatin', truth be told."

Not every drop was as smooth for *Ladyhawke* as Burton. In Harden, Lara Perez couldn't find a clean way out.

"Best I can do is a light cruiser, Emmet."

"Will he have range on us, Lara?"

"With missiles. Yeah. And within their powered envelope. They'll be evading our fire, or trying to."

"But we haven't seen any ECM yet?"

"No. Not yet."

"OK. Well, we'll see how it goes."

Ladyhawke overshot her orbit, as always for a drop, and fifteen Erians jumped out of the airlock. Then *Ladyhawke* went to two-point-two gravities and headed for the hyperspace limit.

"Watching that light cruiser, Sir. She hasn't reacted yet."

"How long do you think my bullshit to Harden Space Control will hold?"

"Not long, Sir. Light cruiser is thrusting now. She's heading for intercept."

"Captain to Grey Wing."

"Grey Wing Leader."

"Can you guys launch under this gravity?"

"Of course, Sir."

"All right. Stand by for launch."

"Grey Wing Leader to Grey Wing. Stand by for launch under acceleration."

"Grey One ready."

"Grey Two ready."

"Grey Three ready."

"I don't want to get into his powered envelope if I can help it, Lara. I want to take him out before he gets there."

"We shoot first, Sir?"

"Sure. Why not? I was told Febo's done caring about their feelings."

"Roger that, Captain. Best launch is coming up then. Two minutes."

"Captain to Grey Wing Leader. Launch in two minutes."

Durst nodded to Perez, and she released the *Ladyhawke*'s latches. The attack ships were still on the docking hooks, but launch was now under their control.

Perez nodded back to Durst.

"Captain to Grey Wing Leader. You are cleared to launch on the mark."

"Grey Wing Leader cleared to launch on the mark."

The timer counted down the two minutes warning, then the call came back.

"Grey Wing Leader. Grey Wing away."

"That ship – *Bald Eagle* – she's launched four parasites, Sir. Accelerating now. Making nine-point-three gravities. They're heading our way."

"Point defense. Four incoming."

"Aye, Sir. Tracking four incoming."

"Evasive maneuvers."

"Evasive maneuvers, aye."

Grey Wing Leader hung back as clean-up. Grey One, Two, and Three made attack runs on the light cruiser. She was trying evasive maneuvers, but the attack ships were so maneuverable, she could just have sat there immobile and been no easier a target.

Grey Wing released one rack of missiles per ship, for nine missiles launched. Point defense on the light cruiser took out five of them.

But four missiles was more than enough to doom a light cruiser.

Grey Wing Leader had no clean-up to do.

"Grey Wing Leader to Grey Wing. Nice shooting. Return to mother ship."

The four attack ships sped off after *Ladyhawke,* catching her easily, and docked while *Ladyhawke* maintained acceleration.

"What the hell is that thing?"

"We have no idea, Admiral."

"Missile-launching parasites? She's not a carrier. All of those we saw in the Vauxhall and Earth battles were heavy cruisers."

"Yes, Sir. A pocket carrier, maybe?"

"Send the whole sensor package to Navy Intelligence. Maybe they can figure it out."

"Yes, Sir."

"Damn. That was something. I hope whatever the hell it is, they don't have more of them."

Nine hours later, *Ladyhawke* reached the hyperspace limit and was gone.

The demonstrations started on Burton within the month. They grew more raucous over time. When he judged the time was right, the Erian facilitator joined the king, King William VI, in his office.

Of course, he didn't go through the formal meeting

scheduler. He had no clout with which to wrangle a meeting. He simply appeared in the king's office one day, stepping out from behind a drape.

The QE radio surveillance rig had already been placed.

"Good morning, Your Majesty."

"Who the hell are you?"

The king grabbed at his desk drawer and pulled out a pistol. He shot twice, center of mass. The facilitator smiled at him, then spat out the spent rounds.

"I'm afraid that won't work, Your Majesty. To answer your question. I am Gary Manners. I am a facilitator."

"A facilitator of what?"

"A facilitator for you, Your Majesty. To facilitate your stepping down from power and becoming a figurehead monarch. You give up power to an elected parliament, but you get to stay the nominal King of Burton, continue to live in this nice house, with the staff and everything. The only difference is that you no longer rule."

"Never. I'll never surrender to the mob."

"As you wish, Your Majesty. As I say, I am your facilitator. No one else's. If you do not wish to survive, that is up to you. But it makes no sense to stand against the tide of history."

"The mob will never take over. I'll see to that."

Manners bowed.

"Of course, Your Majesty. If you ever change your mind and have need of me, just say, 'I want the facilitator.'"

"Just say it?"

"Of course, Your Majesty. I'll know."

With that Manners walked behind the drape. When the king went to look behind the drape, he wasn't there.

Security, having heard the gunshots, was banging on his office doors now. He unlocked the doors and they inquired as to what was going on.

"Just some target practice. I'm fine."

William Burton – King William VI, ruler of the Kingdom of Burton – never did call for the facilitator.

He also did not survive the revolution on Burton that installed a parliamentary democracy.

"A failure," the facilitator's aide said to Manners in their hotel suite in Burton City.

"Perhaps. Over time, I expect the ruling monarchs to become more amenable to such an arrangement."

"You do?"

"Of course. As more and more of their fellows refuse it and end up dead, it becomes a more, shall we say, positive option."

The Fire Spreads

The new attack-ship carriers – the first round of forty-eight of them – were going operational, and Isabela Febo considered how best to use them.

Staffing them was itself a problem. That was a lot of ships, in the context of the current size of the individual cluster navies and the cluster consortium navy of fifty heavy cruisers, now with attack-ship capabilities.

The solution was obvious, and she put her proposal through the admiralty council of the consortium. It took some cajoling, but Febo and Corliss were persuasive, and the individual cluster navies were miniscule in force projection compared to the new ships shoving off the docks.

Very simply, the solution to manning the new ships, in addition to a cluster-wide recruitment drive, was to decommission the individual cluster navies. Those older ships were manpower-intensive and had little to add to the force-projection capabilities of the new ships.

The new ships, by losing the missile tubes, had much-reduced manpower requirements. The older ships had effectively been mobile missile platforms. Much like the wet-water navies of the past, whose guns had been the whole point of their existence, the missile tubes had been the focus of older navy ships.

With the new attack-ship carriers, however, the attack ships were the point of their existence. Carrying attack ships to the battle was now their mission.

The elimination of the missile tubes reduced the manpower requirements more than the addition of the attack-ships increased it. Reduced manpower on its prime mission also reduced all of the support services that manpower required. Galley, recreation, sanitation all got smaller. All of the other departments on the vessels shrank.

For this first round of attack-ship carriers, manpower requirements were met by decommissioning the manpower-intensive ships of the individual cluster navies. That left the cluster nations without individual navies, which was an emotional political problem that took some selling.

But the overall naval power of the cluster went from five hundred attack ships on fifty platforms to twenty-four hundred attack ships on ninety-eight platforms.

"Good afternoon, Isabela."

"Good morning, Michael. Thank you for taking my call."

"Of course, Isabela. How can I help you this morning?"

"First, I wanted to thank you for working through the staffing problem with me, with the other cluster chief executives."

"I was happy to do it, Isabela. You were right. We just needed to get the others to see it."

Febo nodded.

"The other thing, Michael, is to talk out some of the implications of this new capability. Basically, now that we have them, how do we use them?"

"I'm assuming you have some thoughts in this regard, Isabela. Please, continue."

"Thank you, Michael. Our current squadrons have eight ships each, with a launch capability of eighty attack ships. On Earth and Vauxhall, we split one squadron into two divisions of four ships, with launch capabilities of forty attack ships per division. Those divisions were able to prevail against two squadrons of battleships in one case, and three squadrons of heavy cruisers in another.

"But each of these new attack-ship carriers has launch capability of forty attack ships. A current squadron of them can launch three hundred and twenty attack ships. That is ludicrous, given the performance of fifty attack ships in the Second Battle of Vauxhall and forty in the Battle of Earth.

"I propose therefore that a squadron of the new attack ship carriers be four vessels, and a division be two vessels, and that we typically deploy them in divisions."

Corliss thought about it as Febo was content to wait. It certainly made sense to him. The whole point of organizing ships in squadrons and divisions was to be able to deploy them in those groups, and eight of the powerful things was a deployment structure he couldn't envision.

"I agree, Isabela. That makes tremendous sense to me. Now what are we to do with them all?"

"I have some ideas there as well, Michael. Consider. We have defended the cluster with six squadrons of heavy cruisers for some time now, and never felt particularly vulnerable until King Albert targeted us with his naval development.

"Thanks largely to our treaty with the Erians, we now have the most powerful ships in human space. By a lot. I propose we deploy six squadrons of the new ships to protect the cluster, as before."

"But those are now four-ship squadrons, Isabela?"

"Yes, Michael. Four-ship squadrons that usually space as divisions."

Corliss nodded.

"That takes twenty-four of the new ships, Isabela. Half of this first round. What about the other twenty-four, and the forty-eight heavy cruisers with attack-ship capabilities?"

"We deploy them to the core, Michael. All of the heavy cruisers and half the carriers. We space them around in divisions, to visit our new friends, the fledgling democracies there. We have them rotate around the democracies, have them spend port time in some of them. The ones that give good coverage to the whole of the core in minimizing spacing times, for instance."

Corliss chuckled.

"And, of course, if someone calls us to tell us they are being attacked by a monarchy navy, we would be close by to lend assistance."

"Yes, Michael. If we find one of the democracies under attack, we would, of course, assist the people of that planet in repelling such an attack by a foreign power."

"The monarchies would soon find that the only way to protect their navies from being wiped out would be to keep them at home, Isabela."

"A positive development, I think, Michael."

"Agreed. I like it, Isabela. I like it a lot. I will support you in making this the policy of the cluster. It can only reap benefits for us, in extending our free-trade environment and in keeping the monarchies too busy at home to threaten us here."

Febo and Corliss spent quite a bit of time selling this new idea to the other four cluster chief executives, but the outcome was inevitable. Replacing a division of four heavy cruisers with a division of two carriers doubled the attack-ship capability from forty attack ships to eighty.

The financial aspect was the one thing that came up as an objection. But the expanding trade with the core worlds as the X-3 drive propagated had the economy of the cluster booming.

And a booming economy supported a stronger defense.

Febo also insisted that the core worlds they visited support the ships visiting there. No, the cluster would not pay for fuel, or reaction mass, or restocking of provisions in the core worlds they visited or spent port time at. The world visited would provide those things gratis to the visiting ships.

If not, the cluster consortium navy could instead visit other, more hospitable, worlds.

None of the new core-world democracies objected. In fact, they competed with each other to provision the ships at premium levels, to entice the division commanders to stay at their planet longer.

Crews on planet leave found they were buying their drinks at cost, and even the prostitutes were giving discounts.

It got to the point that visiting consortium navy crews were in danger of getting tired of filet mignon and lobster tail in their galleys.

Several times, the consortium navy ships arrived at a world only to find monarchy navy ships in possession of it. They were in orbit of the planet, and a day's spacing from the hyperspace limit.

They were trapped in the planet's hyperspace shadow.

The consortium navy commanders had their orders, and engaged the enemy ships with attack ships launched from the hyperspace limit.

Those engagements were short, and brutal.

A couple of times, the consortium navy ships dropped out of hyperspace to find two monarchy navies fighting over the newly democratic planet.

Consortium attack ships raced to the battle, and wiped out both sides.

The Chairman

"Hey, Bert?"

"Yes, Sam?"

"Chairman Febo asked me if the ten of us would be available at some point to meet with her at the executive building. Some afternoon."

"Sure, Sam. We can do that. The ten of us?"

"Yes. Claude and Phyllis, Serp and Marge, Gloria and Davian, you and Elina, and Jules and I."

"We're going to need a bunch of babysitters. We don't go out much, and you or Jules normally help us out."

"I can handle that with Erians, Bert. I have plenty of help available."

"And they're all capable in this regard?"

"They will be, Bert. I will instruct them when they show up. A few minutes, not more."

Mangum knew the Erians could transfer a lot of information quickly over their neurological link.

"OK, Sam. Get everybody else's schedule together and pick a day. Elina and I are pretty open, I know."

"Thanks, Bert."

Gloria and Davian and the three kids came in to Ashur from their house on the beach the night before the meeting. They stayed at the Ashur Park Plaza Hotel down the street. Well before the meeting, two Erians showed up at their hotel room. Dent answered the door.

"We're the babysitters, ma'am. Sam Hawker sent us."

"Two of you?"

"Yes, ma'am. We think it's safer for the children. If one of us is busy with one, the other still has an eye on the others."

"I see. Well, that makes sense. Come on in."

"Thank you, ma'am."

When Gloria and Davian were ushered up to Mangum and Elena's unit in The 909, just down the street, everyone else was already there.

"We have a few minutes before the cars arrive," Portnoy said. "Does anyone know what this is all about?"

Mangum looked at Sam.

"Chairman Febo did not tell me her purpose, or the topic of this meeting," Sam said. "She simply asked as to our availability."

"Interesting," Stickney said.

"Well, we should probably move downstairs," Mangum said. "The cars should be here soon."

There were two of the big government cars for the ten of them, and they all piled into one or the other. They were all close friends by this point, and there was no rhyme or reason to how they loaded.

When they arrived at the executive building, a security supervisor waited for them at the top of the steps of the portico.

"This way, please, everyone."

They went on in, and he led them past the security screening and down the hall to the elevators. They rode to the top floor, bypassed the more intensive security screening there and went down the hall to the outer office of the Chairman of the Council of the Association of Planets.

The receptionist stood up from her desk and opened one of

the doors into the inner office.

"Go right on in, everyone."

Mangum, Stavros, Dent, Varley, Sam, and Jules had all been here before, but for Portnoy, Stickney, Kendall, and Schofield it was all new.

They all trouped into the chairman's office, not knowing what to expect.

Chairman Febo was standing in the middle of her office when they arrived. She greeted each of her visitors individually by name, shaking their hands.

"Please, have a seat, everybody."

Mangum noted the furniture had been moved for this meeting, with eleven comfy armchairs arranged more or less in two rows of a half circle facing a wall.

Mangum and Elena sat in the back row, as Agency supervisors often did, leaving the front row to the operatives. Sam and Jules sat together, in the center of the front row, as protocol dictated for the ambassador, the senior person there.

Febo herself sat at one end of the front row. She could see everyone from there.

"I wanted to call you all here today, you ten, to show you something. Staff prepared it for me, and keeps it updated."

Febo manipulated a control she took from a pocket of her suit, and the wall panel they faced revealed itself to be a large three-dimensional wall display. It had previously been displaying a section of wall.

Sprawled across the display was a map of human space, both the core worlds and the cluster. In the core, a thousand inhabited systems were indicated with blue dots, while in the cluster a hundred were indicated with green dots.

"This was the situation when I took office. In fact, it has been the situation for a millennium or more, right up to the second mission to Vauxhall that resulted in the overthrow of the monarchy there. The first monarchy to fall. Blue dots are monarchy systems. Green dots are democracies."

Febo advanced the picture. Now only the core was shown, and the detail was easier to see. A thousand inhabited worlds, all under the rule of hereditary monarchs.

"Here we see the core worlds alone. Again, this was the situation before the second mission to Vauxhall. Now let me show you the situation today."

Febo advanced the picture again. It was the same view of the core worlds, but now the dots were blue, yellow, orange, red, and green. There were still a lot of blue dots, perhaps the majority. There were a lot of yellow dots, some orange dots, and a very few red dots. There were quite a few green dots. Dozens of them. Perhaps hundreds.

"The blue dots remain undisturbed monarchy worlds," Febo said. "The yellow dots are those planets where we have, with the help of the Erians, distributed the cure for RDT. The orange dots are those worlds that have gone further, in which there are now large demonstrations against the monarchy. The red dots are currently in open rebellion.

"And the green dots, my friends, the green dots are democracies."

Febo paused to let that sink in. Mangum studied the display. There was Vauxhall, there Earth. Both green. There were other green dots within the old Kingdom of Vauxhall. There, that dot, was Burton, an early recipient of the cure for RDT. He picked out other systems here and there.

"You did that, my friends. You ten, more than anyone else alive, and I wanted you to see it."

"We had a great deal of help, Madam Chairman," Sam said.

"Yes, of course you did, Mr. Ambassador. But it was your ideas, your plans, your involvement at the critical junctures, that made that happen. Remember, I read all the raw reports. Not just the executive summaries. The raw reports. Often *your* raw reports. I know who did what, and when, and how, and at what terrible risk.

"And terrible loss, too. Peggy Dawson couldn't be here, obviously, but she should be.

"I don't need to spell out all the details of what each of you did to make that happen. You all know. You were there. You lived it. But I wanted you to know that I know, too. I can't ever acknowledge what you did publicly. It can't ever become widely known.

"But you ten have changed human history, for the better. After a millennium and more, the monarchies are falling, one after the other. I don't think any of them will survive, except perhaps as figureheads.

"And that wouldn't have happened without each and every one of you."

Febo pointed to the map.

"You did that. You more than anyone else. It is something to be tremendously proud of, for the rest of your lives."

Changes

Time passed.

The children grew. The adults aged, too.

And there were changes.

Sam – Ambassador Sam Hawker – moved out of Mangum and Stavros' unit at The 909. He established the Erian Embassy to the Association of Planets down the street. Jules Hawker worked there with him. Some activities of the embassy, both present and past, were extremely confidential, but Jules was already in the know.

Of the four human couples, three lived in The 909 and got together regularly. Sam and Jules often joined them.

The children all got along, the eight in The 909, Dent and Varley's three, and Jules' three. When Dent and Varley came into town, and all fourteen of the children got together, they were a bright, active bunch, and took some watching.

They went to the beach, too, for their get-togethers. In particular, they took an annual vacation at the beach. It became something of a tradition.

At some point, Mangum and Stavros decided Franklin and Harriet – Frankie and Harry – needed separate rooms. This was a bit of a problem. Their unit at The 909 had four bedrooms. One was the master, one was their office, one had been the guest room and was now the kids' room.

The fourth was Mangum's gun room. Steel-lined and with a bio-lock on the door.

But neither Bert Mangum nor Elina Stavros was any longer

an active operative for the Agency. They were management. Desk jockeys who managed the Agency's operatives across all of human space.

But they no longer needed an arsenal.

Mangum bought a large gun safe for the master bedroom, one with a bio-lock on the door. There were children living in the unit after all. As the kids grew up, he taught them gun safety and marksmanship in the private gun range in the basement of The 909.

But he still kept the guns locked up.

Mangum and Stavros selected the weapons to put in the gun safe. The weapons they would keep. Mangum kept a dart gun and his 8mm semi-automatic pistol with integral suppression. He kept a shotgun and a varmint gun, an SBR and a select-fire assault rifle. Stavros kept her carry and backup guns, and a spare of each of those.

Mangum also kept one of the two Marchesi 'Duchessa' breakdown sniper rifles. The other he gave to Jules – an excellent shot – in case of need. Anyone Jules felt necessary to shoot was probably OK with Mangum.

For the rest, Mangum called the armorers at the Agency. Perhaps his operatives in the field could use some of what he had collected over the years. Or perhaps there was a firearms museum at the Agency.

It turned out there was a firearms museum at the Agency, basically a collection of things that had been stocked by the armorers at one point but which had been superseded by new acquisitions.

Mangum contacted them, and they said they would be happy to come out and look at his collection. They would be able to separate what was suitable for the armory and what was better off in the museum.

The bellhop showed the curator of the Agency's firearms museum up to Mangum and Stavros' unit in The 909.

"Mr. Mangum, I'm Martin Pell."

"Yes, Mr. Pell. Come in."

"Now, where is this collection?" Pell asked, looking around.

"This way."

They walked across the living room to the hallway to the bedrooms.

"Nice view," Pell said.

"Thanks."

They walked down the bedroom hallway to the gun room, and Mangum swiped at the bio-lock. Pell nodded approvingly.

Mangum waved Pell into the room.

"Heavens," Pell said when he walked in, looking around. "This is marvelous."

Mangum had removed less than five percent of the collection into the gun safe in the master bedroom, so the bulk of his collection remained in the gun room.

Pell walked around the room, looking at the pistols, rifles, shotguns, grenade launchers, rocket launchers. It went on and on. And one whole wall of ammunition, organized by caliber.

Pell picked up one of the rockets for the rocket launchers, inspecting it carefully.

"This round is live!" he said.

"Yes. Of course it is. Everything in this room is functional, Mr. Pell. Live rounds, functional guns."

Pell looked around again, eyes wide now.

"You could arm a rebellion with this room, Mr. Mangum."

"In a long career with the Agency, Mr. Pell, I have had many needs for firearms. Starting a rebellion was just one of them."

"I don't even know where to start in valuing this collection, Mr. Mangum. Fully functional, and quality items all. It is worth a small fortune on the open market."

"Yes, Mr. Pell, but I don't want it on the open market. I don't want any of our operatives to have to face these firearms in the field."

"Oh, yes. Quite."

"Instead I want to give it to the Agency. To the museum or the armory. The one condition is that you must take it all."

Armorers and curators of the armory and the firearms museum of the Agency came to The 909 for several days to pack and take all of the guns and ammunition in the gun room. They packed all the ammunition in metal cases against any possibility of accident.

At Mangum's insistence, they took the display cases and shelving units as well. When they had left, the gun room was completely empty.

Frankie liked his new bedroom. He especially liked the steel walls. He could hang things on the walls – anywhere on the walls – with magnets.

When he got a dart gun with magnetic darts, he was in heaven.

Ten Years On

It was their annual vacation. For two weeks every summer, everyone who had been involved in the momentous events of a decade and more ago got together at the beach. They rented the last half dozen beach houses along the beach, away from the rest of the resort.

This year, the twelfth anniversary of the Vauxhall revolution, everyone was there. Bert Mangum and Elina Stavros. Claude Portnoy and Phyllis Stickney. Serp Kendall and Marge Schofield. Davian Varley and Gloria Dent. Sam Hawker and Jules Hawker.

Even the recently retired Isabela Febo and her husband Paolo attended.

And, of course, the children. Bert and Elina's two, Claude and Phyllis' four, Serp and Marge's two, Gloria and Davian's three, and Jules' three.

Given the money involved and the identities of some of the vacationers, the resort actually closed their end of the beach to the rest of the resort, with signs declaring it a private beach. The vacationers took full advantage of the privacy, eschewing swimsuits for their swimming and sunning. A simple beach wrap was the preferred mode of dress.

Paolo and Isabela Febo were a generation older than the other adults on this vacation, and it could have caused some awkwardness, but for one thing.

Bert Mangum had told his children they were going on vacation with all their friends, like last year, but this year Grampa Paolo and Gramma Isabela would be there, too. The children, most of them resident at The 909, shared that information among themselves.

The first day of the vacation, on the beach, one of the children found a complete shell, and ran up to Isabela Febo, holding it up proudly.

"Gramma Is'bela, look what I found."

There was no awkwardness after that.

The biggest beach house had a large lanai, on which the resort had set up two banquet tables sized for twelve. The twelve adults sat at one and the fourteen children squeezed into the other. The group took most of their meals there together, ordered from the room service of the resort.

Of course, the conversation often turned to the events of a decade and more ago, and the ongoing consequences.

"I saw that the monarchy on Persh has fallen," Mangum said.

"Actually, Bert, the king stepped down as ruler," Sam said. "Gave power to an elected parliament. He and his family will stay on as the royal family, but it will be a ceremonial role. He has no actual power now."

Febo nodded.

"And the other planets of the kingdom have been allowed to go their own way," she said. "The lesser nobility on those other planets is following the king's lead."

"That seems preferable to becoming a dangling ornament on a lamp pole, as the King of Earth did," Mangum said.

"Were you guys involved in Persh, Sam?" Elina asked.

"We have had some facilitators out there working the issue for a while, Elina. They ironed out the details and managed to put it together."

"I think it's another good precedent," Febo said. "Like Norton. Now embattled royal families have examples of other ways out than to fight the inevitable."

"It's a sea change in government in the core worlds," Dent said.

"I'm happy to see it, though I never could have imagined it finally happening," Varley said.

"But you're the one who made it happen, Davian," Portnoy said. "It was amazing how fast things turned on Vauxhall once we started distributing your cure for RDT."

"Oh, yes," Stickney said. "It was mere days. I think it caught the king by surprise. He didn't know what to do."

"We all had a large part to play in the events of a decade and more ago," Febo said. "Something we can all be proud of."

Mangum raised his glass.

"A toast. To democracy, and the end of hereditary nobility."

"Hear! Hear!" Kendall said. "A bad end for a bad lot."

Everyone laughed and drank.

After lunch it was, once again, time for the beach.

The adults for the most part sunned and chatted.

The throng of children – all between the ages of five and fourteen – played in the water and the sand, with the older kids keeping an eye on the younger.

Jules' kids swam merrily in the water, their natural habitat. They had fun at one point by taking on the shape of sharks and swimming through the splashing children, but the other kids were on to that old trick by now, and laughed.

It was a very pleasant vacation.

For dinner the last evening, Mangum surprised them all. He had their final dinner at the beach catered by Marceau's.

"However did you manage this?" Febo asked, watching the resort staff lay out the exquisite spread.

"It turns out many of the shuttle pilots in our military are Erians, Isabela."

"But how did they get the food from Marceau's to the shuttle?"

"It also happens that it's not that hard to get the police to close a block of street. Even Park North Boulevard," Stavros said. "Especially if your last name is Stavros."

Febo laughed.

"Well, this is delightful. What a wonderful final dinner for such a lovely vacation."

Dinner from Marceau's was, as always, excellent.

One Hundred Years On

Sam Hawker and Bert Mangum made their way through the cemetery. It was a well-known path to them. They came here every year on the same date.

The anniversary of Bert Mangum's death.

Sam Hawker was still the Erian Ambassador Plenipotentiary to the Association of Planets. During the past century, he had slowly progressed his appearance from the age of about sixty to the age of about seventy.

Sam had worked with eight different Chairmen of the Council by this point, the first being Isabela Febo. She had retired over ninety years ago, and died eighteen years later.

His companion today, Bert Mangum, was not Norbert Ignatius Mangum, of course, but rather Norbert Franklin Mangum, named after both his great-grandfather Norbert Ignatius Mangum and his grandfather Franklin Mangum Stavros.

They found their way to the gravesite, where two stones marked the graves of this Bert Mangum's great-grandparents, Bert Mangum and Elina Stavros.

"Thanks for coming, Bert," Sam said when they got to the graves.

"As every year, Sam."

Sam nodded, and laid a bouquet of flowers on each of the graves.

"He was a great man, Bert. The things he accomplished. The full story has never been told, you know. He was allowed to fade into obscurity."

"That's a shame."

Sam shrugged.

"Not really, Bert. He had a long and enjoyable retirement, without repercussions. It would not have been the same if he had the notoriety he deserved. He would have been a target. Instead, he and Elina were allowed to live out their lives in comfort. Not being hunted."

Sam turned to Bert.

"It wasn't always that way, you know."

"So you've said, Sam. But you've never told me the full story."

"Perhaps I should, Bert. Perhaps I should. I am not long for this life anymore myself, and, when I die, the story will most likely die with me if I don't pass it on. Only Jules knows most of it."

"But you're immortal, aren't you, Sam?"

"Oh, no. We're mortal, though much more long-lived than humans. It's because we don't have differentiated organs. We are less prone to failures of that kind. And I was not a young man when I met your great-grandfather."

Bert was surprised by all of that. Sam was just Sam, had always been Sam. Had always been there.

"I always wondered why you stayed such good friends with the family, Sam. Were such a benefactor – in advice, in connections – to my grandparents, my parents, to me and my siblings. You were always there for us."

"Reciprocity, Bert, and loyalty. Your great-grandfather was a huge boon to Erians generally and me personally. He supported and protected Jules when he was young, introduced me to Chairman Febo at the critical time, fought quietly, through his connections, for Erian rights within the Association of Planets and the other cluster nations. Even within the core worlds. People – important people – owed him a lot, and they knew it. He used that influence on behalf of me and my kind."

"I didn't know that, Sam."

"Oh, yes. In some sense, he did even more for the core worlds. For the humans there. He was a key player – *the* key player, you might say – in the fall of the monarchies. He, Elina, and their friends set the dominos falling."

"I would love to hear the whole story, Sam."

"Perhaps. Perhaps I should tell you the whole thing, from the beginning. Though I'm not sure you will believe much of it, Bert."

In the end, as Sam felt his own death approaching, he did tell Bert the story. He retired from the ambassadorship, then spent long days telling the whole incredible story to Mangum.

They used a variety of favorite venues. The top-floor condo of The 909, where Bert Mangum now lived, his parents having down-sized to a smaller unit on a lower floor. The beach where that earlier Bert Mangum had vacationed with his wife Elina Stavros and their friends. A bench in the park across from The 909, where a much younger Sam and Jules had played fetch, taking turns being the young boy and the golden doodle.

The story itself was incredible, in the true meaning of the word: unable to be believed. But Sam was so matter-of-fact about it all, in the manner of Erians, that Mangum did believe it. Most of it, anyway.

With the story finally told, Sam's summary of all that came after really caught Bert's attention.

"Yes, the fall of Vauxhall was, after all, Bert's project. He pushed for it, he planned it, he designed it for the maximum impact on the other core worlds.

"And it worked, Bert. Once Vauxhall fell, once the family that controlled all the kingdoms of the core worlds was deposed on one of the core worlds, and they transitioned successfully to democracy, people on the other core worlds knew it was possible. Knew there was a way to kick the nobility out and successfully reclaim their own self-determination. Their freedom.

"Much like the revolutions in Europe in 1848 of Earth's old calendar, coming sixty years after the French Revolution, and the Great War sixty years later that brought about the fall of the great monarchies of Europe, the fall of Vauxhall precipitated the fall of the core-world monarchies."

"But it happened much faster, Sam."

"Oh, yes. Less than sixty years. That was because of the cure for RDT. The Association of Planets kept propagating the cure across the core worlds. They sent the cure itself initially, then manufacturing modules, and finally the plans for the manufacturing modules. The technology spread across the core worlds. That accelerated the whole thing.

"And now you know that even the cure for RDT was Bert's project. It was Bert and Gloria Dent who uncovered Evelyn Barnes' unique treason. It was they who proposed the formation of the consortium navy, which united the cluster militarily against the core worlds.

"It was Bert and Elina who uncovered the RDT ring that was being run out of the Crossroads space station. They and Gloria Dent and Claude Portnoy brought that whole thing down. And in the doing, they discovered that, in the core worlds, there existed a cure for RDT.

"It was Bert's mission to Earth that discovered the inventor of the cure, Dr. Davian Varley. That rescued him and brought him to the cluster, where he invented the even more potent cure. The one that also granted immunity against the drug.

"It was Bert, acting through Jules, who confronted the King of Vauxhall over the letters of marque that had him and Elina, Dent and Varley, and Claude Portnoy hunted in the cluster. Dozens of innocent bystanders died in the indiscriminate attempts to kill them.

"Finally, it was Bert's plan to overturn the monarchy on Vauxhall that set the dominoes falling, so that now, across all of human space, every human lives under some sort of democracy. Oh, some are better than others. No doubt about that. But all are better than even the most benign of the hereditary monarchies."

"That mission was the end of my great-grandfather's involvement, Sam?"

"Oh, no. It was Bert who came up with the idea of the cluster sending out Erians as facilitators. Chairman Febo picked up that ball and ran with it, as did her successors. We negotiated arrangements in which the monarch could give up power to an elected parliament, but remain a figurehead. The head of state nominally, but more of a tourist attraction actually.

"That is why there are so many parliamentary monarchies remaining among the core worlds. It avoided the bloody wars and revolutions that initially followed the fall of the monarchy on Vauxhall. The later transitions were generally less violent."

"And now there are Erians in all the nations of human space."

"Yes, Bert. That was also your great-grandfather's idea. We Erians generally like living among humans. We find them interesting, much as humans enjoy watching videos, I assume.

"Bert encouraged us to spread out. Not be isolated. Become participants in human society, even while keeping our own planet a nature preserve, untouched by development.

"It's worked out well, and we are trusted and our contributions valued across human space."

"It's an amazing story, Sam."

"Yes, Bert. I didn't really realize it at the time. As it was happening. I was just having fun, hanging out with my friend Bert.

"But we changed the world."

Bert Mangum recorded those conversations with Sam, and listened to them all again after. He thought it would be useful to put them all together in book form, but Sam had been adamant. No publication until after he, Sam, had himself passed.

It would complicate his role as a diplomat.

The funeral was over. All the dignitaries and friends had left. Remaining standing at the fresh grave were just two people, Jules Hawker and Norbert Franklin Mangum.

There was a new stone there, prepared in advance. Now three stones stood in a line.

[SAM HAWKER] [BERT MANGUM] [ELINA STAVROS]

"Thanks for arranging this, Bert," Jules said. "It was important to him."

"It was important to me, too, Jules. Together again, finally. Bert, and Elina, and Sam."

"Yes. They were quite a team."

"Were they really, Jules? When Sam spoke of all the things that went on, he concentrated on my great-grandfather. He didn't mention my great-grandmother as much."

"Oh, yes, Bert. They were very much a team. Don't forget,

Sam had been with Bert ten years by the time Elina came along. It wasn't even another ten years from Elina's arrival to the fall of Vauxhall. More like five. And after that my father was very busy. With the integration of Erians into human space. With sending out facilitators to negotiate peaceful transitions in the core worlds. Lots of things.

"I have a different perspective, as I came along just after Bert and Elina got together. From my point of view, they were always Bert and Elina. I had no experience of Bert alone.

"During those critical years, Elina was very much involved. She and Bert were so close, and they worked so closely together, at times they seemed almost Erian. They would finish each other's sentences, or come up with the same idea at the same time, or work an idea back and forth between them, almost like one person thinking it through. I didn't think it remarkable at the time, as Sam and I did that sort of thing. I didn't realize until later that most humans didn't."

"I see. That makes sense, Jules. Thank you for that."

"No problem, Bert. And thanks again for arranging my father's burial here. I think it's the first time an Erian has been buried in a human cemetery. The first time permission has been granted to do so."

"Yes, Jules, but if there had not been permission granted for Sam, it would have been a travesty. A terrible injustice."

The two old friends walked away from the gravesite, chatting about family.

Behind them, the team was back together at last.

Please review this book on Amazon.

Author's Afterword

I have attempted, in these five volumes, to lay out the stories Sam Hawker told me about my great-grandparents, Norbert Mangum and Elina Stavros. It has not been an easy task.

Sam Hawker was an Erian, and his understanding of some human topics was sketchy at best. He tended to concentrate on the factual parts of the story, and the decision-making process of various leaders, especially Association of Planets Chairman of the Council Isabela Febo and Gaston Alliance Speaker of the Assembly Michael Corliss.

These legendary figures, with whom any student of history will be familiar, come across in Sam's telling somewhat sterile, as if their decision-making was their major feature, and their human feelings were secondary. Yet Chairman Febo's own memoir and Speaker Corliss' biographers all say differently, stressing, for example, the trust and respect both leaders had for each other and the role that played in events.

Similarly for other figures in Sam's story. My great-grandparents themselves come across as larger-than-life figures. Who knows? Perhaps they were. Certainly they and their friends were involved in the momentous events that occurred a century ago. Were they as centrally involved as Sam indicated in his stories? We will never know.

Yet Sam was present for all of these events, and certainly some of what he related is factually true. In the Palace Museum on Vauxhall, in the foyer, there is a large marble sarcophagus, with the inscription 'Peggy Dawson, Hero of the Revolution.' That is a fact.

It is also a fact that there are no birth record or school

records for a Peggy Dawson of the correct age on Vauxhall, while there are on Mardouk. And one Peggy Dawson was for a number of years an employee of the Ashur City Zoo on Mardouk, as a large predator specialist, as Sam related. Was she also a professional assassin for the Agency?

How would I know? But, if not, we must ask how did she get to Vauxhall, during the critical events there, and how did she die? In her thirties she simply disappeared from the records on Mardouk. There is, for example, no death record here.

Similarly, we know the transit times between the cluster and the core worlds, and how they decreased over time. We know about the addictive drug RDT – no longer manufactured anywhere in human space – and its eventual permanent cure by Dr. Davian Varley. We even know about the death of Prince Michael aboard the Vauxhall heavy cruiser HMS *Prince Alfred,* the letters of marque the king of Vauxhall issued in response, and the carnage that resulted from those.

Those records exist. And those facts and others – things we *know* to be true – featured prominently in Sam's stories.

Other things we have to wonder about. Did Peggy Dawson kill the entire royal family of Vauxhall, basically single-handedly? Did Jules Hawker – another Erian and Sam's son – repeatedly walk in and out of the Vauxhall royal palace grounds using deer paths? Did Bert Mangum assassinate Nina Lato on Abelon at the request of the government's then-Coordinator, Jacques Martin? Did Mangum discover and befriend the Erians in a crash landing on their home world?

We have only Sam's word for it.

In these volumes, then, I have taken Sam's word for the turn of events. He was very fond of my great-grandparents and their friends, and spoke well of them all, but he did not glorify them. So I have taken the events he described as he told them.

I have also had to impute the human emotional background for some of what Sam described. As an Erian, he did not understand human emotions very well. He did not understand love or sex, or irrationality of any sort. That's just not who Erians are. It's not how they think.

Sam did understand honor, duty, and loyalty, perhaps even better than most humans, and those values played an important part in his story. On those subjects, I did not need to impute anything, as Sam's insight on those topics was unerring.

I suppose it is best then to consider these books as historically accurate fiction, and not pure history. I did consult primary sources for those things I could, and I remained true to that contemporaneous documentation, but much of what Sam described was not well documented at the time, and for good reason.

The existence of the Agency itself is still denied by the Association of Planets government. Did it exist? Does it still? How would we know? Did it actually engineer the overthrow of the Kingdom of Vauxhall, the seminal event in the ultimate collapse of the core-world monarchies? Sam's story is compelling, but it cannot be considered proven.

In any case, I hope you enjoyed my five volumes of Sam Hawker's stories about my great-grandparents, Norbert Mangum and Elina Stavros, and their friends. I enjoyed preparing them.

Norbert Franklin Mangum
Ashur, Mardouk, Association of Planets
May 8, 875 (Association Calendar)

www.ingramcontent.com/pod-product-compliance
Lightning Source LLC
LaVergne TN
LVHW010052110826
845155LV00028B/297